St. Martin's Paperbacks Titles by

Heidi Betts

Tangled Up in Love

Loves Me, Loves Me Knot

Loves Me,
Loves Me Knot

Heidi Betts

St. Martin's Paperbacks

This is a work of fiction. All of the characters, organizations, and events portrayed in this novel are either products of the author's imagination or are used fictitiously.

LOVES ME, LOVES ME KNOT

Copyright © 2009 by Heidi Betts.
Excerpt from *Knock Me for a Loop* copyright © 2009 by Heidi Betts.

For information address St. Martin's Press, 175 Fifth Avenue, New York, NY 10010.

ISBN: 0-312-94672-4
EAN: 978-0-312-94672-2

Printed in the United States of America

St. Martin's Paperbacks edition / August 2009

St. Martin's Paperbacks are published by St. Martin's Press, 175 Fifth Avenue, New York, NY 10010.

10 9 8 7 6 5 4 3 2 1

Without a doubt, this one has to be for my "Darlings of the Dungeon." I toyed with the idea of dedicating *Tangled Up in Love* to you because of Ronnie's "Domiknitrix" screen name, but no, it had to be *Loves Me, Loves Me Knot*. Why? Well, because of your amazing support and enthusiasm—*always*. And because you've been with me through every word of this story and know (almost) all of its behind-the-scenes secrets. But most of all because I know how much you, more than anyone, will appreciate the creative use of restraints in this story . . . and probably come up with a few more inventive ideas for their use, as well. *vbg*

And to the rest of my wonderful readers: If you're not a Darling of the Dungeon, but think you might like to be, click your stilettoed heels over to **HeidiBetts.com/ WIPSandChains**. We've got a whip (and handcuffs and some whipped cream) waiting just for you! *wink*

Cast On

With a final shove, Charlotte Langan managed to heave the heavy, centuries-old spinning wheel up the last two attic steps and onto the dusty floor.

When she'd hauled the thing down to her bedroom six months before, she certainly hadn't anticipated the need to carry it back up so soon—at least not by herself. But with her niece due to arrive any minute, she didn't have much choice. Jenna would be staying at the house for the next two weeks while Charlotte was on the road for one of the country's largest traveling craft shows.

She'd been preparing for this trip for years. Raising and shearing her own alpacas—who had become practically like children to her, given the amount of time she spent with them. Dying their fiber and spinning it into yarn. Knitting scarves and hats and mittens and sweaters—everything she could think of that might sell, until she had boxes upon boxes of items ready to go.

Some of her creations she sold at her booth in a local indoor craft and flea market, but since she spent most of her time either knitting or spinning, she had plenty left over for the traveling show. Or rather, she had enough left over from her stockpiling for the traveling show to also keep the small local booth.

Breath wheezing from her lungs, Charlotte tugged the hem of her floral polyester top down over her wide hips and continued to slide the spinning wheel across the floor toward a far, shadowed corner. She planned to lock the attic door, and couldn't think of any reason her niece might have for poking around up here, but she didn't want to take chances.

If Jenna found the ancient spinning wheel in a corner of the attic, covered by a thick white sheet, she might wonder why Charlotte wasn't using it. Why she'd gone to the expense of purchasing a brand-new one when she had a perfectly good and probably much more valuable one in her possession.

Oh, Charlotte could lie to her. She had no compunction about that sort of thing, not when it was for the greater good. She could tell her niece she hadn't wanted to risk anything happening to the family heirloom . . . or that it had a squeaky wheel . . . or that it didn't spin quite as well as the other one.

And Jenna would probably believe her. The dear, sweet child would never even consider that her eccentric old aunt might be up to something. Something secret, something devious, something . . . well, something Jenna would likely not appreciate if she knew.

Because the spinning wheel she was even now covering with the sheet, hiding like a fat kid squirreling away a last slice of birthday cake, wasn't just old. It wasn't just a family heirloom or a possibly priceless antique.

It was magic.

Charlotte hadn't believed it in the beginning. When she'd first remembered the old spinning wheel in the attic, she'd also begun to recall the tales her mother and grandmother used to tell her during her youth about its enchanted properties. How it was a true-love spinning wheel, and that the yarn it spun could bring two people together for their very own happily ever after.

At the time, she'd thought they were simply stories created to lull her to sleep or fill her head with Rose Red dreams. But when Ronnie Chasen, one of the young women in her Wednesday-night knitting group, had found herself at sixes and sevens with a fellow journalist, Charlotte had decided to put the spinning wheel to the test.

As hopeful as she'd been that the soft black yarn she'd spun with Ronnie and Dylan in mind would work to draw the two together, she wasn't sure she'd actually believed it would. Not until the sparks had begun to fly and the animosity between the two newspaper columnists had turned into something equally combustible, but far more . . . naughty. The details Ronnie had shared with the group since then were enough to turn Charlotte's hair carrot orange . . . if it weren't already, thanks to a copious supply of L'Oreal's limited-edition *I Love Lucy* do-it-yourself hair-coloring kits.

The good news, though, wasn't that Ronnie and Dylan were apparently extremely sexually compatible, but that the spinning wheel had worked! The yarn it spun really did seem to be magic and able to generate love where it hadn't been before.

Of course, one positive result couldn't really be considered conclusive evidence, could it? No. As impressed as Charlotte was with the results of the first skein of yarn she'd spun on the antique wheel, she thought that another test or two might be in order.

And if anyone needed a little love in her life, it was her dear niece, Jenna. The poor girl just hadn't been the same since her divorce from Gage Marshall a year and a half before. The two had been meant for each other— or so Charlotte had thought. She'd been completely shocked when they'd split up, and she still wasn't sure she understood the reason for it. Not all of it, anyway.

But just because Jenna's marriage to Gage hadn't worked out didn't mean the girl had to spend the rest of her life moping. And no matter how many dates she'd been on recently, that's exactly what Jenna was doing.

She needed a boost. A lift. A little fairy dust to raise her spirits and get her back in the game.

Confident the spinning wheel was adequately covered and hidden behind several large boxes of odds and ends, Charlotte dusted her hands together, patted her brow with the edge of one sleeve, and moved back down the stairs to the doorway that opened directly into her bedroom. She closed and locked the door behind her, tucked the key at the back of her underwear drawer, then took a second to glance in the mirror.

Her mop of bright orange hair was still perfectly coiffed, thanks to the industrial amount of hairspray she'd used on it only a few hours before. Her white blouse with its tiny blue flowers was still pristine, not even a smudge of dust from her excursion to the attic on it or her navy blue slacks.

Satisfied with her appearance, she headed downstairs and into the sitting room to collect her handbag and a thick skein of bright purple yarn. Her niece's penchant for knitting sexy, slinky boas to go with just about everything she wore meant that Charlotte had had to spin a light, feathery yarn that Jenna would be likely to start using right away.

It hadn't been easy. Certainly not as quick or straightforward as the thicker, sturdier yarn she'd spun for Ronnie, and which the young woman had ended up using to help teach Dylan—albeit reluctantly—to knit. A competitive challenge that had developed into something much more personal and significant.

Thanks to Charlotte's covert matchmaking efforts, of course. Oh, she hadn't picked Dylan for Ronnie or anything as ordinary as that. No, she'd simply handed Ronnie the special yarn and let the enchanted spinning wheel's powers do their thing.

Which was exactly what she planned to do with this ball of yarn. The rest would be up to Fate and magic . . . and hopefully Jenna's willingness to experience love again.

At the sound of a vehicle pulling into the drive, Charlotte grabbed her things and hurried to the front door in time to see her niece climbing out of her sunflower-yellow VW Beetle. Falling in line with Jenna's somewhat quirky personality, large magnets in the shape of white and yellow daisies decorated the doors and hood of the adorable vehicle.

Flowers weren't Jenna's only mode of decorating her beloved bug, though. At Easter, she used a nose, tail, and ears to make the car look like a bunny rabbit; at Halloween, a broom and the back end of a witch's robe would appear as though sticking out of the rear hatch; at Christmas, it was antlers and a bright red Rudolph nose.

Charlotte loved to see Jenna's happy yellow Beetle

coming up the drive, never knowing what amusing guise the little VW would be wearing.

Today, Jenna herself was dressed in dark blue jeans that flared at the calf and sparkled at the thighs and pockets with a mixture of rhinestones and silver studs. Her blouse was sage green and cut in a tank-top style, made of some soft, flowing, almost diaphanous material that was so popular these days. Never mind that one could almost see a girl's bits and pieces and skimpy brassieres underneath.

And as usual, Jenna also had a boa wrapped loosely around her neck in blending hues of green, yellow, and brown that perfectly matched her blouse.

"Hello, dear!" Charlotte called as she pushed through the front screen door and bustled down from the porch.

Jenna smiled and raised a hand to wave before reaching into the back seat for her overnight bag.

"You ready to go?" Jenna asked as Charlotte crossed the yard to greet her.

Charlotte's head bobbed up and down. "The station wagon and U-Haul are both stuffed to the gills. As soon as you're settled, I'll be on my way."

"If you're in a hurry to get going, don't let me hold you up," Jenna said. She cocked a hip into the car door to slam it closed behind her and turned to face her aunt, rainbow-striped valise in one hand. "I know my way around, and some of the girls are coming over tomorrow night to keep me company."

"Oh, good! And you know where everything is, right? Even in the barn?"

Jenna's lips curved indulgently. "Don't worry, Aunt Charlotte, your babies are safe with me. I'll take good care of them, I promise."

A small weight lifted from Charlotte's chest. "Of course you will. I'm sorry, it's just that I don't leave them very often, and I'm too used to taking care of them all by myself, I guess."

"Except when I come over to help you out, which is how I know all of their names, their little quirks, and where everything is that they could possibly need."

Jenna leaned in and Charlotte hugged her back, then let her niece herd her toward her late-model station wagon. It was sort of a buzzard barf brown, according to Jenna, with the prerequisite faux wood side panels. A "woody," as they used to say . . . though the last time she'd called it that, her niece's cheeks had turned bubble-gum pink and she'd been quietly informed that "woody" was a term currently reserved for a rather private, highly aroused portion of the male anatomy. Charlotte hadn't referred to her station wagon in that manner since.

Jenna often told her she should trade the outdated rattletrap in—if a dealer was even willing to take it—and find something a little more modern and reliable to get around in. But Charlotte liked her wagon. It had plenty of space and got her where she needed to go, which was all she required of her mode of transportation these days.

Vinyl seat squeaking as she climbed behind the wheel, Charlotte deposited her purse on the passenger-side floor before fitting the key into the ignition.

"Oh, I nearly forgot." She hadn't, of course, but the more spontaneous her gift seemed, the better.

Taking the skein of purple yarn from her lap, she held it out to Jenna. "I made this for you. Thought it might give you something to do while I'm away and you're in that big old house all by yourself."

Jenna took the yarn, running a few of the fringe-like strands between her fingers. "It's beautiful, thank you. Purple is one of my favorite colors."

She leaned in to press a kiss to her aunt's cheek, then straightened and pushed the door closed.

"Drive carefully," she said through the open window. "And good luck with the show. I hope you sell out of everything."

"Me, too, dear. Of course, if that happens, I'll just have to start all over again."

One corner of her niece's mouth quirked up in a grin. "Yes, but you love every minute of it."

"You know I do," Charlotte returned with a grin of her own. She cranked the engine and waited for the low throb to vibrate along the car's long metal frame all the way to her posterior. "All right, then, I'm off. You take care, and if you need anything . . . Well, I don't have a cell phone, so if you need anything, you're going to have to run to someone else. But I will call as often as I can to check in."

"I'll be fine. And so will the alpacas. You just go and have fun."

With a nod, Charlotte put the car in gear and rolled slowly out of her drive. She eased the wagon and U-Haul onto the dirt road, kicking up dust and waving into her rearview mirror at Jenna, who stood where she'd left her, enchanted yarn clasped tightly in one hand.

Charlotte hoped for a lot of things for this trip. Safe traveling, high-volume sales of her hand-spun yarns and knit goods . . . but most of all, she hoped for a very special man to appear in her niece's life. One who would take the shadows from her eyes and make her smile—really smile—the way she hadn't since her separation from Gage.

It was a lot to ask of one tiny skein of yarn.

But the spinning wheel had worked its magic before, and Charlotte was confident it would do so again.

Knit 1

The Rob Thomas/Santana collaboration "Smooth" rocked from the small radio/CD player Jenna had set up on her aunt's kitchen counter, cranked up high enough to be heard and thoroughly enjoyed over the loud whir of the blender. The girls would be here any minute, and she wanted to have the margaritas mixed and ready to go.

Hips twitching in time with the heavy Latin beat, she punched the blender's off button and popped the lid, dipping her finger in for a tiny taste.

Mmm, perfect. Mango was definitely a good choice to start. She also had lime, lemon, pineapple, and watermelon-flavored mixes on hand, and all the tequila they could possibly need to make Mexican Night *mucho, mucho ay caramba*!

Even over the bass of the song and her own humming, Jenna heard the insistent pounding on the front door. She slid the volume dial to a slightly less molar-rattling level and ran to answer it.

The minute she turned the knob, Grace and Ronnie spilled into the house, arms loaded with paper sacks, fabric totes, and bottles dangling from their fingers.

A dozen delicious aromas wafted around them, making Jenna's stomach growl. She'd barely eaten a thing all day, knowing they'd be stuffing themselves this evening with enough calories to make the local circus come looking to recruit them to take over the Fat Lady's tent.

"We're here," Grace announced somewhat breathlessly. "Let the fiesta begin!"

Laughing, Jenna took a few items from each of them to lighten their loads and led the way to the kitchen.

"I've got a pitcher of mango margaritas mixed already, but that's about it."

"Well, that's why we're here," Ronnie said, dumping her bags on the island countertop. "To do whatever it takes to get this party started."

Out of long practice and many Girls' Night get-togethers, they moved around the kitchen as a unit, opening drawers and cupboards, organizing things just the way they wanted them.

Blond and stunningly beautiful, Grace Fisher was everything Jenna wished she could be—tall and lithe, confident, successful, happy . . . She was the host of her own local cable talk show, recently renamed "Amazing Grace" in honor of the nickname viewers had bestowed upon her practically from the very beginning. On camera, at least, Grace seemed capable of just about anything, from baking and decorating a three-tiered wedding cake to changing the oil and spark plugs in her car.

She also happened to be engaged to another national celebrity, Zachary "Hot Legs" Hoolihan, star goalie of the Cleveland Rockets hockey team. The two made a sickeningly attractive couple—the Ken and Barbie of the media world.

If Jenna didn't love them both so much, she'd have been thoroughly green with envy. Especially considering how short and plain and boring she was in comparison.

A humble grade-school teacher, Jenna had short black hair, plain features, and was lucky to reach most people's armpits unless she decided to suffer the pains of four-inch heels, which she did only on extremely rare occasions.

Ronnie was just as beautiful as Grace, but in a more down-to-earth, approachable manner, Jenna thought. Equally tall and shapely, Ronnie's hair was a gorgeous chestnut brown that reached halfway down her back. She wrote a weekly column for the Cleveland *Sentinel*, and until recently had been caught up in a down-and-dirty, anything-you-can-do-I-can-do-better competition with Dylan Stone, her arch-nemesis at a rival paper.

Antagonism had quickly turned to passion, however, and the two were now cheerfully involved, living together and maybe, possibly, perhaps one day willing to take the next step toward a ring- and vow-related commitment.

Considering Jenna's own failed marriage and current romantic dry spell, it wasn't always easy to see her two best friends happily involved. She'd wallowed in her own misery long enough, however—and boy, had she ever. So now whenever compare-and-despair depression threatened to swamp her, she tried to remind herself of how very much she cared about Grace and Ronnie, and that someday she, too, might find someone and fall in love again.

Hey, it could happen.

"I'll take care of the food," Grace offered, loading up a tray with mass quantities of Mexican take-out that she pulled from multiple bags and containers.

"Ronnie," she continued, "you take the radio into the living room and find somewhere to plug it in. We must have music to make Mexican Night *fantastico*."

Ronnie bustled around, unplugging the radio and hoisting it off the counter.

"Jenna, don't just stand there," Grace, ever the take-charge kind of gal, ordered, shaking a lock of hair away from her face. "Grab some glasses and start pouring. I've been waiting all week to get plastered."

With a chuckle, Jenna grabbed three jelly jars—the only drinking glasses her eccentric aunt had to offer—from a nearby cupboard. Carrying them in one hand and the pitcher of thick margaritas in the other, she headed for the living room.

"See you in there," she threw over her shoulder, knowing Grace wouldn't be far behind.

Moments later, all three women were sitting cross-legged on the floor behind the low coffee table, backs resting against Charlotte's faded red old-fashioned brocade settee. Jenna poured them each a healthy dose of the thick, frothy, pale peach concoction while Ronnie and Grace took turns loading up plates with a little bit of everything their favorite Mexican restaurant had to offer.

As was typical of their Girls' Nights, ~~~~~~ overboard with both the food and the d~~~~ were cheese quesadillas, chicken enchila~~~~ bean burritos, crispy fish taquitos, side ord~~~ beans, and for dessert, mini churros. Th~~~~~

of those sweet cinnamon snacks waiting at the end of the meal made Jenna's mouth water.

"So how are you doing out here all on your own?" Ronnie asked after they'd each taken several bites and downed half of their slushy drinks.

Jenna swallowed before answering. "Fine. Caring for the alpacas means no sleeping in, but I'm used to being up early for school. And it's quiet with no one else around, but I'm used to that, too." She took a sip of her margarita. "Thanks for coming all the way out here, by the way. I could have just as easily driven back into town."

Grace flicked a taquito-filled hand. "Don't be silly. It's nice to meet somewhere new for a change, and I have to admit it's kind of fun to be here without Charlotte around."

Ronnie's face blanched as she choked on a mouthful of Mexican rice.

"Oh, I didn't mean it that way," Grace quickly corrected herself with a small eye roll. "I just meant that it feels sort of . . . wicked, like when I was a kid and my parents would leave me home alone. I'd poke around for secret hidey-holes, hoping to find hidden birthday and Christmas presents."

"And did you?" Jenna wanted to know.

"Sometimes. But I sort of lost interest after I snooped one time too many and ended up discovering their sex drawer." She shuddered with revulsion, sending Jenna and Ronnie into peals of laughter.

"Oh, my God," Ronnie gasped, "what did you find?"

Grace shook her head as though it were too horrific a memory to put into words, but then said, "Some maga-
~s and . . . toys."

"*Eeew!*" The three of them cringed and shuddered, simultaneously doing their best to shake off the mental image.

"I didn't fully understand what everything was at the time, but I sort of knew instinctively that I shouldn't be seeing them. It was traumatizing, believe me, especially later when I *did* start to figure out what they were for. There are some things a child just *should not* know about her parents, no matter how old she gets."

"Did they ever find out?" Jenna asked.

"God, no!" Grace's normally unflappable demeanor slipped, showing a flush of color on her cheeks. "Can you imagine? I'd have had to shoot myself or move to Siberia or something out of sheer embarrassment."

"Well, you're not the only one trying to block out childhood trauma," Ronnie said, pulling a slice of quesadilla apart to eat section by section. "I once walked in on my father just after he'd stepped out of the shower and was still naked. I don't think we looked each other in the eye again for about six years."

They all howled again, continuing to eat and imbibe great gulps of mango margarita.

"How about you, Jenna?" Grace pressed. "Any 'walked in on Mommy and Daddy doing it doggy-style' issues that it took many years in therapy from which to recover?"

Jenna shook her head adamantly, grateful she'd survived her childhood blessedly unscathed, at least where parental nudity and bedroom habits were concerned. Then again, her parents hadn't exactly been known for their overt sensuality or spontaneity.

She'd been an only child, and her parents had been rather quiet and austere. Her father had h tie-and-pocket-protector type, more interested in his work at a local accounting firm than in his wife or daughter. And her mother had never worn a skirt that fell above the knee or a blouse that didn't button all the way to her chin.

"Definitely not. As tightly wound as my folks were, it's a wonder I even exist. I swear, I'm not sure Marvin and Bernadette Langan even took their clothes off to bathe, let alone actually had sexual intercourse."

She pronounced the last "*sesh*ual intercourse" in a prim, near-British accent, nearly causing Grace and Ronnie to spit their Mexican fiesta halfway across the room.

"Maybe your dad accidentally rolled over on your mom on the way to the bathroom one night," Grace offered, completely straight-faced.

"Or maybe you were an immaculate conception." This from Ronnie.

Jenna bit extra hard into her cinnamon churro, savoring the crunchy sweetness before finally swallowing. "I wouldn't be surprised. And if that's the case, I sincerely hope it runs in the family, because divine intervention is about the only way I'm ever likely to get knocked up myself."

"Awwww." Ronnie put down her now-empty glass, wiped her hands on a paper napkin, and scooted a couple of inches closer to wrap an arm around Jenna's shoulders. "Don't worry, sweetie, you'll find someone soon and probably end up with a dozen fat, happy babies toddling around at your feet. You'll have so many kids, you'll think you're running an orphanage, and you may even attempt to adopt some of them out just to get a good night's sleep."

Where a moment ago she'd been feeling happy and festive, now a lead weight seemed to be pressing down on Jenna's chest, causing her eyes to water.

"I don't think so," she admitted, sounding pathetically whiny even to her own ears. If she weren't so emotionally miserable, she'd be tempted to smack herself upside her own head.

"I've tried," she told her friends. "You know I have. I've gone out with so many different men these past six months, I'm starting to feel like my entire life is one of those pathetic speed-dating sessions."

"And there was no one you'd consider seeing again?" Grace asked.

Jenna shrugged. "They were okay. A couple of them were cute, a couple of them were funny, but none of them . . ." She trailed off, not quite sure how to describe her almost total lack of interest in the male species of late.

"Flipped your switch? Rang your bell?" Ronnie suggested.

"Put the zip in your Miracle Whip?" Grace added with a teasing wink.

Jenna stuck her tongue out at her friend even as two small tears spilled past her lashes to run down her cheeks. "No, not even close. I think I'm turning into an old maid, drying up inside and losing interest in men altogether."

"What about Gage?" Ronnie asked.

The mention of her ex-husband, so unexpected and out of the blue, caused her stomach to flip-flop and sent a wave of heat flooding through her entire system. A lump formed in her throat, keeping her from being able to respond . . . a reaction her friends noticed immediately.

Ronnie's arm around her shoulders tightened and she pressed her brow to the side of Jenna's head. "See, you're not a dried-up old maid. You're just still caught up in wanting Gage, and until you're really and truly over him, no other guy is going to be able to get close to you."

"Oh, God, I'm damaged goods!" Jenna wailed, drawing her knees up to her chest and burying her face against the material of her flowing, tie-dyed skirt.

"Honey," Grace said flatly, shifting until she was closer, too, and they were all hip to hip, arms linked, "we're all damaged. We all have baggage. Your problem is that instead of being packed up and tucked away in a closet somewhere, your issues are still fresh and raw and strewn all over the bed."

Jenna lifted her head and Grace took a napkin from the coffee table to dab the tears from beneath her eyes. When she was finished, Jenna took the tissue from her and blew her nose.

"Now, I know I can be bossy and opinionated sometimes," Grace said, "and if you want to ignore me entirely, you go right ahead. But I'm going to say something I've never said before. Something I've been thinking for a long time."

The air hitched in Jenna's lungs and she let it out on a sigh. "Do I want to hear this?" she asked softly.

"I don't know if you want to, but I think you need to," Grace said, her tone brooking no argument.

Reaching for the margarita pitcher, Ronnie refilled Jenna's glass and handed it to her. "Here, have some more to drink and then let Grace have her say. It'll be like tearing off a Band-Aid . . . it will only hurt for a second and then it will be over."

Grace's lips, still shaded with the long-lasting gloss they put on her at the television studio, twisted. "Gee, thanks."

"Okay," Jenna said, her voice only slightly watery, "lay it on me."

"I don't think you're over Gage. I think you're completely hung up on him being the father of your children, whether the two of you are married or not, and that no other man will ever even come close to filling your extensive mental list of criteria for a DNA donor."

Jenna wished she could be angry with her friend's brutal assessment, but the sad truth was that Grace was right. She'd never really wanted to divorce Gage in the first place, so how could she be expected to stop loving him, to just get over no longer having him in her life?

With a groan, she let her head fall back until the short strands of her dark hair dusted the seat of the sofa behind them.

"So what am I supposed to do?" she asked them. "Go through the rest of my life miserable and childless and alone all because my husband changed his mind about loving me and wanting to start a family with me?"

A beat passed while she waited for one or the other of her closest friends to come to her defense, reassure her, say something, anything to disparage her rat of an ex-husband.

Of course, he was only a rat when she was really mad at him and feeling particularly sorry for herself. Otherwise, she at least had the moral fortitude to admit that he was a decent guy.

Better than decent; he was one of the best. When they'd first been married, she'd thought he was Prince Charming, Sir Galahad, and Superman all rolled into one. It was only later, when he'd started to pull away from her, that she wondered if she'd ever really known him at all.

"Well," Ronnie said, drawing out the word so that it took up about six syllables, "I guess that depends on what kind of woman you are."

Jenna's heart thumped painfully and her eyes went wide. "What's that supposed to mean? Are you saying I'm less of a woman than either of you are? That I was a bad wife or I'd make a bad mother?"

She was shaking now, her tone edging toward hysteria, as every deep, dark, subconscious fear she'd ever had about the breakup of her marriage reared its ugly head.

"Of course not," Ronnie replied calmly. She reached for the pitcher again and drained the last of the slushy mixture into their three glasses. "But you've been divorced for almost two years now, and I think it's time to make some hard-and-fast decisions about your life. That, however, is a conversation better had with more colorful, girly, tequila-based liquids coursing through our veins. Come on, let's go to the kitchen and whip up another pitcher of margaritas."

"And then what?" Jenna wanted to know as the three of them pushed to their feet.

"And then," Grace supplied, "we hatch a brilliant and daring plan for your future."

Jenna didn't know about "brilliant," but the plan was definitely daring. So daring, she wasn't sure she could go through with it.

Sitting around the island in the kitchen, they'd gone through two more large pitchers of margaritas. They'd opted for the lime and then watermelon, mixing in more and more tequila with each batch, while Grace and Ronnie grilled her like a salmon until she'd been forced to come to terms with exactly how she felt and what she wanted.

Did she want to be single or married?

Did she want to date a lot or just a little? Locally, or maybe online or through a service?

Did she really want a child, and if so, was she prepared to be a single mother?

Did she want to be impregnated by a living, breathing male, or would a test tube sort of deal do the trick?

And what she'd quickly realized—much to her somewhat nauseating chagrin—was that she didn't want to be a serial dater. The only man she'd ever really been interested in, or could see herself being involved with in the very near future, was Gage. And if she couldn't have him, then she'd rather be alone.

That particular revelation had come as something of a surprise, considering how hard she'd fought over the past year and a half to convince herself she was over Gage and fine being a happy and independent divorcée.

She really did want a baby, though. She always had. And though she was still young, she didn't know how many truly good years—or farm-fresh eggs—she had left.

Having grown up as an only child in a household where there was very little demonstrative interaction and almost no laughter or merriment, Jenna had always wanted her own family to be a big, boisterous one.

She wanted a husband who loved her and loved their children, and a passel of kids running around, making the windows rattle and floors quake. She'd spent years dreaming of holding her own babies to her breast, watching them learn to crawl and then walk and talk, of getting them ready for school in the mornings . . .

And when she'd met Gage, he'd folded perfectly into those hopes and dreams. She'd been almost giddily eager to start making babies with him, and then to see those little replicas with his Hershey bar brown eyes and mops of black hair similar to both of their dark locks.

They would take walks in the park, swinging a toddler between them, or go on weekend excursions to the lake where they'd deal with inner tubes and water wings, sunscreen and sand castles. She could so clearly picture Gage tossing their son or daughter into the air and catching him or her—or maybe one of each—in his strong arms, eliciting squeals of childish glee.

The day he'd told her he didn't want kids after all, and had no intention of getting her pregnant, had been the darkest day she could ever remember. Her whole world had come crashing down around her, sending her life and everything she thought she'd known spinning out of control.

Ronnie and Grace knew all that. They'd been the first people Jenna called after the fight to end all fights that had resulted in Gage's life-altering pronouncement and her eventual petition for divorce. They'd come running immediately, then held her hand, patted her back, let her sob on their shoulders for weeks on end, and alternately sympathized with her or railed at the duplicity of men in general and Gage in particular.

Which was why Grace's announcement that she thought Jenna had been wallowing for the past year and a half had come as such a surprise. Jenna had tried to work up a good mad at her friend, but any sense of betrayal went down the drain when she realized Grace was right. She hadn't been herself in months, and she darn well knew it.

But what had shocked her even more was what Ronnie and Grace thought she should do to get herself out of her recent funk.

Maybe it was the margaritas talking. Hell, there was a ninety-five percent chance it was the margaritas talking. But it was what she wanted, what she'd always wanted, and the idea of going through with it gave her a warm, fuzzy feeling deep in her belly that put the tequila-laced smoothies to shame.

So now the kitchen and living room—which twenty minutes ago had looked like a frat house on party night—were spotlessly clean. The dirty glasses, plates, silverware, and blender were all stuffed in the dishwasher. Leftover Mexican food had been boxed and put in the refrigerator. And any signs that Grace and Ronnie were in the house had been completely hidden or removed.

"Okay, I think we're set." Ronnie ran a rag over the island countertop one last time before tossing it in the sink. "Are you ready?"

A blip of panic sparked in Jenna's chest, causing her

lungs to freeze and her heart to skip a beat. "I don't think I can do this."

"Of course you can," Grace said matter-of-factly. "We did the whole pros and cons list, you did your little self-examination psychoanalysis, and this is what you said you wanted. You said you were sure."

"I am sure, I'm just . . . not sure."

Grace rolled her eyes. "Stop worrying. Stop second-guessing yourself. This is going to work like a charm, and when it's over, everyone will have exactly what they want."

"Everybody but Gage, anyway," Ronnie put in.

With a shoulder shrug, Grace said, "He should have thought of that before he lied to her and wasted three years of her life. Now it's Jenna's turn to call the shots and make the big decisions, and he'll just have to deal with it."

Grabbing the cordless phone from the wall, she passed it to Jenna. "You've got the story straight, right?"

Jenna nodded.

"Good. So dial."

Taking a deep breath, Jenna focused her slightly blurry gaze on the key pad and very carefully punched in the series of numbers she had memorized, even though she shouldn't have known them at all.

While she listened to the ring and waited for an answer, Grace pinched Ronnie's elbow and lured her out of the kitchen and into the other room. At the muted giggle that followed, Jenna closed her eyes, covered her face with her hand, and seriously considered hanging up before the humiliation that was about to befall her kicked in and became absolute.

But then the ringing stopped and a deep male voice sounded in her ear, sending her stomach plummeting toward her toes and making Phase One of their plan complete.

There was no turning back now.

Purl 2

When the phone rang at ten minutes after ten, Gage Marshall had already been asleep for about forty minutes.

It didn't say much for a thirty-three-year-old man to be passed out in front of the television so early on a Friday night, but his life hadn't exactly been a thrill a minute lately.

If his friends had been in town, he probably would have met them for some beer and fries down at The Penalty Box, but since they were both on the road for the next couple of weeks for an off-season charity event with some of the other players from the Cleveland Rockets, he was on his own. And on his own meant cold pizza, the last remaining Rolling Rock from a six-pack in the fridge, and whatever half-interesting ten-year-old action flick he could find on the tube.

Even work didn't seem to do it for him these days. He still enjoyed going undercover for the CPD, but he wasn't on an active case right now, which gave him more downtime and more time to devote to paperwork than he would have liked.

Downtime meant a lot of time alone and too damn much time to think. He didn't want to think, and he sure as hell didn't want to be alone.

But he'd made his bed, he supposed, and now he couldn't even bring himself to sleep in it.

Scrubbing a hand over his face, he pushed himself up from the couch and searched for the remote to mute the TV. The phone continued to ring, shaking his brain like a snow globe until he grabbed up the handset and barked, "Yeah?" into the receiver.

A second passed with nothing but dead air and he was about to hang up—after muttering a few colorful invectives the prankster wouldn't soon forget—when a soft, tentative voice played over the line.

"Gage?"

He knew that voice, dreamed of that voice, and it went straight to his gut.

"Jenna?"

For a minute, he thought he might still be asleep. Maybe he was dreaming, because there was no earthly reason he could think of that she would voluntarily call him. Not after the way they'd parted and the length of time they'd been divorced.

"I'm sorry to bother you," she said hesitantly while he continued to rub his eyes and tried to make sense of the alternate universe he'd apparently fallen into sometime between arriving home from work and then waking up after passing out on the sofa.

"But I'm at Aunt Charlotte's house all alone, and there's something wrong with the pipes under the sink upstairs. There's water everywhere, and I'm afraid it's going to start soaking through the floor into the downstairs ceiling."

Her words trailed to a stop, but only so that she could take a deep breath and dive in again.

"Normally, I'd ask Dylan or Zack to come over and help me out, but they're both out of town right now. And I'd call a plumber, but you know how expensive they are for evening and weekend visits, and it makes me a little nervous to think about inviting a stranger to come out here with no one else around. Could you . . . I mean, would you mind . . ."

She paused again, and he could picture her licking her lips and shoring up her confidence before continuing.

"I hate to inconvenience you, but is there any chance you could come out and take a look? I'd just die if Aunt Charlotte came home from her trip to a house that looked like it barely survived a hurricane."

Gage's brain was still slogging along, trying to process the fact that his ex-wife was on the phone and that she'd called him willingly. Not only willingly, but to ask him for a favor. It was like an episode of *The Twilight Zone*, and that *do-do-do-do do-do-do-do* theme started to echo in his head.

Scratching his chest through the worn cotton of his T-shirt, he cleared his throat and said, "Yeah, okay. Sure."

He checked his watch, calculated the distance to Charlotte Langan's isolated farm house from his apartment in the city, and added, "Give me half an hour."

When Jenna responded, the words seemed to come out in a rush. "All right, I'll be here. Thank you."

There was a loud click and then he was left with nothing but a dial tone buzzing in his ear.

Ten minutes later, boots and jacket on, Gage walked to his older-model, nondescript, gray unmarked car, small metal tool box in hand. He didn't know a lot about plumbing, but he figured he could tighten a few fittings or replace a pipe or two, if needed, just to get Jenna through the rest of the weekend.

The real problem wasn't how he'd manage to fix a leaky faucet, but how he was going to handle being alone with Jenna for the first time in two years. Away from their small group of friends; away from the boisterous crowd at the bar where they hung out; even away from her odd, mop-headed little aunt.

And he didn't know who he should be more concerned for. Jenna . . . or himself.

Jenna slammed the phone down, feeling like she might throw up. "He'll be here in thirty minutes."

Grace made a sound that was half squeak, half giggle, and both she and Ronnie bounced up and down on the balls of their feet.

"Okay, let's get moving. Ronnie, you go park your car out of sight. Jenna and I will run upstairs and get the bedroom ready."

Oh, God, the bedroom.

This was crazy. It was insane. How had they ever come up with such an off-the-wall idea?

Unfortunately, Jenna agreed that it was the only way she was ever going to get what she truly wanted. It was either this, or be miserable for the rest of her life. And at twenty-nine, she just wasn't ready to give up and play dead yet.

So she would have to go forward with Phase Two of

Operation Knock-Me-Up as planned. Even if the very thought made her feel nauseous, lightheaded, and scared witless all at once.

Thank goodness Grace and Ronnie were there to help her out and walk her through everything that needed to be done—and for the margaritas. Otherwise she would have wimped out hours ago.

Finished in the bedroom and bathroom, she and Grace hurried back downstairs just as Ronnie returned from moving her car behind the barn where Gage wouldn't notice it when he arrived.

"Everything set?" Ronnie asked, slightly out of breath. Her leopard-print raincoat was misbuttoned, two of the fastenings crooked and one in the wrong hole, leaving a flap of extra material where it didn't belong. A thin layer of mud caked the bottoms of her wedges, sprigs of grass sticking out of the light brown sandal straps that criss-crossed over her otherwise bare feet.

Not the least bit anxious about what they were doing, Grace gave a cheerful, "Yep," and skirted around them back to the kitchen.

Digging through her purse, she pulled out a flat plastic tray of tiny white pills. "Get me a couple bottles of beer and two teaspoons," she ordered, beginning to pop the pills one after another through the foil backing.

Ronnie and Jenna quickly gathered the items Grace needed and set them on the island in front of her, watching as she ground a dozen pills into a pile of dust on the counter. With almost scientific care, she deposited half the white powder into each of the two bottles of Corona they'd never gotten around to drinking for Mexican Night and slowly swirl, swirl, swirled them until she felt they were adequately dissolved. Then she

screwed the caps back on and returned them to the refrigerator.

"Remember," she told Jenna, "you uncap the bottles
and hand them to him. Don't let him take the caps off
himself or he might notice they're not on quite right.
And if he starts to get woozy after the first one, don't
bother with the second. We want him passed out and
compliant, not comatose or dead."

Jenna swallowed hard, but nodded. She'd been running the details of the arrangement and exactly what
she was supposed to do over and over in her head. Everything had to be perfect. Everything had to go according to plan.

If she messed this up, if anything went wrong . . .
Well, she would never get another chance like this one,
she was sure.

The rumble of an engine coming up the road sent
her heart into palpitations. "Oh, boy, I think he's here."

Almost as a single entity, the three women froze,
then drew ragged breaths into their lungs.

"Okay, this is it," Grace said, giving Jenna's arm a
squeeze. "You can do this. It's going to be great. And if
you need anything . . . I don't know. Call us, or send up
smoke signals, or scream or something."

Jenna nodded, wringing her hands together as the
worst case of nerves she'd ever experienced assaulted
her.

Ronnie ran up and gave her an encouraging hug.
"We're going to sneak out the back, and if we don't
hear anything from you after a bit, we'll call a cab. But
like Grace said, if you need anything, scream bloody
murder and we'll be back in a snap."

While Jenna stood rooted to the spot like she was

stuck to fly paper, Ronnie and Grace slipped around her and out the door at the rear of the house. A minute later, the front door rattled with Gage's heavy knock, and Jenna wondered if there was still time to run to the kitchen and throw up.

A second later he pounded again, and she decided puking up her guts would have to wait. Forcing herself to move, she headed for the door and yanked it open, hoping her face didn't look as flame-hot as it felt. Hoping her mouth would work even though it felt stuffed with cotton. Hoping her heart wouldn't pound its way out of her chest at the mere sight of Gage standing there, looking better than a winning lottery ticket, a hot-fudge sundae, and steamy, all-night sex all rolled into one.

No matter how long they'd been separated or how many other men she'd gone out with before or after him, he was still the handsomest man she'd ever seen. Towering over her at around six-foot-three, he was built like a great oak, all broad planes and thick muscles.

His face was a collection of hard angles and gorgeous, masculine features. Brown eyes that could go from pleasant to murky and back without warning, surrounded by lashes longer and softer than any man deserved. A hint of five o'clock shadow outlined his jaw, making him look more menacing than usual.

If that were even possible. With his black biker boots, worn leather jacket, and a physique that would put The Rock to shame, the man all but oozed danger from every pore. He might as well have had a blinking red WARNING! label stamped on his forehead.

Which, of course, she'd always found amazingly attractive. Maybe it had something to do with his being almost twice her size, or how safe and protected he made her feel, but the qualities Gage possessed that made most people quake had always turned her on. Big time.

At the moment, his dark brown hair was military short, just starting to grow in from having been shaved to the skin. He'd been known to let it grow out well past his shoulders, too, though, tying it back with a rubber band or thin strip of leather.

It depended, she knew, on what type of case he was working. When they'd first met and married, he'd been a uniformed officer for the Cleveland Police Department. Soon after, though, he'd transferred to vice and started working undercover. Short stints at first that gradually grew longer and longer.

If he was infiltrating a biker gang, his hair was long and sometimes straggly. If he was infiltrating a white-supremacist group, it was the shaved skinhead look. And if it was something in between, then his hair would be somewhere in between.

The funny thing was that Jenna had liked it all. She'd enjoyed tickling her fingers over the slightly stubbled curve of his skull just as much as running them through the long, silky strands when they'd reached halfway down his back.

What she hadn't liked were the changes to Gage's personality. The distance that seemed to grow between them more and more each time he returned home after being away.

Gage cleared his throat, drawing her attention back to the present.

"You going to let me in, or have you changed your mind about letting the house flood?"

It took a second for Jenna's snookered brain to send

the message to her limbs that she needed to move, especially with the way the deep timbre of his words turned her spine to jelly. But finally she stepped back, pulling the door with her, and waved him inside.

"Sorry," she said, having to lick her lips and swallow to clear the squeak from her voice. "I'm just tired, I guess. I didn't expect to still be up this late or to have to deal with household emergencies."

As stories went, it wasn't exactly a *New York Times* bestseller, but it was the best Jenna could do on the fly, with a roiling mass of nerves wiggling around in her belly. She just wasn't as good at this sort of thing as Grace and Ronnie . . . or as good as Grace and Ronnie assumed she would be, at any rate.

"Can I take your jacket?" she asked.

He set the dented red metal toolbox in his hand on a bench just inside the front door, and while he shrugged out of the mammoth black leather coat, Jenna ran to the kitchen and grabbed one of the bottles of Corona from the fridge that Grace had so carefully spiked. She gave it a little swirl and twisted off the cap on her way back into the other room.

Having been in Jenna's aunt's house many times before, Gage didn't need her to show him around and had already hung his jacket on one of the wooden dowels running along the wall above the matching bench by the time she returned.

"Here," she said, thrusting the cold bottle toward him in what was not the smoothest motion in recorded history.

Gads, she hoped he didn't figure out what was going on . . . or that she'd had one or two—maybe six—drinks too many with her so-called dinner. Let him chalk up her odd behavior to the discomfort of having to call her ex-husband in the middle of the night to help with some supposed plumbing problems. Or even to simply being alone with him again after their less-than-amicable breakup and two years of avoiding each other as much as possible given their mutual social circles.

Gage's warm, slightly wary brown eyes took in the beer in her hand before moving back up to her face.

"I thought you might appreciate a little compensation for coming all the way out here in the middle of the night. I know it's not your favorite brand, but . . ."

She shrugged one slim shoulder, hoping he'd buy what she was selling, because Lord knew she didn't have a clue what else to say to convince him to accept the offering.

Thankfully, he lifted the pressure by reaching out for the bottle and taking a quick first swig. A small wave of relief washed over her as she mentally checked that step off her list. If she could just keep him drinking, then this plan might actually have a shot at working.

"So where's this leak?" he asked, picking up his toolbox. The hand holding the beer lowered to thigh level at his side and he clutched the neck between two fingers.

Realizing there wasn't much chance of getting him to imbibe more of the doped Corona right this minute, she dragged her gaze up from his strong, tanned hand to his equally strong, tanned face . . . and slurped up her tongue long enough to tilt her head and turn for the stairs.

"This way." She spun around to lead him in the opposite direction . . . and nearly did a three-sixty as the

room whirled around her and her feet failed to stop
when they should have. Catching herself, she took a
second to regain her balance, then started forward,
hoping he hadn't noticed her imitation of Drunken Bal-
lerina Barbie.

She'd never considered herself inherently sexy, and
she'd lucked out when she'd met Gage, because he'd always seemed to find her attractive enough just the way
she was. She hadn't needed to doll herself up or bat her
lashes or slap on layers of makeup and lip gloss to catch
his attention. There'd been an instant and unmistakable
zap of electricity between them that had never required
play-acting or embellishment.

Even so, as they made their way up the narrow stairwell to the second floor, Jenna found herself purposely
swishing her hips, taking exaggerated Mae West steps
that put her a couple of feet ahead of Gage and hopefully kept her rear end at his eye level.

Until the sleeping pills mixed with his beer kicked in,
she had only her feminine wiles to lure him. And since
they'd been divorced for almost two years now, she wasn't
certain her appearance or flirting skills would have the
same effect on him as when they were married.

At the top of the stairs, she took her time rounding the
newel post, keeping her hand on the carved wood and
drawing her fingers slowly—seductively, she hoped—
along the railing. It also helped to keep her steady, but he
didn't need to know that.

Gage didn't say anything, simply followed along behind, his big boots thumping first on the creaky old
stairs, then along the creaky hallway floor.

That was the thing about two-hundred-year-old houses,

she thought absently as they approached the upstairs bathroom. Everything tended to be squeaky, rickety, and in constant need of repair.

Jenna liked her aunt's old farmhouse, though. It had a comfortable, homey feel to it, and was filled with a million childhood memories. Not just her own, but those of all the generations that had come before.

Keeping with Charlotte's unique—okay, quirky—sense of style, the upstairs powder room was crazy and colorful. The walls were a watermelon pink so bright, it almost hurt to look at them. There was no window in the room, but both an overhead lamp and rows of tiny bulbs on either side of the mirror above the sink provided plenty of light.

With her own overzealous hand, Charlotte had made a shower curtain of fabric that contained both neon checks *and* huge, oddly shaped flowers in colors that were equally bright and didn't quite match the blocks, but didn't clash, either.

Alone, the curtain might not have been too bad. But, of course, her aunt hadn't stopped there. She'd added a rubber duckie soap dish, a giraffe toothbrush holder, a SpongeBob SquarePants Dixie cup dispenser, and a rainbow trout towel rack that held a black towel and washcloth set. (Black, of all colors, when there was nothing else black—save perhaps some miniscule outlining on the shower curtain design—in the entire room.)

But that wasn't all. Charlotte had also knit several Southern belle toilet paper covers and had them strategically displayed. Three lined up along the back of the commode, two on the floor on either side of the toilet, and one across the room on the floor at the opposite end of the white porcelain tub. Just in case, you know, there was a major toilet paper emergency. Like maybe a Girl Scout troop dropped by and all needed their tushies wiped at the same time.

Martha Stewart, her aunt definitely was *not*. Although, ironically, Charlotte's bedroom and the rest of the house was actually rather normal and mundane. There were a lot of antiques sprinkled around, and a few unusual pieces here or there, but nothing that would put someone in fear for their life.

Gage wasn't afraid, though. Jenna doubted much of anything scared him, frankly, and he'd been around Charlotte and Charlotte's old farm house enough while they were married that he probably wouldn't have been surprised if a litter of rabid squirrels jumped out of the linen closet.

Before he'd arrived, Grace and Jenna had raced around the upstairs, putting things to wrong. She'd told Gage there was a plumbing leak when there really wasn't, so they'd had to create one.

To that end, Grace had loosened a pipe fixture under the sink, and they'd used a couple of the SpongeBob Dixie cups to splash water here and there as though the pipes had been dripping for quite a while, then sopped it up with extra towels. The towels were still on the floor, wadded up and wet and screaming for a cleanup crew.

"Sorry about the mess," Jenna said, kicking at one of the towels with the toe of her shoe. "I tried to keep the water from spreading too far."

"No problem," he murmured, setting his beer on the sink and his toolbox on the floor, then kneeling down to study the vanity's inner workings.

Worrying a thumbnail between her front teeth, Jenna stood in the doorway and watched, praying he wouldn't figure out that she and her friends had staged the leak to lure him out to the house. He didn't seem suspicious as he turned the knob to shut off the flow of water to the pipes, twisted this and felt around that.

"I don't see any cracks or corrosion," he said.

She didn't respond, afraid that anything she said might blow the whole charade.

Gage flipped around, lying down on his back to stare up at the bottom of the sink basin. "Can you hand me—"

Before he'd even finished his sentence, Jenna had the bottle of Corona shoved into his hand.

"Um . . ." He looked at her oddly. "Thanks, but I was actually going to ask for a wrench."

"Oh." She gave a nervous, too high-pitched laugh. "Sorry about that. But you might as well enjoy it," she added, crouching down beside his toolbox to search for what he needed.

When she found it, rather than handing it to him, she stood back and waited. He continued to eye her strangely, but she held her ground.

Finally, he took a slow sip of beer before setting the bottle aside. As soon as he did, she handed him the wrench.

"Thanks," he muttered, reluctantly pulling his attention away from his exhibiting-blatant-signs-of-psychosis ex-wife to once again tinker beneath the sink.

She liked to think that after this was all over, he'd believe her when she said she hadn't gone off the deep end and wasn't in need of a Thorazine Big Gulp, but something told her that wasn't going to happen.

It was a shame, too, because as she stood there, staring down at him lying on the floor, she couldn't help but wish things had worked out between them. That she had a right to ogle his body, admire the play of muscles beneath his tight T-shirt and the way he filled out a pair of Levis.

And he filled them out well. Really, really well.

"You've got a loose fitting under here, so I tightened it, but I don't see anything else that should be causing a leak."

Sliding back out from under the vanity, he used a corner of one of the towels to dry the pipes, then turned the water back on and tested his work. When everything remained dry, he slapped his hands together, wiped them on the front of his jeans, and returned the wrench to the toolbox.

"I don't know how that got loose, but you should be okay now. At the very least, it will hold until you can get a professional out here next week."

"Thanks. I don't know what I would have done without you."

That sounded good, right? Now she just had to figure out how to get the rest of that Corona—and maybe a second one—into him before he could leave.

To that end, she rushed around him, plucking up the wet towels and tossing them into the bathtub, then grabbing the bottle of beer while he collected the toolbox.

Gage stepped out of the small powder room, moving toward the stairs, and a shaft of panic stabbed through Jenna's heart.

"Wait!" she cried, reaching out with both arms as though that gesture alone could draw him back and keep him there a bit longer.

Cocking his head to one side, he did exactly as she asked—he waited. For her to say something, do something, give him a reason not to climb back in his car and drive back to town.

And she was trying, she really was. Her mind was doing its best to race, to grasp for an excuse. But a couple pitchers of margaritas and enough Mexican food to feed Santa Anna's army had made her brain sluggish.

A dozen responses would have rolled off Grace's tongue by now, with a dozen more lined up and ready to go. Ronnie would have simply grabbed him by the collar and kissed him into submission.

But, for better or worse, Jenna wasn't like either of her friends. She may have been married to Gage for three years before things had started to go downhill, but that didn't mean she knew what to say or how to handle him. She wasn't sure she ever had.

"Jenna?" he prompted when she stood there like a crash test dummy. "Was there something else?"

Eyes wide, mouth open and working like a guppy's, she made a high, squeaking sound that caused Gage to blink. He probably thought she was having a seizure and was about to swallow her tongue.

Then she blurted, "The bedroom!"

He blinked again.

"There's a . . . um, lamp in the guest bedroom that hasn't been working quite right. I'm afraid the wiring might be faulty and I worry about it starting a fire."

Lifting a hand to his chin, he rubbed his jaw, his

fingers making a slight scratching sound as they scraped against the dark beard stubble growing there. He shook his head slightly, and she knew she had him about as confused as a man could get.

"Jenna, I'm no electrician. I—"

"Please?" she asked, instilling her tone with what she hoped was just the right amount of pleading. "I'm out here all by myself for two weeks. I don't want to lie awake nights worrying about the house burning down around me."

Gage sighed. "Fine. Lead the way."

"Great." She beamed at him and moved down the hall, pushing open the door to the room where she was staying.

As he brushed past her, she once again shoved the bottle of Corona into his free hand. "Here, finish your beer before you start, though. You deserve it."

Instead of following him inside as she probably should have, she slowly moved away. "I've got another one in the fridge. I'll just go get it for you. Be right back."

Sidestepping along the railing that ran the length of the upstairs hallway with a too-bright, too-wide smile stretching her lips, she quickly spun around the banister and danced down the stairs . . . *not* breaking her neck, thank goodness, although there were a couple times when her feet slipped and she nearly took a header.

This wasn't part of the plan, she knew. Grace would crown her if she knew Jenna was running *away* from the bedroom where she'd finally managed to corner Gage.

But she needed that beer, darn it. She needed Gage to drink it, and drink it fast.

If he didn't . . . Well, if she couldn't get it into him, then she'd just drink it herself and be done with this whole stress-inducing, blood pressure-raising, faint-worthy mess.

Knit 3

While Jenna was off God knew where doing God knew what, Gage touched the bottle of Corona to his lips and took a long swallow, wondering what Jenna was up to. It didn't take a detective—which he just happened to be—to figure out that she was drunk off her ass, he just didn't know *why.* Or what had apparently caused her to drunk-dial him after more than a year of no direct contact or one-on-one conversations between them.

He'd bet a month's pay she was up to something.

Or maybe she wasn't up to anything, but was simply nervous about having him around when they normally made a point of keeping Zack, Grace, Dylan, and Ronnie around as buffers.

But he still got the feeling there was more to it than that.

The minor bathroom issue that could have been resolved with a single twist of a wrist.

The sudden need to have a lamp looked at in her bedroom, when she could have just unplugged it and told her aunt she should have an electrician check over the house's wiring when she got back.

The cold bottle of beer shoved into his hand the minute he walked through the door, and the second one she literally ran downstairs to retrieve.

That was the strangest thing of all. Even while they'd been married, he could count on one hand the number of times Jenna had greeted him at the door with a cold beer. Or brought him a beer at all, unless he'd asked her to.

If he didn't know better, he'd suspect she was trying to get him drunk, too.

Of course, he shrugged off that thought as soon as it popped into his brain, because even Jenna could figure out that it would take a heck of a lot more than two beers to put him under the table. He was a big guy; two six-packs might not even have done it.

He couldn't remember the last time he'd been three sheets to the wind, let alone flat-out, ass-on-the-ground drunk, but if it was going to happen, it would take something stronger than Corona.

Taking another pull from the bottle in his hand, he set his toolbox down beside the bed and flipped the switch to turn on the lamp Jenna had complained about. It came on smoothly, with no flickers or sizzles that might signal an electrical problem.

He shook his head and lowered himself to the corner of the bed, facing the doorway. Continuing to sip the beer that had no chance of making a dent in his blood-alcohol level, he listened to the sounds of Jenna moving around below.

The muted shuffle of her rapid steps as she crossed the floor. The smack of the refrigerator opening and closing. The echo of her moving back the way she'd come. He heard her bouncing up the stairs, heard her stumble and mutter a mild curse (because for Jenna, they were all mild) as her shin hit a runner, and knew the second she rounded the corner even before she reappeared at the door of the bedroom.

Then again, he had a feeling he'd have been able to sense her movements anywhere. Not only in a big, empty house, but in the middle of a crowded city street . . . a busy bar . . . an ear-splitting rock concert. Something about Jenna had always gotten to him on a level that didn't necessarily require her presence. He smelled her, heard her, felt her, even before she walked into a room.

Living without her these past eighteen months had been a fun and inventive form of pure torture. He'd brought it on himself, he knew that. And he'd wished a thousand times, or maybe more, that he could go back and handle things differently.

But even if he had, it wouldn't really have changed anything. They'd still have been in the same boat as when she'd filed for divorce in the first place.

So as much as he might have hated it, it was probably better that he'd been forced to move into a small, two-room apartment. A place where, even though Jenna had never set foot there, he still sometimes heard her or imagined her moving around.

He wasn't crazy. His friends might have thought he was if he'd ever admitted to them just how much he missed his wife, but he figured it was no worse than an amputee who continued to feel their missing limb and think it was still there, even when it clearly wasn't.

And that about summed up his relationship with Jenna perfectly. She'd been a part of him, a part he'd never wanted to live without, and when she'd left, it felt like she'd ripped his heart out and refused to return it to the big, gaping hole in the center of his chest.

Yeah. That was something he'd prefer no one—especially his best friends and his ex-wife—knew. He sounded like a damn Lifetime movie-of-the-week. Sappy. Broken. Pathetic.

Much more of this and he'd have to check his nads at the door.

Eyes locked on Jenna—and hers locked on him—he downed the rest of his beer.

No sooner had he set the bottle aside on the same nightstand as the lamp he was supposed to be fixing than Jenna was right there beside him, shoving a second bottle into his hand.

"Is there something I should know about this beer?" he asked her, eyeing the cold Corona quizzically. There was something going on here, getting fishier by the minute.

"No, why?" she replied just a little too quickly and with a little too much pitch to her tone.

He remained silent for a beat before shrugging a shoulder and raising the bottle to his mouth. "Just wondering."

His throat flexed convulsively as he swallowed, taking in a full three-quarters of the fresh beer. He didn't have a reason for taking so long to drink, except that it bought him some time to think, to contemplate what might be going on here, since he didn't believe for a minute that she'd called him over just to help with a few random household tasks.

"So tell me again what the problem is with the

lamp," he said, setting the second bottle of beer next to the first and beginning to rise from the bed.

A wave of dizziness washed over him and his vision went from black to fuzzy to black again.

"Whoa." Blinking in an effort to bring the room into focus, he stretched an arm out toward the carved oak headboard and slowly lowered himself back to the mattress.

"Gage? Are you all right?"

Jenna's voice, filled with concern, came to him as if through a wind tunnel, hollow and reverberating. He lifted his head to glance at her only to have her face go all blurry and indistinct.

"I'm fine. I just—" He continued to blink, trying to shake off whatever had suddenly taken hold of him. His eyes were dry and tired, his tongue feeling about three sizes too large for his mouth, making it hard to talk. Not that it mattered much, considering his brain seemed to be having a difficult time putting two thoughts together.

"Why don't you lie down," Jenna offered.

She was beside him now, one arm around his back, helping to lower him to the mattress, the other pressing against his chest to make sure he went down.

"What did you do?" he thought he asked, though it might have come out as more of a slur.

"Nothing, you're just tired. Lie back and go to sleep."

But he wasn't tired. Or he hadn't been when he'd gotten here. He'd been wide awake—or darn near—after her phone call woke him from a dead sleep. How could he be tired again already? Unless . . . ?

It was right there, on the tip of his tongue. The reason he was so groggy all of a sudden, the reason he felt like he needed a nap and might not have much say in whether he took one or not.

But then it was gone as his grogginess grew. It didn't help, either, that Jenna was sitting on the bed beside him, her hip pressed against his, her fingers brushing lightly through his short hair and over his scalp in a soothing motion that was growing hard to resist.

He let his eyes drift closed, let her lull him in a way she hadn't since they were first married. When they were still crazy in love, and before he'd fucked it all up.

Gage couldn't remember a time in his life when he'd been this happy, this content.

Then again, what sane man wouldn't be?

The way he figured it, things didn't get much better than this. Waves lapping just outside the room. The warm island breeze blowing through the open balcony door. And the most beautiful woman in the world tucked securely at his side, her slim, sleek body rubbing sensuously against his own.

Oh, yeah, this was the life. If he'd known it could be this good, he'd have swept Jenna away to the Caribbean long before now. As it was, he was beginning to wonder if there was any way to stretch out their two-week honeymoon and stick around St. Thomas and its surrounding islands for the next . . . oh, fifty years or so sounded good to him.

The short, spiky strands of Jenna's dark hair tickled his bare shoulder as she began to stir. Her leg, hitched over his own, bent and slid up his thigh until her knee came dangerously close to unmanning him. Instead of disturbing him, though, the soft brush of skin on skin

heated his blood and generated thoughts of making love
to her, even though it hadn't been that long since their
last passionate encounter.

Not that it mattered. He'd realized almost from the
moment they'd met that he couldn't get enough of her.
He could still be inside her, limp and wrung out from
one of the earth-shattering climaxes he always found in
her body, and want her again. Find himself growing
hard again.

He was one lucky son of a bitch.

And he knew it. Knew there wasn't another woman
on the planet who could set him ablaze the way Jenna
Langan—now Marshall, thank God in heaven—did.
Knew no other woman would ever match him as well.
It sounded hokey, but she was like his other half, seeping in and filling all the holes in his spirit that had been
empty and cold before she'd come along.

She understood him. Understood his love for his
job, and didn't freak over the fact that it sometimes
put him in danger. She'd admitted that she worried
about him, but had been quick to add that she trusted
him, trusted his training, and knew that he'd do everything he could to come home safely at the end of
the night.

She wasn't like some cops' wives who whined and
cried and complained about the dangers of having a
loved one on the force, about the long and unpredictable
hours, about their husbands caring more about their
jobs than they did about them.

And though she wasn't classically beautiful, Gage
couldn't imagine another woman flipping his switch
the way Jenna did.

Until he'd met her, he'd always been attracted to tall,

leggy women with long hair and big boobs. The *Sports Illustrated Swimsuit Edition* types with more T and A than I and Q. Women who, frankly, tended to look more like her best friends, Ronnie and Grace.

He'd actually had his eye on Ronnie initially, thinking about culling her from the rest of the herd and hitting her with one of his tried-and-true come-on lines when he'd run into Jenna, and thoughts of asking out any other woman had flown straight out of his head.

She was tiny, the top of her head barely reaching his chin, her compact build looking almost shapeless and boyish beneath the plain, Bohemian outfits she gravitated toward. Faded jeans and colorful, flowing blouses. Long skirts and peasant tops.

And scarves. Or boas, as she'd recently trained him to think of them. She loved to knit long boas out of fancy, fluffy, brightly colored yarn and then wrap them around her neck to coordinate with whatever she was wearing that day.

At first, he'd thought she was using them as a shield to cover an embarrassing birth mark or scar, or maybe just some hickeys she didn't want anyone to know about. Then, after he'd learned they were simply a part of her own personal fashion sense . . . and after they'd started getting hot and heavy . . . he'd gotten a secret thrill out of putting some hickeys on her neck himself that she really *did* need the scarves to cover. It had turned him on to see them and know that his sexy little marks on her body were hidden beneath.

He also enjoyed unwinding them, drawing them slowly from her neck, sometimes using them to loosely bind her arms behind her back or teasing other tender, sensitive parts of her body while he undressed her.

Oh, yeah, there were lots of fun, interesting things he liked to do with those boas.

Jenna's slim fingers twitched where they rested on his bare chest and he lifted her hand to his mouth, pressing a firm kiss to her knuckles. She made a low, purring sound in her throat that went straight to his gut and squirmed against him.

Wrapping an arm around her waist, he dragged her from his side to lay on top of him, covering him from neck to ankle. She blinked like a sleepy owl, a wide, contented smile spreading across her face.

"Hi," she whispered.

His own lips curved upwards. "Hi. Wanna get dressed and go down to the beach? Maybe grab some dinner?"

He knew what *he* wanted to do, and it didn't involve food or leaving the room. But since it had been several hours since breakfast and the island offered plenty of shopping and sightseeing opportunities, he thought he should at least offer to show her as much of a good time out of bed as he was determined to show her in it.

She considered his question for a minute, her dark brows drawing together adorably over her tiny, wrinkled button of a nose.

"I'm thinking room service," she finally responded.

His own brow quirked as he studied her. "You sure? The concierge recommended some restaurants she thought we should try. We could take the ferry over to St. John, maybe visit a few places over there."

"Are you sick of my company already? Bored with your new bride?"

She propped her chin in the palm of her hand, her elbow digging into his pec. A small puff of air huffed from his diaphragm, but he didn't say anything, didn't move to relieve the pressure. He was too amused by his little wife to care about a minor twinge of pain.

"That's not a good sign, you know. It doesn't bode well for the rest of our married life if one of us starts feeling like the honeymoon is over during the actual honeymoon."

"Honey," he drawled, smoothing his hands up and down her bare arms, "I have a feeling our honeymoon won't be over even when we're ninety and swinging on the front porch, watching our great-great-grandkids playing in the yard."

Her ripe pink lips pulled into an adorable bowlike moue. "You think you'll still be up to honeymoon activities when you're nearing the big nine-oh?"

Gage waggled his brows, cocking his hips to let her know how *up* he was to honeymoon activities at that very moment. "With you, I have a feeling I'll be up to it even when I'm six feet under."

A shadow passed over her face, but was just as quickly gone. "Let's not talk about that sort of thing. In fact . . ." She slid her hands to the mattress on either side of his waist, did the same with her legs on either side of his thighs, and pushed herself into a sitting position. "Let's not talk at all."

His heart was pounding in his chest, his cock throbbing between his legs and pointing like a compass toward due North.

"What do you suggest we do instead?" he asked. And he was pretty sure he was only imagining the strangled wisp in his voice. He was heartier than that, right? He was a big, strong man; it should take more than a petite fairy of a woman to take his breath away.

Sitting back on her haunches, the globes of her ass cushioned on the tops of his thighs, she let her fingers trail along the tight, concave plane of his abdomen. "I think we should order room service," she said.

With her gaze latched firmly on the path her nails were making as they raked across his flesh, she tipped her head to one side. "And while we wait for it to arrive, I think we should do dirty, naughty things that we can't tell our friends about when we go home."

"Sounds good to me." Hell, it sounded like freaking paradise. And her hands drifting from his stomach to the Little General felt even better.

But instead of wrapping around his hard length, her hand skimmed past to gently cup and fondle his balls. Air hissed through his teeth, and any blood that had been keeping the rest of his body functioning immediately gave up the fight and headed straight for his groin.

"What about room service?" he grated, since she didn't seem inclined to follow through with her suggestion.

"You dial," she said in a sultry, brown-sugar voice. "I have a feeling I'll be hungry, so order me one of everything."

He started to lower his arm, wondering briefly how it had gotten over his head to begin with. He didn't remember gripping the headboard, only stroking Jenna's shoulders and arms.

She chose that moment to scoot back even farther and lower her head until her lips grazed the tip of his cock. A shock of electricity rolled down his dick and flashed like lightning through the rest of his system.

"I'm not sure I'm going to be able to dial, let alone talk, with your mouth on me."

"Mmm." She parted her lips a fraction and let her tongue dart out to lick his sensitive flesh. "That could be a problem. Maybe we should wait until after we've eaten to participate in more . . . interesting activities."

But instead of stopping, instead of pulling away, she opened her mouth even wider and engulfed him by a full inch.

Though he didn't know how he retained the ability to speak, he managed a wobbly, "I like the sound of that."

Tugging once more at his arm, he tried to touch her face, tried to run his fingers through her hair, but his hand wouldn't budge.

He frowned. What the hell was going on? Why couldn't he move his right arm?

He gave up on the right and tried to lift the left. Same problem. Same dogged resistance.

Okay, this was getting ridiculous.

He rolled his head on the pillow, first to one side, then to the other, in an effort to see what was holding him back. There was something there, he knew it, but his eyes wouldn't seem to focus. And the more he tried to clear his vision, the worse it got.

He returned his gaze to Jenna, who still hovered above him. Their surroundings were different now, though. He could no longer hear the waves lapping outside the open balcony door or smell the fresh scent of the island breeze. The four walls surrounding him didn't look like those of the hotel room where they'd honeymooned, but were darker, plainer, and closing in on him.

Mind searching for an explanation, he turned his attention back to Jenna. Something felt strange. Wrong.

And suddenly Jenna didn't just look sexy, wanton, and desirable, she also looked . . . guilty.

"What did you do?" he asked, brows knitting as the words came out slurred. "What did you do?"

Purl 4

Jenna didn't know whether to continue or run off in a panic. The pills in the beer had worked just the way Grace said they would, but now Gage seemed to be coming around.

On the one hand, that was good—it meant he would be more physically able to respond to her touch.

Not that she had much doubt about him in that respect; she knew Gage's body well enough to know he could be in a coma and would still likely react to her caressing his junk.

On the other hand, being awake and lucid meant he might begin to put two and two together, figure out what she was up to . . . and take the house apart in a blind rage. She'd seen Gage angry before—never at her, thank goodness—and it hadn't been pretty. But she knew his strength, and she knew he wouldn't take kindly to being tricked or manipulated.

Swallowing hard, she ignored the trickle of self-consciousness that niggled at her and double-checked the ties at his wrists.

"I didn't do anything," she lied in what she hoped

was a soothing, believable whisper. "Now relax, the fun is just beginning."

He shook his head where it rested on the white pillow, his arms pinned above him, tied to either side of the headboard with a couple of her hand-knit boas. One of them was purple and not quite finished, started with the homespun alpaca yarn Aunt Charlotte had given her before leaving. The other, and the two binding his ankles to the footboard, were ones she'd brought along from home. Grace had helped her set them up and then tuck them unobtrusively under the bedding before taking off with Ronnie, so that all Jenna had to do after drugging Gage and luring him into the bedroom was secure him with the already prepared restraints.

It all felt so bad and manipulative and . . . *wrong* to Jenna on several levels, but she and Grace and Ronnie had discussed the situation *ad nauseum*, with no other solution coming to mind. Add to that the nearly two years of wishing, dreaming, regretting, and basically circling around to the very same conclusion . . .

This might not make her a good person, but it was what she had to do in order to move on with her life rather than wallowing in sadness and regret for the next fifty years.

With that thought firmly in mind, she took a deep breath and moved on to the task of stripping them both bare. She started with herself, crossing her arms over her abdomen and lifting her blouse off over her head. Then she did the same with her long, flowing skirt, because it was easier than shifting around to get it down and off past her feet.

She sat back, perched on Gage's denim-clad knees in only a conservative white bra and panty set. It had been so long since they'd been together—so long since she'd been with anyone—that even just the act of undressing felt awkward and naughty.

But naughty in a good way. She could feel the blood turning thick and warm in her veins, and her nipples were beginning to bud inside the padded cups of her bra.

It should be just like riding a bike, though, right? Climb on, grab the handlebars, and start peddling. How hard could it be?

Glancing up into Gage's face, she noticed that his lips were pressed into a flat line and his intense brown gaze was locked on her. "What are you doing?" he grated.

Oh, he was awake now. Whatever effect the pills had had on him, they'd obviously run their course, leaving him wide-eyed and alert. Wary, but alert.

Tugging the tail of his shirt from the waistband of his jeans, she pushed the soft cotton upwards, revealing the gorgeous expanse of his broad, tanned chest inch by luscious inch. Since his hands were sort of . . . otherwise occupied . . . there was no way to remove the shirt without untying him, so she settled for slipping it over his head and leaving it there, caught at the back of his neck and under his arms.

It wasn't ideal, but it would do. The same as leaving his pants bunched around his ankles would have to do.

Hmm. Perhaps she should have thought this through a bit more before tying him to the bedposts. Either that, or stripped him naked beforehand, leaving only her own nudity to worry about.

"Don't be angry," she told him in a hushed voice. "I know this is a little unusual, but it's the only way I felt safe inviting you over here."

Her fingers moved to his belt, releasing it and the top button of his jeans before slowly sliding down the tab of his zipper. Dragging the thick denim past his hips was made more difficult by his spread-eagle position, but she didn't let that stop her. A good yank did it, and she was able to shimmy them down his legs to bunch around his calves.

The thin material of his black boxer briefs didn't leave much to the imagination, and she could clearly see that he was interested in what she was doing to him—or at least his body was. Not throbbing, frothing, fire-poker interested, but not impervious, which made her feel a little better about the entire situation.

Climbing back into position over his thighs, she took in all the sleek golden flesh her disrobing of him had revealed and felt a flutter of longing low in her belly.

At his throat, his Adam's apple bobbed and his tongue darted out to lick his lips. "What are you doing, Jenna?" he asked again, the words even more strained than before.

She knew what he was asking—not the what of her actions, but the why. Something she wasn't nearly ready to confess. So she simply leaned forward, pressed a soft kiss to the corner of his mouth, and whispered, "Making love to you."

Thankfully, three years of marriage and hundreds of bouts of hot, sweaty, ultra-passionate lovemaking had clued her in to his likes and dislikes. If not all of them, then certainly enough to move them toward that fire-poker thing and get her through this evening.

Laying her hands flat at the sides of his waist, she trailed them upwards, sliding slowly along his tight abdomen, his ribcage, over the T-shirt bunched at his

armpits, and up his arms until she'd reached his hands.
She enjoyed every inch of warm flesh and compact
muscle, just as she had while they'd been married.

To steal a line from one of her favorite songs, Gage's
body was a wonderland. Even if he hadn't been a cop,
needing to stay in shape to keep up with the rigors of
his job, she suspected he still would have been at the
gym five or six times a week. Running, swimming, lifting weights. He did a bit of everything, and it showed.

And she appreciated his diligence. She always had,
even if his big, muscle-bound, in-shape body tended to
make her feel small and somewhat out of shape in comparison.

She'd also always loved his tattoos. She wasn't inked
herself . . . she wasn't sure she was brave enough to let
someone permanently mark her body with a thousand
razor-sharp needles . . . but she could certainly appreciate the beauty of good body art on the canvas of Gage's
spectacular physique.

While they'd been together, he'd only had a couple—
a tribal rope design around his left bicep and a strip of
barbed wire around his right wrist. He'd talked about
getting more, but to her knowledge had never started
the process.

Since their breakup, however, it looked like he'd not
only been busy, but perhaps spent the majority of his
free time in a tattoo artist's chair. She could see the nose
of a dragon breathing fire at the top of his right pectoral. Full of bright color and angry passion, it trailed up
under the black of his bunched-up T-shirt, presumably
to cover the slope of his shoulder. She assumed it blan-
keted a fair expanse of his back, as well, because the
creature reappeared below the line of his waist, its tail

wrapping around his left hip while the tip curled over his pelvic bone and ended just above his groin.

Licking her lips, she linked her fingers with his and leaned down to press a soft kiss on his mouth.

"You remember this, don't you?" she asked quietly.

She rested her breasts on his chest, the rough, springy hairs there tickling her sensitized nipples. Lower, beneath her belly, she felt him stir and knew her attentions were beginning to have the desired effect.

"You remember me," she added, and this time it was a statement rather than a question.

His fingers flexed around hers, and she couldn't read whether it was in desire or anger.

"I remember you." She grazed his cheek with her lips. The stubble of his jawline tickled, but in a good way, so she did it again.

"I miss you," she murmured, feeling secure enough to admit the truth only because he was tied up and—in theory, anyway—at her mercy.

She nipped the lobe of his ear with her teeth and was rewarded with a small, low groan. Her lips traveled down the side of his neck, pressing soft, languid kisses along the way. Every once in a while, she let her tongue flick out to taste and dampen his skin.

She'd always loved the way he tasted—salty and masculine, like a man who worked hard and played hard, and wore both scents as his own personal fragrance. High-priced colognes and aftershaves had nothing on *Eau de Gage*.

When she reached his shoulder, she gave the muscle there a tiny love bite through the material of his shirt, almost as though she were attempting to French kiss the dragon itself. A shiver of excitement swept through her at the mental image before she moved on to outline the sharp edge of his collarbone, the base of his throat, and down to the positively mouthwatering twin rises of his pectorals.

His nipples were tight little beads at the centers of perfectly round brown areolas. Sexy circles over a mostly smooth, broad chest that tapered to a flat, narrow stomach.

Sliding her hands down the insides of his arms, she toyed with the piercing tips, first rolling them beneath the pads of her thumbs, then the palms of her hands. Letting her fingers wander off to explore other parts of his chest, she replaced them with her mouth. Kissing, licking, biting lightly before using her tongue again to wash away any possible sting.

His breaths were coming in shorter pants now, his body stirring under her sensual ministrations. Beneath her breasts, his belly went concave as his diaphragm tightened.

Her own nipples pebbled at the knowledge that she was turning him on. He might not have expected to land in her bed, but he was going to enjoy himself—of that she had no doubt.

She kissed her way down his sternum, her breath whispering over the light streak of hair that led from his navel to his groin. His penis was fully erect now, responding to her every touch and caress, and hungry to be freed from the confinement of his briefs—an appeal she was more than happy to satisfy.

Pushing them down to join the tangle of denim near his ankles, she shifted to straddle his knees rather than his thighs. It was a shame he was on his back and had to stay that way for the duration because she would have liked to see his rear end, maybe give it a squeeze or take a nice, ripe bite out of it the way she used to.

He'd always had a world-class butt. The kind you could bounce quarters off of—something she knew as fact because she'd tried it a time or two while they were married. He'd put up a fight, acted embarrassed by her fascination with his backside, but had eventually given in.

Forever after, when he was feeling particularly frisky, he'd hand her a quarter and ask if she wanted to put it to good use. Only once, when she'd been mad at him and he'd been arrogantly pressing his luck to begin with, had she threatened to do more with the coin than simply bounce it off his tight ass.

Then again, the view from the front wasn't exactly a scene out of *Fright Night*. There were no two ways about it—Gage Marshall was a god. An Adonis in blue jeans and tight black tees. Or in this case, nothing but his birthday suit, a few gorgeous tattoos, and the long, feathery restraints wound around his wrists and ankles.

She took in all of that, every plane and angle, every bulge of muscle and inch of sun-bronzed skin. It was ridiculous for her to be nervous about making love to him considering how many times she'd been with him in the past, but that didn't keep cocoons of anxiety from unfurling low in her belly.

Maybe it had been too long.

Maybe she'd been missing and wanting him all this time more than even she had realized.

That wasn't something she particularly wanted to contemplate at the moment, however. It was too deep, too raw, and if she hadn't figured out her feelings for him in the last year and a half they'd been divorced or the months before when she'd been torn over whether to file or not, then she wasn't likely to have some amazing epiphany in the next five minutes.

So she pushed that aside, tamped it down and buried it away once again, bringing her attention back to the matter at hand. And speaking of hands . . .

She gently cupped his testicles, cradling them in her palm, exploring their soft contours. Gage was already tense, his long frame rigid with anticipation. But if possible, he stiffened even more, every muscle drawing tight beneath her touch.

His cock twitched and she used her other hand to stroke it from base to tip and back again. She heard him suck in a breath and lifted her head to find him watching her through dark, heavy-lidded eyes. Neither of them said a word.

Holding his gaze, she lowered her mouth and took him inside. His teeth clicked together and the tendons of his throat jutted out in stark relief. Between her lips, he burned, he throbbed, and she tasted the evidence of his arousal against her tongue.

She would have liked to stay there, licking, sucking, driving him crazy and doing her best to make him come in her mouth. But she wasn't here for sexual pleasure. Or not *only* sexual pleasure.

Giving him a blow job, as enjoyable as it might be for both of them, wasn't going to get her any closer to her goal. And there was no time—or sperm—to waste.

With a last long, slow swirl of her tongue, she released him and rose, shifting so that she hovered just above his upward-pointing erection.

She didn't have to check her own readiness; she was

already wet, almost embarrassingly so. Wrapping her fingers around the base of his erection, she centered the large, plum-shaped head at her opening and slowly lowered herself down his entire length.

He was big, filling her completely, and she bit her lip while her body stretched to accommodate him. It didn't hurt exactly, but she'd been celibate for so long that there was a modicum of discomfort, a moment when she needed to remind herself to relax and let him in.

He'd had that effect on her the first couple of times they'd been together, too, she remembered. It had taken a while for her to get used to the sensation of having him inside her, but she'd liked it. He'd hit her in all the right spots, the same as he was doing now.

"You don't want me to stop, do you?" she asked, her voice shaky and breathless and not much louder than a whisper.

She rose up on her knees, letting him slide partially free. The friction alone sent the air stuttering from her lungs and she nearly whimpered. Gage, she was satisfied to notice, curled his fingers into fists, pulling slightly at the ties that held his wrists.

"Untie me," he rasped.

Her hair bounced when she shook her head. Gliding back down, her internal muscles squeezing and thrumming around him, she barely managed to say, "I like it this way. And you do, too. I can tell."

She continued to move on him. Small, almost imperceptible motions that brought her up and down, forward and back, side to side. She could feel him flexing beneath her, bucking in time with her movements.

Given his strength and bulk, Jenna had no doubt that if he really, truly wanted to break free, he could. She'd wrapped the feathery boas around his ankles and wrists several times, making them as strong as she could without cutting of his circulation, but they were still just strips of yarn, and he was six-feet-three-inches, two-hundred-plus-pounds of pure muscle.

He was fighting the urge, though, she could see it in his eyes. Whatever he thought of her little game and the tricks it had taken to get him here, he was more interested in letting her finish what she'd started.

Thank goodness, because at this point, she just might cry herself if he left her.

Pressing her mouth to his, she kissed him, startled when he kissed her back.

What this man could do to her without the use of his hands she suspected other men couldn't do with a dozen.

When their mouths parted, they were both out of breath, and she was pretty sure she knew what his answer was going to be. She asked anyway, her lips continuing to brush against his.

"Do you want me to stop, Gage? Or do you want me to keep doing what I'm doing? Riding you. Fucking you."

His cock flexed inside her, showing its approval of both her language and her continued gyrations on his lap.

For the most part, she was a good girl. Not quite Pollyanna, but close. She swore only occasionally in the presence of close acquaintances and was exceptionally careful of her word choices when it came to working with her young students.

But sex with Gage didn't count. With him, she'd always been a little wild and a lot uninhibited. He liked it when she talked dirty . . . and she liked it because of the response it evoked in him.

A muscle ticced in his jaw. His molars ground together. He continued to clench and unclench his fists where they were bound above him. When he spoke, his voice was sandpaper rough, but firm, and she knew there would be no turning back.

"Don't stop," he grated. His body echoed his sentiments, hips lifting to spur her on.

She smiled and kissed him again, letting her breasts rub seductively along his chest, and purposely gave him a small Kegel exercise that made him groan.

"Good answer," she murmured before pushing herself up on his chest and into a sitting position.

Knees locked tight on either side of his thighs, she slowly began to angle her hips so that she moved forward and back on his hard length at the same time she rose and fell just slightly.

"And it feels even better," she told him. Her hands were still flat at his waist, and she used them for leverage as she increased the speed of her movements. Just a bit. Just enough to add to the friction.

Gage licked his lips and swallowed, Adam's apple bobbing like a fishing lure in his throat.

"I forgot how big you are. How you fill me like no one else ever could."

His pelvis rose up at the same time hers came down and she gasped, biting her bottom lip to keep from crying out.

"And how right it feels."

Her eyes slid closed as sensations continued to swamp her. Oh, how she'd like to believe she was in control. That she could maintain control no matter what.

But she wasn't a fool, and she couldn't lie to herself, even if she tried.

With Gage, she was never in control. Not entirely. Not when he touched her, kissed her, moved inside of her.

"I forgot how good this feels. How good *you* feel."

He gave a low grunt and thrust his hips upward in a quick, stabbing motion as high as he could go. "Then for Christ's sake, speed it up," he growled.

A flare of heat burst low in her belly and spread out to every extremity. She wished he would do that again but was afraid if he did, it would all be over too soon.

He hadn't been inside her for five full minutes yet, but already she was teetering on the edge. Completion was right there, within reach, and she could get there in a blink if she put her mind to it.

But then it would be done, and she'd really rather make it last. Maybe not all night . . . after all, she was kind of hoping for an encore later, if he was up to it and the boas held . . . but something that lasted more than five or ten minutes would be nice. If only to give her a longer memory to carry with her through the rest of her life.

"You don't want to rush, do you?" Without even trying, she sounded as though she were channeling Marilyn Monroe.

Gage's voice, however, was anything but soft, anything but yielding. "I want you to finish what you started. Finish what you dragged me in here and tied me up to do."

A spurt of guilt thumped through her heart and caused it to skip a beat. "Please don't be angry," she said. Later he would be furious and demand answers, but until then . . .

Trailing her hands from his waist, she let them slide along her own thighs, then inside to lightly skim the triangle of dark curls surrounding him, over her belly and up to her breasts. They weren't large, but they were perky and Gage had always claimed to find them fascinating.

He'd also liked to watch her touch herself, and she did so now, feeling his gaze lock on her like a heat-seeking missile. On her fingers where they cupped the small globes. On her thumbs as they coasted over her hard, raspberry nipples, making them pucker even more.

His chest rose and fell with his sharp, shallow breaths, and he was struggling beneath her now. Not to get free, but to get her to move, to drive deeper, to bring them both to a fast, fiery climax.

Bringing her right hand to her mouth, she licked the pads of her thumb and forefinger, then returned them to the same nipple to roll it between the damp digits. "Tell me what you want," she ordered, her voice little more than a lacy wisp of breath. "Tell me what you want me to do."

Knit 5

Gage knew exactly what he wanted. He wanted Jenna to untie his hands and let him touch her. Let him cup those delectable tits himself and lean up to take a ripe, pebbled tip into his mouth. Let him grip her hips while she rode him, helping to set the pace, moving her just the way he needed to bring them both to a crashing, violent climax.

He didn't know what the hell was going on here, but one thing was for sure—a band of South American guerrillas armed to the teeth and threatening unspeakable torture couldn't get him to call a halt to the delectable pleasures Jenna's body was offering right this second.

She shifted slightly and his balls tightened. He locked his jaw and dug his heels into the mattress to keep from coming off the bed.

Later, he'd spank her ass—and not in the way he'd like to at the moment, which would heighten the sexual anticipation already bouncing off the walls.

But for now, he had every intention of taking her up on her erotic invitation.

"Touch yourself," he rasped.

Her eyes sparkled and her mouth turned up in a self-satisfied grin, making her look for all the world like a devilish little pixie up to no good.

"But I am touching myself," she replied, tugging at her nipples as she continued to bounce lightly on his lap, just enough to make him sweat through his teeth.

Air puffed from his lungs in short, heavy bursts and every muscle in his body strained toward her. The ties at his wrists and ankles chafed his skin where he'd struggled against them, because he couldn't *not* move. He couldn't *not* pull at the restraints that kept him from being able to touch his ex-wife the way he wanted to. *Needed* to, dammit.

His throat went desert dry as he studied her, took her in from the top of her head to her knees braced on the bed and straddling him.

Shit, she was beautiful. She always had been.

From the first moment he saw her, he'd been half in love and all in lust with her. He'd been a beat cop then, out on a routine patrol. Her car had been pulled to the side of the road with a flat.

She'd been in the process of calling Triple A, but that wouldn't have given him an excuse to spend a little time with her, so he'd offered to change the tire himself. He'd ruined his uniform and hadn't been as smooth in the process as he might have liked, but it did the trick.

Jenna chatted with him the entire time, and he'd quickly learned that she was a grade-school teacher on the way to pick up supplies for an end-of-the-year pizza party she'd promised her students as a reward for a district-wide recycling campaign she'd instituted and they'd helped to spearhead. It had also given him the perfect opportunity to show his interest in the youth of America . . . an interest she'd jumped on, soon asking if he might be willing to talk to her class the following school year.

Oh, yeah, he'd been willing. He wasn't a big fan of public speaking, especially to a room full of kids who were either picking their noses in boredom or making faces in an attempt to distract him. But for the chance to impress her and to see her again, he'd have eaten live African cockroaches.

By the time he'd finished replacing her tire, he had her phone number and a date for lunch the next week so they could "discuss topics for his talk with her classroom."

They'd ended up seeing each other a lot more than just that once throughout the summer. He'd discovered that she liked to knit and had mentioned the knitting group he knew Grace and Ronnie attended, which was how the three women had become such close friends.

And when the school year started, he almost spent more time talking to her class than he did on duty. By the time Jenna took the lid off the cookie jar and let him into her pants, he'd lectured her group of third-graders on everything from playground safety to saying no to drugs.

They'd also heard her call him by his given name so often that he became "Officer Gage" and started to get recognized by the eight-year-olds on the street and introduced to their parents. Many times as "the police officer who kisses Miss Langan when he doesn't think we're watching."

It had all been worth it, though. More than worth it. Before the end of the following school year, Gage had known he wanted to spend the rest of his life with Jenna and had popped the question.

And from that, they'd come to this.

No matter how he cut it, this *was* the good stuff, but it wasn't happily married good stuff. It wasn't *She's mine and no other man will ever put his hands on her unless he wants to lose them* good stuff.

Even as long as he'd had to get over that, it still pissed him off, but he was willing to suspend his annoyance. Just for tonight. Just for a while.

After that, all bets were off.

"Put your hand between your legs," he ordered, feeling his temperature continue to rise at the sight of her fondling her breasts.

She continued to wear the cat-that-ate-the-canary smile that turned his insides all hot and molten.

"Like this?"

With deliberate slowness, she let the fingers of one hand fall away from her nipple and trail down her front, over her midriff, around her navel, and into the springy black curls at the apex of her thighs. When she got there, she stopped, simply letting her hand rest there, not moving.

"Now what, Gage? What do you want me to do now?"

"You know what," he ground from between tightly clenched teeth.

She shook her head, sending the short wisps of her dark hair dancing. "I don't. You have to tell me."

His heart beat against his ribcage like a battering ram, and the muscles in his shoulders and forearms bunched with the effort not to bust the bedframe to get loose.

"Touch yourself, dammit. Slide your fingers between your folds and touch your clit."

She did as he said, and when she moaned, closing her eyes and throwing back her head, he just about came. He was hard as a spike, hard enough to pound through concrete, he was sure.

"Mmm, that feels good," she told him as though she were commenting on the taste of a particularly ripe strawberry. And then she raised her head again to look at him. "Now what?"

"Goddammit, Jenna, you know what," he ground out.

One corner of her mouth twitched with cocky, confident amusement. "I do," she admitted, "but I'd rather hear you say it. Tell me what to do now that I'm touching my clit. Tell me what to do to make you come."

Jesus. She didn't have to do much more than just sit there on his cock, wearing that angel-fallen-from-Heaven grin, and talking about things that would make a saint kick in a stained-glass window.

Panting, writhing beneath her, he said, "Move your fingers. Stroke your clit and make yourself hot."

"You make me hot," she murmured, but she did as he asked. While one hand continued to toy with her breasts, she used two fingers from the other to slide around between her folds.

She was wet, the evidence of her arousal glistening on her fingertips and melting around him from where she clasped him tight inside her body. And she used that moisture to ease her motions, to slick the tiny bud that caused her breath to catch and a pale pink flush to climb over her chest and throat.

"Faster," he commanded. "And move your hips. Ride me like you promised."

He bent his knees as far as he could, given the restraints threatening to pull his joints from their sockets. It didn't do much, but it gave him a small amount of leverage to cushion her soft buttocks and aid the upward thrust of his hips.

Blood thrummed through his veins, white-hot and on the verge of overflowing while he took in the sway of her breasts, the bounce of her slim frame, and the increased speed of her hand pressed between their two bodies as she fingered herself.

"God, yes," he rasped, not caring that he was completely at her mercy and fading fast. "Can you feel it?" he asked, knowing she could, reading the signs clearly on her face and in the way she ground down on him, harder and faster with each passing second. "Can you feel me inside you, ready to burst?"

And, God, was he. His balls were tight, his cock swelling with approaching orgasm.

"Gage," Jenna panted. Her eyes were open now, wide, bright, and focused directly on him. "Yes. Please. Come with me, Gage. Come with me now."

And she went, toppling over the edge with a sudden cry of pleasure that reached into his gut and wrapped around his soul. Her slick inner walls gripped and released, gripped and released, and he couldn't hold back any longer. Didn't even want to try.

With his own shout of completion, he stiffened and poured himself into her. Wave after wave of pure ecstasy washed through him, through both of them, until he was finished.

Sated. Done for. Wiped out. A five-alarm fire burning the old farm house down around his ears couldn't have made him budge.

And from the looks of it, Jenna felt much the same. Collapsed across his chest, her cheek fell into the crook of his shoulder while her ragged breaths echoed in his ear.

If his arms were free, he'd wrap them around her, hold her close, but all he could do was turn his head and press a soft kiss against her crown.

Deep down, he was still pissed about what she'd done to get him here, but damned if he had the energy right now to get to the bottom of it. Later, he'd make her untie these restraints and give him some answers.

But for now, it felt too good to have her lying on top of him, covering him . . . trusting him again, at least for a short while.

When the phone rang at eight a.m., Grace Fisher groaned, rolled over, and stuffed her pillow over her head in an attempt to drown out the hideous jangle that ripped through her brain like a chainsaw. After a full sixty seconds, blessed silence reigned once more, but before she could sigh with relief, the ringing began again.

"Dammit," she muttered, tossing the pillow aside and rolling in the other direction until she could grab the handset from the nightstand.

Contrary to popular belief, she was not always in a good mood and she most certainly did not wake up chipper. Especially not after a long Girls' Night of eating, drinking, and making mischief.

Punching the talk button, she snapped, "What?"

"Please tell me we didn't do what I think we did," Ronnie said by way of response.

Grace rubbed her eyes and pushed into a sitting

position, propping herself against the headboard while she struggled to shake off the last remnants of sleep.

"That depends. Did we scarf enough Mexican food to resurrect the Hindenburg and drink until we passed out?"

"We always do that," Ronnie replied, sounding somewhat short-tempered herself. "I'm talking about abducting Gage and holding him against his will."

For a minute, Grace nearly scoffed. What a ridiculous idea. Like anyone could abduct six-foot-three, two-hundred-plus-pound Gage Marshall, who loosely resembled a less green, less pissed-off Incredible Hulk.

But the more she thought about it, the more flashbacks started to spiral through her head.

Downing margaritas and enchiladas and laughing with her two closest friends.

Hugging Jenna when she got depressed about her broken marriage and lack of a man or children in her life.

Crushing tiny white pills and spilling them into a bottle of beer.

Hiding outside in the shadows with Ronnie and then hiking down a dark gravel road until her cell phone got enough reception to call a cab.

"Oh, my God," she breathed. Reality struck with the intensity of a lightning bolt, shocking her to the soles of her feet. She sat up, poker-straight, clutching the phone even tighter. "Oh, my God."

"No kidding," Ronnie muttered. "And it was your idea. If we go to prison, I'll expect you to protect me and claim me as your girlfriend before any Big Bad Berthas start eyeing me like a nice, juicy steak."

"Oh, my God," Grace said again, because it was the

only thing she could think of beyond an unending shriek of unadulterated panic.

"Welcome to my world. And if we're freaking out, think what Jenna must be going through."

At the reminder of their other friend, the one they'd left alone with the Incredible Hulk, Grace shot off the bed and began to pace.

"Oh. My. *God*. We have to get back there. We have to rescue her before Gage gets loose and kills her, then comes after us."

Because though Jenna's ex wasn't normally a monster of giant green proportions, Grace was pretty sure he'd be frothing at the mouth and tearing the house apart board by board when he woke up and discovered himself tied spread-eagled to the bed.

"Let's try calling her first," Ronnie said in a voice of reason. The only one currently occupying the phone line.

Grace's viewers all thought she had it so together. To them, she was a little Jackie O, a little Oprah, a little Martha Stewart, and maybe even a little Mother Theresa all rolled together.

Ha! She wondered how they would react when she was hauled away in shackles and a traffic-cone orange jumpsuit. And no belt, because the cops would worry she might commit suicide.

Rightfully so. She was thinking about going to the bathroom and drinking a bottle of drain cleaner right now just to save the state the expense of her trial and execution.

"What if the phone wakes him?" Grace asked. To her, that seemed a bit too much like poking a bear with a stick.

"We'll call Jenna's cell. She keeps it in her purse, and her purse was on the dining room table when we left. If he's still tied to the bed, he won't hear it—or at the very least, it won't ring loudly enough to bother him."

"What if *she* doesn't hear it?"

"That might mean Jenna and Gage are still snuggled up in post-coital bliss and we shouldn't be bothering them one way or the other."

"Or maybe it will mean he broke free, went into a rage, and chopped her up into tiny pieces that he's even now dropping to the bottom of a deep, dark well."

"Nice visual, Little Miss Sunshine." Ronnie made a disgusted noise low in her throat. "Just call her on her cell."

"Why do I have to call?" Grace yelped.

"Because this whole mess started with one of your *brilliant* ideas." She drew "brilliant" into three or four syllables and made it sound like a dirty word.

Grace rolled her eyes. For the most part, her ideas *were* brilliant and *did* tend to work out.

So she'd had a bad night—sue her.

"Fine. I'll call you back when I know something."

After hanging up with Ronnie, she lowered herself to the edge of the bed and dialed Jenna's cell phone. As her friend's classical ringback played in the background, Grace prayed that everything had turned out fine.

She prayed Gage was still unconscious.

She prayed Jenna had gotten herself knocked up sometime around midnight and was now safely back at her own apartment in the city, leaving Gage in the country to chew through his bonds alone.

Lifting her head, she caught a glimpse of herself in the wide mirror above the bureau.

And she prayed the authorities wouldn't come for her until she'd had a chance to fix her hair and makeup. She looked like something the cat had dragged in, then batted around for a few hours, and it wouldn't do for her viewing public to see her hauled off to prison in such a sorry condition.

Gage was in the middle of another helluva erotic dream. This time, though, the swim toward consciousness went faster and reality dawned much sooner.

It wasn't a dream—or not entirely.

He was in bed with Jenna. *Tied* to a bed in her aunt's farmhouse.

As soon as he remembered that, he came wide awake, automatically yanking at his bonds.

Shit, what was *with* her tonight?

She was still on top of him, he was still lodged firmly inside of her, and she'd once again managed to work him into a bit of a lather before he was even fully awake.

Tamping down on his desire, he locked his jaw. "Untie me, Jenna," he told her in a voice that brooked no argument. "I mean it this time."

She shook her head, determination etched in the flat line of her lips and the downward arch of her brows. "Not until I've gotten my fill. Come on, Gage," she wheedled, her expression lightening a few degrees. "Be a sport. Let me have some fun."

Fun, my ass. She'd never been interested in this kind of fun while they'd been married, and he sure as hell didn't believe she'd developed a fondness for Bondage for Beginners since their divorce.

"Untie me and I'll show you fun. I'll show you all kinds of fun."

The last round had been nice. More than nice—it had just about blown the top of his head clean off. But if she wanted a night of adventurous sex with the ex, he could show her more creative positions than just "Ride 'em, Cowgirl."

He wanted her on her back, on her knees, bent over the dresser . . .

"I like things just the way they are. It makes me feel sexy."

She gave a little swirl of her hips and he sucked in a breath, scrambling for statistics from the Rockets' last season to keep from shooting off the bed—in more ways than one.

"Besides, I let you tie me up once, remember?"

He hadn't until she mentioned it, but now he did, and no amount of thinking about hockey or mentally reciting game scores was going to put a halt to the throbbing of his dick.

"Of course, you didn't really *tie* me to the bed, did you?" She spoke in a low, cajoling tone, leaning down to skim her lips along his chin and cheek. "You cuffed me with those cold, heavy metal handcuffs you carry around all day at work. And you know what? I liked that, too."

As hard as he fought it, he couldn't hold back the groan that rolled up from his solar plexus.

"Do you think about that, Gage? Do you think about what we did that night every time you pull out your cuffs? Every time you slap them around someone else's wrists?"

His body bucked beneath her. Fuck, yes, he thought

about it. Nightly, while he tossed and turned and tried to fall asleep without her in bed beside him. It was often the leading fantasy that played through his head when he needed to jack off just to find a little satisfaction and rid himself of the frustrations of not having her near.

But this was better than fantasy, wasn't it? At least for the most part.

Oh, if he had his hands free, he'd have flipped her over by now—onto her back or maybe her stomach. He'd have her legs hooked into the crooks of his elbows and be fucking her until her eyes rolled back in her head. But beggars couldn't be choosers, and he was damn close to getting ready to beg.

She rode him expertly, moving against his desperate motions rather than with them so that the friction between their two bodies grew and sparked like fresh-lit kindling.

"I'm going to remember tonight every time I wrap one of those boas around my neck. Every time I see them, every time I feel them brushing along my skin, I'm going to think of you, think about you filling me and driving me to orgasm over and over."

She kissed her way across his face and upper chest, but what she was doing with her mouth was nothing compared to the words pouring out of it.

"If I'm alone, I'll probably get so turned on that I'll have to go to my room, get undressed, and use my hands to satisfy myself."

The image of her doing just that, of what she'd done earlier in the evening to heighten her pleasure while she rode his cock, flashed through his brain and put every cell of his being on red alert.

"If I'm not alone, I'll just have to hope no one notices how flushed I'm getting or suspects how damp my panties are."

His nostrils flared and if he wasn't careful, he'd end up grinding his molars to dust.

Her tongue outlined the shell of his ear, sending tremors down his spine. Her hands followed the path of his long arms until her fingers dusted the feathery strands of the knitted yarn binding his wrists.

"And every time you see me wearing one of these, you'll know exactly what I'm thinking about. You'll think about it, too, and we'll both be back here, teetering on the edge of bliss. Unless you want me to stop," she added.

Her breath skated across the back of his neck, raising gooseflesh, while her nipples dragged sharply along his chest.

Yeah, he wanted her to stop. About as much as he wanted to contract a flesh-eating disease on his pork and beans.

"When I get out of this," he growled, "I'm going to turn you over my knee and blister your behind."

Pushing vertical, she stared down at him with one brow arched over a moss-green eye. "You know I'm not into the 'spank me, Daddy' punishment thing, but if you want to look at my ass . . ."

With that, she lifted off of him and swung around so that she faced the other direction. Glancing back over her shoulder, she shot him a grin and grabbed him by the root.

Air hissed through his teeth at the harsh treatment. Not that he was complaining. She wasn't really being rough enough to hurt him, but he was already so hard and so sensitive that even the lightest brush of her fingers threatened to make him go off like a rocket.

"You used to like it this way, too," she said before repositioning herself and driving herself back down onto his burgeoning erection.

"Christ on a cracker!"

His body bowed, driving his heels and skull into the mattress. She stiffened on him as the motion sent him thrusting deeper inside her, but ended on a sigh.

He was panting now, hanging on by a thread, not sure whether to pray she'd slow down or beg her to finish him off.

"Since when did you add torture to your repertoire?"

Her short black hair danced at her nape when she shook her head. "This isn't torture," she replied.

Easy for her to say. She didn't have a hot, wet woman lodged on her cock, clasping him like a vise.

"*This*," she murmured softly, "is torture."

Her slim, smooth back blocked his vision, but a foot-thick wall of concrete couldn't have kept him from feeling her very special brand of torment as she reached down to cup his nuts.

She palmed them, but no matter how gentle the touch, the sensation went straight to his hypothalamus, sending his nerves screaming. Screaming, thudding, bucking for release.

The side of her thumb stretched to the tight flap of skin connecting his testicles to the base of his dick and began to caress, and he knew he was a goner.

"Move, Jenna," he bit out, the words laced with as much animal lust as he'd ever heard in his own voice. "Move now and bring yourself off, or I'm going over without you."

He'd always been one to take care of a woman's fulfillment—especially this woman's—before his own, but this time he didn't have a choice. Try as he might to fight it, he was about to come, and she was on her own.

Instead of letting go, she continued what she was doing, the nails of her other hand digging into his thigh as her hips sped up. She lifted and fell, slid forward and back, the soft globes of her ass bouncing against his abdomen. The heavy beats of her breathing filled the room, and all the while she continued to fondle him.

His balls tightened and shrank in her hand, and pressure built. He thrust as hard and fast as he could from his prone position, wanting to fill her, go deep, give her a portion of the satisfaction she was giving him.

And then it was too late. The boas cut into his flesh as his entire body jerked, strained, convulsed . . . and emptied itself in a shower of pleasure so intense, he thought he might black out.

Through his haze of completion, he heard Jenna's mewling cries and felt her spasming around him, and knew she'd reached her pinnacle, too.

Purl 6

The next time Gage came awake, it was with a clearer head than before, and his immediate thought was, *Third time's a charm.*

He fully expected to open his eyes and find Jenna still straddled across his lap, still trying to stir his poor, abused willy to porn-star proportions, still trying—and succeeding—to ride him hard and put him up wet.

And this time, God help her, he *would* get loose and he *would* exact his revenge. He was downright looking forward to it.

But when he opened his eyes, the room was empty. Well, except for his bare-naked ass strapped to the four corners of the bedframe.

The sheets were a tangled mess beneath him and trailing onto the floor. A thin strip of sunlight shone through the partially open blind on the window behind him, bringing out the individual colors of the thin, worn rug covering the floor—and his clothes, strewn about in piles where Jenna had tossed them after stripping him down to his birthday suit.

His abductor, however, was nowhere in sight.

So she planned to use him for her own selfish sexual gratification and then take off, did she?

A knot of annoyance tightened in his stomach. He didn't much appreciate being the object of her *wham, bam, thank you, man* mentality.

He didn't much appreciate still being roped up like a calf during branding season, either.

Craning his neck, he took in the ties at his wrists. He'd done more than his fair share of yanking last night, and all he'd managed to do was pull the boas tighter. So he wouldn't waste any more time with that.

Instead, he studied his bonds, lingering until he found what he thought might be an end piece. From the looks of it, the lengths of tasseled yarn weren't so much knotted as wound around his wrists and the bedposts, then tied into tight bows.

Twisting his body, arm, and hand—and not all in the same direction—he got two fingers around one of the ends and slowly began to tug.

Slowly.

Slowly.

The end started to move. Mere centimeters at first, but it was coming.

He kept at it, making sure he didn't rush and lose his grip or end up with tighter bindings than he'd started with. When the first boa loosened and fell from around his wrist, he let his head fall back on the pillow and bit back a shout of success.

Lungs burning from lack of oxygen while he'd held his breath in concentration, he rolled to his other side and yanked the end of that boa until his right wrist sprang free. A second later, his feet were undone and he was off the bed, grabbing for his clothes.

Hopping on one leg and then the other, he jumped into his pants on his way to the door and was tugging his plain black T-shirt over his chest as he hit the hall.

Feet bare and fly still open, he cocked his head to listen for sounds of Jenna. No telling where she was in this big old house, and he didn't want her springing any more surprises on him. If anything, he intended to spring one or two on her.

When he didn't hear anything on the second floor, he headed for the stairs, zipping up as he took the steps as quietly as possible one at a time.

As he reached the bottom, he heard someone talking and knew it was Jenna. Her voice was low and intense, coming from around the corner.

Careful not to make a sound, he stopped on the last step and leaned a shoulder against the wall. She was close, probably only a few feet away, even though he couldn't see her.

He pictured her standing near the dining room table, speaking in hushed tones to . . . someone. Apparently on the phone, because he hadn't heard a second voice even though there were plenty of pauses long enough for someone else to fill.

"Yes, I'm sure," she insisted just above a whisper.

He imagined she was keeping her voice low in hopes of not waking him. Little did she know . . .

"Ohmigod, it was amazing. I can't thank you two enough for all your help."

Silence. Though he suspected—hell, he knew—she was talking to either Ronnie or Grace.

"No, he won't," she went on matter-of-factly. "He'll be furious. I'm kind of hoping I can cut him loose while he's still asleep and then run off to hide until the coast is clear."

And now he was sure about something else—she was talking to one of her friends about *him*. About tying him up and having her wicked way with him. Over and over again.

"But hopefully the deed is done and it won't matter how angry he is with me."

Hmph. She should be so lucky. He didn't appreciate being manipulated, no matter what the reason. Not when she could have just *asked* him to come over and help her scratch her itch.

That, he thought, really pissed him off . . .

Wait. What deed?

Wasn't having sex with him last night "the deed"?

No, that couldn't be right because she'd said "hopefully the deed was done" and that deed was definitely done. It had been done hard and fast and quite thoroughly. Twice.

So what else could she have hoped to accomplish with her little domination-and-submission routine?

"I don't know."

Her voice dropped, and he imagined her chewing the corner of her lower lip the way she always did when she was nervous.

"Don't those over-the-counter tests say you have to wait seven to ten days or something?"

Gage's brows knit. Test? What kind of test took seven to ten days?

Jenna sighed. "Start over, I guess. Start dating again, maybe visit one of those icky sperm banks. But I don't want to think about any of that. I want to stay positive and hope the plan worked. If it does, Gage will kill me when he finds out, but I don't think I care."

The last of her words swirled around him, going in one ear and out the other because his internal organs had all stopped functioning at *sperm banks.*

Son of a bitch.

She hadn't drugged him and tied him down just to have fabulous, forbidden sex with her ex. She'd drugged him and tied him down to get pregnant.

Son of a bitch! Fucking son of a goddamn bitch.

The one thing she *knew* he'd never agree to. The biggest cinder block in the wall that had gone up between them and eventually destroyed their marriage.

Fists clenching and unclenching at his sides, he forced himself to breathe evenly and remain perfectly still. If he moved, it would be to whip around the corner, snatch the phone out of her hand, and shake her until her teeth rattled or worse.

It was the "worse" that kept him rooted to the spot. Because he was afraid if he saw her right now, if he laid a finger on her, he might do serious bodily harm. And no matter how furious he was with her—even now, when she'd betrayed his trust and used his own weak, disloyal flesh against him—he would never truly want to hurt her.

But damn, it was tempting. His jaw ached from holding back a roar of outrage.

Just when he thought his head might explode from the pressure building behind his eyes, Jenna's voice intruded again.

"Yes, I'm sure. If I need anything, I'll call." A beat passed. "I think that's a great idea. I'm sure they'd love to see you, and then I won't be the only one who got lucky this weekend."

Her tinkling laughter filled the room and spilled up the stairwell. Normally, he loved to hear her happy. She had one of those laughs that poured over him like warm honey and burrowed under his skin.

This morning, though, it grated, reminding him that she and her friends had concocted a plan to knock him out and knock *her* up.

She said good-bye and he heard a small beep as she disconnected. He braced himself, expecting her to round the corner and run smack into him, but instead her footsteps moved in the opposite direction, toward the kitchen.

And she was humming. Humming, dammit, happy as a lark at the little scheme she and her friends had concocted and managed to pull off—brilliantly.

God, he felt like a schmuck.

Oh, sure, I'll come over and fix your dripping sink. Duh.

Gee, thanks for the cold beer, it really hits the spot. Der.

You want to fuck like bunnies even though we've been divorced for more than a year? Awesome!

Idiot, idiot, idiot!

A fresh wave of anger hit and he pushed away from the wall, intent on finally facing her and letting her have it. He wouldn't bruise her, he wouldn't shake her, he wouldn't toss her through an upstairs window.

But he couldn't promise not to shout the rafters down around her ears.

Walking softly, he was careful not to alert her to his presence. She was in the kitchen now, still humming as she moved around, running water for coffee, filling a filter with grounds.

He didn't let himself notice the snug fit of her cut-off denim shorts or the long, slim legs they left bare. The bright red tips of her toes or the sleeveless white top tied just beneath her breasts to expose her taut midriff.

He didn't want to see any of that or think about the fact that she looked almost as good in clothes as she did out of them.

Oh, no, not today. He was not going to let his attraction to her get in the way of his fury over her betrayal.

She had her back to him, and it was almost too easy to sneak up on her. When she turned, he was less than a foot away. Her eyes went wide, she shrieked in surprise, and the coffee pot she was holding slipped from her fingers, smashing to the floor in a shower of water and glass.

Gage cursed. He'd meant to intimidate her . . . and yeah, maybe scare her a bit . . . but he didn't want her to hurt herself.

Cupping his wide hands under her elbows, he lifted her straight up off the floor and swung her around, well out of range of the dangerous mess. He set her down on the other side of the kitchen doorway and backed her into the dining room.

Her cheeks were flushed as she gaped at him, her pupils mottled pinpoints of astonishment and wariness. She opened her mouth, but the only sound she emitted was a low, strangled hiss.

"What's the matter, sweetheart, cat got your tongue? Or maybe you're just braver when you've got me trussed up like a Christmas turkey to your bedframe."

She swallowed, tongue darting out to wet her lips. "How did you get untied?"

"What?" he asked, his tone sharp. "Did you think you could keep me trapped up there forever? Were you going to fuck me until I was all used up, or just until you were sure you were pregnant?"

If possible, Jenna's already pale porcelain skin turned even whiter.

"How did you . . . ?"

Her eyes darted toward the hidden stairwell and then to her open handbag, where her cell phone rested on top of everything else she carted around on a daily basis.

"Did you think I wouldn't find out?" he charged. Despite his earlier determination not to rattle the daylights out of her, his teeth clicked together and he gave her a tiny shake. "That I wouldn't stop and do the math when your belly started filling out? That I wouldn't figure out what you'd done? That you'd used me, lied to me, forced me into fatherhood when you know that's the *last thing* I want."

Where a second ago her expression was cautious and wan, a flare of color now bloomed high on her cheekbones. She yanked her elbow out of his grip and took a step back, putting what she apparently considered a safe distance between them.

"Do you want the truth?" she charged, her voice steady and tinged with accusations of her own. "The truth, Gage, is that I wasn't thinking about you. I didn't consider your feelings or wishes. I was thinking about *me*, and what you stole from me, and how I might— *just might*—get it back."

His brow crinkled as he frowned. "What are you

talking about? What the hell did I ever steal from you?"

She rolled her eyes in what he recognized as a time-honored gesture that basically implied men were obtuse idiots and he was their king.

"You took *everything* from me, Gage." The words were spoken softly enough, but carried an elephant's weight of emotion. "I thought we were happy. I thought we were going to be together forever, but you took all of that away from me. You woke up one day and decided you didn't really want a wife or children, and expected the whole world to fall in line accordingly."

It was his turn to roll his eyes. "We've had this discussion before. And it doesn't change the fact that you drugged me and held me against my will."

"No, we haven't *discussed* this before," she argued, crossing her arms beneath her breasts and taking a stance that clearly said she was just getting started. "Because every time I tried to talk to you about it, you clammed up. I begged. I pleaded. I screamed and cried and threw pillows at your head. But your mind was made up, and that was the end of the story, as far as you were concerned. You wouldn't listen to me and refused to understand my point of view."

"I don't want kids, Jenna," he said, standing his ground. "That's not an opinion that's going to be swayed by a passionate, well-orchestrated argument."

"But you did when we got married," she all but shouted at him, rising on her bare tiptoes in an attempt to meet him eye to eye. "We talked about our future. We talked about having babies and growing old together. *You're* the one who changed the rules in the middle of the game and expected me to go along with them."

She paused only long enough to take a breath, uncross her arms, and poke him hard in the center of his chest with an index finger.

"Well, I *do* want kids. I wanted them with you in the picture, but you've decided to be an asshole, so now I have to switch to Plan B and get them some other way."

He watched her, and despite what she thought, he *was* listening. But this was a battle that was never going to end. They could talk, yell, debate, and play Rock-Paper-Scissors until they were blue in the face, but neither of them was ever going to win.

She clearly wanted one thing, and he wanted another. And it wasn't like they disagreed over what color to paint the guest bathroom; this was big-time, life-altering, mega-important stuff.

"And Plan B was tying me down and raping me?"

She reared back as though he'd struck her. "I'm sorry you feel that way about it," she said. "That wasn't my intention, and except for the circumstances, I thought you were as into it as I was."

For a brief moment, guilt stabbed at him. It hadn't been that bad, and they both knew it. In fact, part of what had him so ticked off was the knowledge that even if he'd understood what she was up to at the time, he still wouldn't have stopped. He still wouldn't have fought hard enough to break free and toss her aside.

"So what do we do now, Jenna?" he asked calmly. "Wait to see if I've been strong-armed into fatherhood?"

"No. We don't have to wait for anything. I did this because *I* want a baby. You don't, and I would never force you to be involved in something you didn't willingly sign on for. I won't ask anything of you, Gage," she rushed to reassure him. "If I'm pregnant, I'll raise the child alone. I'll tell people I was artificially inseminated or that it's the result of a one-night stand or something. It won't affect you at all. No matter what, you can go on with your life and pretend last night never happened."

Gage wouldn't have thought it possible to be more furious than he'd been when he'd overheard her conversation with Grace, but that last statement did it. He felt his temperature rising, his lips pulling back from his teeth in a sneer.

Taking the single step that brought them nose-to-nose once again, he leaned in until she was forced to lean back or risk him touching her. As it was, his hot breath bathed her face and feathered through the hair at her temples.

"If you believe that," he hissed, "then you never really knew me at all."

And with that, he spun on his heel, crossed the room to grab his leather jacket, and slammed out the front door.

Knit 7

Ronnie wrinkled up the empty Combos bag and tossed it over her shoulder into the back seat. Then she reached into the console and dug around for a stick of gum.

"Dylan is not going to appreciate it when I show up at his door with dragon breath," she said, as Grace made a right-hand turn into the Marriott parking lot.

"Dylan is going to be so thrilled to see you, he won't care if your breath smells like Charlotte's barn," Grace reassured her with a chuckle. "And if it's that bad, he'll just bend you over the bureau with your face in the other direction."

Even though her cheeks heated at the image her friend's comment created, Ronnie laughed so hard, she nearly swallowed the gum.

"Or here's another novel idea: I could make him wait five seconds while I borrow his toothbrush."

Grace rolled her eyes. "Well, if you wanted to take the logical route, I suppose that would work."

Ronnie still couldn't believe they were doing this. An impromptu road trip hadn't been on her list of things to do over the weekend, but as soon as Grace had called her back to let her know that Jenna was not only alive and well, but crossing all of her fingers and toes that last night's mission had been accomplished, and then suggested they get the hell out of Dodge just in case, Ronnie had suddenly thought it sounded like a stellar idea.

It was one thing to manipulate events and take some liberties with a man's free will when it came to sex, but it was a whole other thing to stick around and wait for The Wrath of Gage to fall upon them.

If he woke up pissed, Ronnie just knew she and Grace were going to be at the top of his list of people to kill. And the man was a redwood. He could snap them in half with his pinky finger, if the notion took him . . . something she would just as soon avoid, if at all possible.

So a road trip for a little out-of-town nookie and temporary witness relocation it was.

The parking lot was packed, but they eventually found a spot about six miles from the main building and pulled in. Both women gathered their purses and small overnight bags, then locked up and made the long trek to the hotel lobby.

Unlike most nearly empty hotel lobbies, this one was packed—and every other person milling about wore a Cleveland Rockets jersey, sweat- or T-shirt, or some other type of hockey paraphernalia. There were even a few giant foam fingers being waved around.

Those who weren't obvious hockey fans were even more obvious puck bunnies, dressed in skintight jeans or short-shorts and tops so snug, one good breath would have their breasts popping out like they were at a La Leche convention.

She probably couldn't spot them as quickly as Grace did, but Ronnie knew a groupie when she saw one. And living with a sports reporter who covered the Rockets almost exclusively meant that she spent her fair share of time at games and practices, and wasn't the least bit surprised by the number of fans hanging out in the hotel lobby praying a player would wander through. Some were hoping for autographs, others pictures. And the bunnies . . . well, they were hoping for the chance to put another notch on their bedposts with some willing player's skate blade.

"Thank God we don't have to bother with going up to the registration desk and asking for room numbers," Grace said as they bypassed the crowd and headed directly for the bank of elevators.

"Yep. It pays to be sleeping with a star goalie and the team's own personal sports reporter," Ronnie quipped in response.

Grace cast a disparaging glance toward the stacked and shellacked bimbettes waiting for a chance to do just that. "Not that you'd ever catch me hanging around like that. I don't care how hot some of the players are, don't those women have *any* self-respect?"

Ronnie followed Grace's gaze just in time to see a groupie with blond hair bleached within an inch of its life lean over . . . and the waistband of her jeans ride down to reveal a bright red thong and a vine-and-roses tramp stamp at the small of her back.

"Good God," Ronnie said, appalled. She blinked rapidly and turned away. "I think I've been struck blind."

Grace chuckled as the elevator dinged and the up arrow turned green. "Do you need me to walk you to

Dylan's room, or do you think you'll be okay?" she asked as they stepped into the car.

"Give me a minute, I think I'll recover."

The elevator dinged again and the door slid open on the twelfth floor. Ronnie patted the buttoned panel and the cool metal frame, feigning visual impairment. "Is this where I get off?" she teased.

Grace put a hand in the center of her back and shoved her playfully into the deserted hallway. "Only if you're lucky," she quipped as the doors slid closed again.

Ronnie stood there for only a second before turning on her heel and heading for room 1218. When she arrived, she raised a hand and knocked hard, doing her best to stifle a grin as she barked out, "Room service!"

She heard shuffling on the other side and pictured Dylan climbing off the bed or sofa and making his way to the door. The locks clicked and the knob turned.

"I didn't call room—"

The door swung wide and he froze in mid-sentence, taking in her seductive pose as she lounged against the jamb.

"Good afternoon, sir," she murmured in her sultriest Kathleen Turner/*Body Heat* impression. "Did you order a little afternoon delight?"

A playful twinkle lit his blue eyes and his mouth curved up in a sexy smile. Warm pleasure burst in her chest and spread outward.

Dylan had only been on the road a week, but Ronnie realized now how very much she'd missed him. For a woman who prided herself on her independence, she sure had adapted quickly to living with a man.

She loved falling asleep at night with him at her side and waking up to him each morning. And when he wasn't there, she missed him. Missed his warmth and his presence and the way the mattress dipped whenever he moved.

If she was the first person up in the morning, she automatically fixed breakfast for him at the same time she fixed her own, and knew that if things were reversed, she could look forward to him doing the same.

She called him to ask if he wanted her to bring something home for dinner, and picked up items at the grocery store that she knew he'd like.

She was, for all intents and purposes, silly in love. And to add insult to injury, she wasn't even trying to fight it.

Six months ago, she would have; she'd have fought it tooth and nail. Now, she simply let go and allowed the sensation to carry her along, like a leaf on the wind. She was happy. Content. Her life was finally full and well-rounded, and she was enjoying the hell out of it.

"I didn't," Dylan answered, "but I'll be more than happy to sign for the delivery, anyway."

"Oh. Well. If you're not interested . . ." she teased, pretending to be offended and turn away.

He grabbed her arm and tugged her into the room, letting the door slam shut behind her while he hauled her up against his chest and laid one on her. His mouth was soft and warm and very welcome after the three-plus hours it had taken to get from Cleveland to Columbus.

When they broke apart long, long, *loooong* minutes later, Dylan pressed his forehead against hers, his hands around her neck, his thumbs stroking her cheeks.

"Why didn't you call and let me know you were coming?" he asked.

"I wanted to surprise you."

He smiled softly. "You definitely managed that. You didn't drive all the way here by yourself, though, did you?"

Ronnie's heart swelled at his concerned question. It just made her feel warm and fuzzy all over to know he worried about her and cared how she was doing, what she was doing, whether or not she was safe.

She shook her head. "I came with Grace. It was her idea, actually." Over his shoulder, she lifted a wrist and glanced at her watch. "She's probably knocking on Zack's door right . . . about . . . now."

"Well," Dylan said, hooking an arm around her waist and all but sweeping Ronnie off her feet as he swung her toward the bed, "I hope he likes his surprise as much as I like mine."

Grace reapplied her lip gloss—the clear, wild-cherry flavor Zack liked so much—and ran her fingers through her hair to boost the light blond curls. Then, pasting on her most seductive Marilyn Monroe pout, she tapped on Zack's hotel room door.

It took longer than she would have expected for him to answer, so she tapped again. She heard a couple of muffled noises and a muttered curse in response, and had to bite back a laugh.

If she knew Zack—and she did—the room was probably a disaster area already, after his being there only one night, and he was probably tripping over his own shoes, pants, shirts, suitcase, and everything else in an attempt to answer her repeated knocking.

When he finally opened the door, however, she was startled not by his messy living habits, but by how incredible he looked half-naked, still dripping from the shower, with only a modest, white towel clutched around his hips.

Oh, yes, there was a reason she'd fallen in love with this man.

More than one, she supposed, but at the moment it was his incredible physique that stood foremost in her mind.

He blinked and ran his fingers through his wet hair.

"Hey," he said somewhat distractedly, obviously struggling to make sense of her sudden appearance. "What are you doing here?"

"What do you think I'm doing here?" she replied, her grin widening as she took a step into the room and sidled up to him. She pressed herself against his tall, solid frame, uncaring of his dampness soaking into her clothes. "I came to rock your world, big boy."

At that, his lips curled and a devilish light brightened his blue eyes. "Well, okay, then. Come on in. Don't mind the mess," he said, shifting them both so the door could swing closed.

"I never do," she replied with a chuckle.

What he'd done to the hotel room was nothing compared to the state of his apartment back in Cleveland. If he didn't have Magda, his housekeeper, come in a couple times a week to clean up, Grace swore the place would be declared uninhabitable. And she put up with that, didn't she?

All right, so she tended to pick up his socks and wipe down a few surfaces any time she was over, but otherwise she thought she tolerated his Pig-Pen lifestyle fairly well.

Pulling away slightly, she leaned back against the wall running between the bathroom and the rest of the suite. She raked him from head to toe with a hot gaze, using two manicured nails to tug at the towel he was still holding low on his hips.

"I think I'm overdressed," she murmured saucily.

His lashes fluttered as he returned the head-to-toe scrutiny, causing her nipples to pucker beneath her bra and a warm longing to gather between her legs.

"I should say so," he replied in a low, suggestive tone. "You need any help remedying that fact?"

"Oh, I think I can handle it," she teased.

Slipping away from the wall, she continued to face him as she walked backwards into the main area of the room. Step by slow step, while her fingers worked to free the buttons running down the front of her blouse.

Her heel caught on something and she glanced down to find herself standing in one of the leg holes of a pair of discarded BVDs.

"Nice," she said, shaking her foot and kicking the briefs aside.

As she lifted her head, something in her peripheral vision caught her attention. A movement, a flash of pink.

Focusing her gaze, she turned her head the rest of the way and zeroed in on a woman sitting in the center of the king-size bed, back against the headboard, naked except for a matching lollipop pink bra and panty set.

Grace blinked. The blond—bleach blond with dark roots, not professionally salon blond in keeping up with her natural hair color the way Grace did—shifted nervously, dragging the sheet up to cover what Grace had already had the misfortune to see.

Turning her attention back to Zack, she speared him with a look that should have shriveled his testicles and had him running like a girl.

"Is there something you'd like to tell me?" she asked,

her previously sultry tone replaced with icicles sharp enough to kill.

Zack's pale brows knit. "Huh?"

Oh, he was good. He had the dumb-jock routine down pat.

She cocked her head to the right, indicating the bimbo still snuggled up in his bed. Zack followed her movement with his eyes, and darned if he didn't go a few shades paler.

Finding herself suddenly the center of his full attention, the woman climbed to her knees and let the sheet drop. "Hi," she said with a too-sweet smile. "I didn't want to interrupt."

"What the hell are you doing here?" Zack snapped.

Grace knew he was addressing the woman in his bed, but she was the first to answer. "You know, I was just asking myself the same question."

Fingers flying, she rebuttoned her blouse, then charged for the door, pushing past Zack before he had a chance to stop her.

"Grace, wait."

With her hand on the knob, she spat back, "Fuck you. Or better yet, let your bimbo do it."

"Grace!"

She heard him calling her, heard his footsteps pounding down the hall after her, but she didn't stop, didn't even slow down. Knowing the elevator would take too long and give him too much opportunity to catch up to her, she raced for the emergency exit and slammed through, filling the stairwell with the sound of her heels clacking down, down, down, around, down, down, down.

She didn't cry. She wasn't quite sure why not, because inside her heart was breaking and a voice was screaming so loudly, her brain felt as though it were bouncing off the walls of her skull.

But over that was a burning, melting, red-hot fury and sense of betrayal that seemed to obliterate everything else.

Zack was lucky she didn't have a gun or knife or any other type of weapon on her person. If she had, she was very afraid he'd be lying in a pool of his own blood by now.

She'd have shot him in his cold, black heart. Stabbed him in the balls and cut off his dirty, stinking, skirt-chasing dick. Bludgeoned him with his own hockey stick.

Finally reaching the twelfth floor, she pushed through the heavy metal door and hurried down the carpeted hallway. She was out of breath from running, but her pulse was jumping under her skin out of pure anger.

She found Dylan's room and started to pound.

"Ronnie! Ronnie, open up! It's Grace, we have to go."

Even knowing she was disturbing them and that it might take them a couple of minutes to get dressed and get to the door, Grace continued to rap.

As the seconds ticked by, everything seemed to come crashing down around her. Her arm grew heavy, slowing her knocks. Her lungs burned, causing her to inhale and exhale rapidly. Her eyes stung and tears finally began to flow.

By the time the door opened to reveal Ronnie and Dylan, both half-undressed and struggling to shrug back into a decent amount of clothes, Grace was sobbing, gasping for breath.

"We have to go," she told Ronnie brokenly. "*I* have to go. I have to leave right now."

"What in heaven's name happened?" Concern laced her words and filled her gaze as she stepped into the hall, immediately wrapping her arms around Grace.

Grace sagged against her friend for precious seconds. "He's a lying, cheating bastard. There's a woman in his room. In his bed! Naked!"

The more details she tried to give, the higher her voice rose, but instead of falling apart—or falling apart any further—they acted to galvanize her, and fury washed through her once again.

"I have to go," she said again, pulling away from Ronnie and straightening her spine. "I can't stay here, I have to go home. If you're not ready to leave, I'll go by myself and you can find a way back later. Or I'll call a cab and you can use my car to get home. I don't care, I just have to go. I have to go. I have to go. I have to go."

On some level, she realized she was out of control and on the verge of a breakdown, but all she could think was that she couldn't stay here—in this city, in this building where Zack had cheated on her, betrayed her, ripped her heart from her chest and stomped all over it.

"Okay, okay, give me a minute," Ronnie replied, still sliding her hands up and down Grace's arms.

Letting go, Ronnie turned, and Grace was vaguely aware of her speaking with Dylan in hushed tones. Later, Grace knew she would feel horribly guilty about her behavior and about ruining her best friend's surprise rendezvous with her boyfriend, but right now the only message her brain was processing was the urgent need to run.

A moment later, Ronnie returned to the hall with her purse under her arm. She kissed Dylan's cheek, shot him a crooked, apologetic glance, and took Grace's elbow to steer her down the hall.

She took Grace's purse and dug out her key ring, keeping it in hand. Though her brain still wasn't processing details as well as she'd like, Grace was frankly relieved to turn the task of driving over to someone else, since she knew she was in no shape to get them back to Cleveland in one piece.

"It's all right, sweetie," Ronnie murmured softly as they headed for the elevators and pressed the button that would get them to the lobby level. "Everything's going to be all right."

But everything wasn't all right, and Grace knew deep down in her soul that it never would be again.

Purl 8

When Jenna heard the low growl of an engine, she was in the barn, filling feed troughs and bowls with grain. At the moment, her aunt's alpacas were still out in the pasture grazing, but before nightfall, she'd be bringing them in, and they needed to have fresh food, water, and hay in each of their stalls.

Aunt Charlotte would never forgive her if she dropped the ball in taking care of her little sweethearts, no matter how distracted Jenna might be with other things.

Which was why she didn't think twice about a vehicle passing by the house. The dirt road running past Charlotte's farm didn't get a lot of traffic, but the occasional car or truck did rattle by on its way here or there.

And right now, she had much more important things on her mind. Baby names and colors for the nursery.

Oh, she knew it was premature to be thinking about that sort of thing already. She'd only finished having sex twelve hours ago; there was no way she could know for sure whether she was pregnant or not.

But she was hopeful. So very, very hopeful.

The fight with Gage that morning had definitely

shaken her, but it hadn't exactly been unexpected. She'd known how he would react once he became cognizant enough to realize what she'd done—and why.

It hadn't been noble of her in the least, that she could fully admit. In some ways, though, it had been necessary—at least to her.

She was lucky, too, that she knew Gage so well. He was furious with her, yes, and he would likely take out his anger and frustration at the gym, pumping iron and pounding a punching bag until his already impressive guns grew even bigger and harder. And he would probably drink a little—a few beers at home in front of the TV and then a few more later, once Zack and Dylan got back into town and could help him commiserate about the deceptive nature of women in general and his ex-wife in particular.

Jenna wasn't proud of the fact that she'd caused Gage that kind of stress and displeasure, but she was still grateful that he was who he was. Because any other man might have chosen to react with physical violence or by taking legal action.

Despite all of that, however, soon after Gage had stormed out, she'd caught herself humming and then realized that she was also smiling . . . and she hadn't stopped since.

She was humming every lullaby she knew, one after another. Her hands continually drifted to her abdomen as she wondered if she really might be pregnant at this very moment, and she kept trying to decide if she should do the baby's room in Sesame Street or adorable jungle animals.

There were so many things to consider. Did she want to know the baby's gender before he or she was born, or did she prefer to be surprised? Did she want to do a nursery in standard boy (blue) or girl (pink) colors, or should she go with something more general, like green or yellow?

It was frightening, but it was also exhilarating, and she couldn't wait. She just couldn't wait to find out if she was or wasn't . . . and she prayed to God she was.

Finishing up in the barn, she wiped her hands on the seat of her pants and turned for the open barn door. The car—or truck or whatever—was still out there, she noticed. Rather than passing by, it seemed to have stopped, idling near the house.

Jenna frowned. She wasn't expecting anyone, and people didn't usually drop by her aunt's for no reason. And if it was someone she did know—like Charlotte or Grace and Ronnie—that would mean their plans had been ruined and they'd been forced to return sooner than anticipated.

Leaving the barn, she headed for the house, but couldn't see the driveway until she'd rounded a small tool shed between the two larger buildings. When she did, when the driveway and the big chrome-and-black Harley-Davidson Low Rider sitting there came into view, she froze.

Her arms fell to her sides and her feet refused to budge. Deep in her chest, her heart began a staccato *thu-thump, thu-thump, thu-thump*, sending blood pounding through every part of her body except her brain. That remained surprisingly inactive and empty of coherent thought.

Gage, who continued to balance the bike while it throbbed beneath him, pinned her with a cold glare, then cut the engine, kicked out the stand, and swung off. He set his helmet on the black leather seat before collecting a large army-green duffel bag that had been fastened behind him, and started toward the house.

The entire time, he barely took his gaze off of her. Halfway across the yard, he stopped, cocked his head, and said, "You coming in?"

Jenna blinked, waiting for the world to right itself and once again begin to make sense.

What was he doing here? Where was he going? Why did he have a duffel with him? Why was he headed for the house?

Why couldn't she seem to get enough oxygen into her lungs or reduce the beat of her heart to something slower than a hummingbird's?

Without waiting for a response, he continued onto the porch and through the front door. And finally, almost as though a firecracker had gone off behind her, Jenna jerked, regained control of her limbs, and took off after him.

Screen door banging shut behind her, she raced into the house, only to find the dining room and kitchen empty. She checked the living room. No one there.

There was only one place left where he could be.

Upstairs.

Taking the steps two at a time, she rounded the newel post and started glancing into open doorways.

She found him at the end of the hall, in her room. The same room where they'd spent last night.

His duffel was on the unmade bed and he was systematically pulling items out, placing them on the nightstand or in the single dresser alongside her own clothes.

"What are you doing?" she asked, slightly out of

breath not from running up the stairs after him, but from the mild panic that was beginning to funnel like a tornado low in her belly and spiral outward to every other organ.

Gage didn't bother to glance up. "Unpacking."

"Why?"

He still wouldn't look at her. "It's what folks tend to do when they move into a new place."

Feeling as though she'd been sucked into an alternate reality, Jenna stood staring dumbly at him. She blinked, but each time she opened her eyes, he was still there, and she could have sworn there was a buzzing growing in her ears.

Fainting would be good. If she could just hyperventilate a little harder, if the lightheadedness could just come on a bit stronger, then she might pass out. And when she came to . . . When she came to, Gage would be gone, she would be back on planet Earth, and everything would be all right again.

But she didn't lose consciousness, and this didn't seem to be a figment of her over-stimulated imagination. Gage remained standing before her, acting for all the world like an invited guest.

Swallowing hard, she found her voice and said, "You're not moving in here. Are you?"

She still felt like she was drowning, and simply could not make sense of what was going on around her.

"Damn straight." He lifted his head then, his coffee-brown eyes drilling into hers. "Got a problem with that?"

"Yes!" she blurted, her hands going to her hips. She had a million-billion-gazillion problems with that, starting with the fact that she didn't want him there and ending with a rather unpleasant mental image of him trying to strangle her to death at some point . . . or perhaps her doing something similar to him.

"Tough shit." He scooped up a medium-sized brown paper sack lying next to his duffel on the mattress, his fingers tightening on the package until his knuckles turned white. "You started this by tying me to the bed and forcing me to knock you up against my will. So until we know for sure whether you are or not, you're stuck with me."

The bag crinkled as he opened the top and reached in, then a small, light-colored box came flying at her. She cringed, but caught it as it arced past her waist on its way to the floor.

"Go take that," he ordered.

She glanced down and saw that he'd tossed her an over-the-counter pregnancy test. One that promised one-hundred-percent accuracy.

"I'm not going to take this," she told him, tossing it right back.

"Yes, you are," he shot back through clenched teeth. "If I have to tie *you* up this time, you will take that test."

"Read the instructions, you big jerk. It's too soon to know anything, and if I pee on that stick, all you'll end up with is a wet stick."

"Fine," he acquiesced, though he looked none too pleased that he hadn't gotten his way. "Then you'll take it later, but you *will* take it."

She wanted to continue arguing. She really, really did. But when Gage got it into his head that he wanted something or something needed to be done, he became more stubborn than a Brahman bull. She'd be better off fighting with a brick wall.

She'd learned that the hard way nearly two years ago, hadn't she?

Squaring her shoulders, she said, "If I'm pregnant, it's nobody's business but my own. But if you'd like to know, I'll be happy to tell you—later, in a month or two, when I'm sure. Perhaps over the phone or through a registered letter."

Okay, so maybe she shouldn't have added that last part. Not only was it snide, but it caused a muscle to jump in Gage's jaw, just below cheeks that were turning red with his rising fury.

For several long seconds, he didn't respond. Then he shook his head and blew air through his nose in what might have loosely been construed as a humorless half-laugh.

"You always could piss me off faster than anyone else," he muttered, almost as though he wasn't even talking to her, but himself.

Then he straightened and fixed her with another of his hard, razor-sharp glares. "You started this, Jenna—you and your friends with your devious little plan. You wanted me to get you pregnant, and I may very well have done just that. But if you think I'm going to walk away and leave you alone now, you're crazier than your aunt Charlotte, Grace, and Ronnie all rolled into one."

"They're not crazy," she defended.

He arched a brow. "No? Do you know of any other *sane* person who would come up with the idea to drug a man and tie him to the bed until he unwittingly fathered a child with his ex-wife?"

"I didn't hear you complaining," Jenna muttered, crossing her arms over her chest.

"I didn't know there was something *to* complain

about. Somebody forgot to give me a copy of the game plan ahead of time."

Jenna bit back her annoyance and any further reply she might have made because he did, after all, have a point. A small one, anyway.

"So what are you going to do?" she challenged, cocking a hip and raising a dark brow of her own. "Hold me hostage here until I agree to pee on your little plastic stick?"

One corner of his mouth lifted in the mockery of a smile that could only be called unfriendly and determined. "Bingo, sweetheart. You got it in one."

Gage's remark was rewarded with the blood draining from Jenna's face and her arms falling limply to her sides. Her jaw dropped so fast, he was surprised it didn't hit the floor.

Good. Maybe now she'd have a clue how he'd felt when he'd been hit by the bombshell of knowing she'd lured him to her aunt's house under false pretenses, then used him to get her pregnant when that's the *last* thing he ever would have wanted or agreed to.

But even though being a father wasn't something he would have signed up for given a choice, if she *was* pregnant, if there *was* a child involved now, then there was no way he could ignore it. Jenna might have thought she could use him as a stud and nothing more, but Gage didn't have it in him to walk away from his child. Wanted or not, planned or not, if he'd contributed his DNA to another human being, then he was in it for the long haul.

It might not come to that, but until he knew for sure . . . Well, he planned to stick to Jenna like superglue.

"You can't stay here," Jenna insisted when she finally found her tongue.

He raised a brow and almost, *almost* grinned. "Oh, yeah? Why not?"

"Because I don't want you to," she blurted. "Because we could barely tolerate living together the last few months of our marriage, and I can't imagine trying to do it again now will be any better. Because you're simply not welcome. Get out."

She took a step to the side and pointed out the open bedroom door, as though that alone would be enough to send him scuttling.

He bit back a snort. "I don't think so. Until I know for certain whether or not I'm going to be a father, you're stuck with me."

She looked like she was about to toss out another of her trivial demands that would bounce off of him like bullets off Superman, so he held up a hand and said, "Give it up, Jenna, you're not going to win this one. I'm staying. And if it turns out you are pregnant, then I'll be sticking around a hell of a lot longer than just a few days or a few weeks. I won't abandon my child or leave him to be raised without a father or by another man."

The very thought sent his blood pressure rising, and it took a second before he could continue.

"Consider yourself lucky," he told her, turning back to his duffel to dig through the few items left inside. "I could be pressing charges against you and your little cohorts for what you did. Instead, I'm just going to be a thorn in your side for a while."

A very long while, if she really was pregnant— something even he wasn't particularly looking forward to.

"Fine," she clipped out, her chin setting into a mulish slant, "you can stay. Just . . . stay away from me."

With that, she spun on her heel and marched down the hall.

Gage didn't laugh. Not out loud, anyway. He didn't want to ruin his ex-wife's proud exit or start another verbal battle she had no chance of winning.

She was wrong, though. He had no intention of staying away from her.

Palming the over-the-counter pregnancy test she'd tossed back at him and the paper sack that held several more exactly like it, he lined them up side by side on top of the dresser along the wall opposite the narrow bed.

A lead weight settled in his gut as he realized his fate rested on a tiny plastic wand and either the plus or minus sign that it would reveal. He knew how he'd feel if the tests turned up negative. Positive was a whole other matter.

The last few hours had been filled with so much anger and disbelief, he hadn't really taken the time to consider how he'd feel if Jenna wound up pregnant. If he was forced into fatherhood.

It was easier to pretend everything would be okay. That in a week or two, this would all be nothing more than a bad memory, and both he and Jenna could go back to their regular lives, their neutral corners.

Now, he lowered himself to the lumpy old mattress of the twin-size bed and let the idea settle in and take root.

The rabbit died and Jenna was, indeed, expecting his child. The woman he used to love, the woman he'd vowed to honor and cherish till death did they part.

Yeah, that had worked out well, hadn't it?

But still, he'd once had feelings for Jenna. Hell, he still had feelings for her. He was man enough to admit that, and to admit that if she hadn't been the one to call it quits and walk out, they would probably still be married.

He'd been happy with her. Maybe not bounce-off-the-walls, every-day-is-a-parade delirious, but content.

Could things have been better between them?

Sure. He'd pulled the rug out from under her with that whole not-wanting-kids thing. He realized that. And he could have opened up more, explained himself, shared things about his job that might have helped her understand his change of heart.

He *could* have, but he also couldn't. He'd loved her too much to unload on her about some of the things he'd seen and done as an undercover cop, working some of the ugliest cases in some of the seediest parts of the city.

In many ways, Jenna was an innocent. She walked around wearing rose-colored glasses, always smiling, always looking on the bright side, always thinking the best of everyone.

How could he share the gory details of what it was like to spend weeks living in a crack den? Or how it felt to sell drugs to school kids to keep up his cover. Or admit that even though it was against department policy, he'd taken the occasional hit of meth, cocaine, weed, and heroin to convince those around him that he was an addict or dealer, and to avoid having his brains blown out his ear.

And he could just imagine her reaction if he filled her in on the number of dead bodies he encountered on a regular basis. There were images in his own head—a bloated corpse pulled from the lake . . . a teenage overdose with the needle still stuck in her arm . . . a new-born baby tossed in a Dumpster in the dead of winter like just another piece of garbage.

It was enough to give anyone nightmares, and he'd be damned if he'd dump that on Jenna's shoulders, expecting her to process the events of his job like he was some pencil-necked accountant with nothing more life-altering to report than a mathematical error in the books.

Gage sighed, letting his shoulders slope and his chin fall to his chest. He ran splayed fingers over his short hair that was just beginning to grow in after his last round of shaving it off.

What if she'd thought differently of him after he told her? he wondered.

As much as he hadn't wanted to burden her with the knowledge of what his job truly entailed, he sometimes thought that was the real reason he'd closed down and refused to talk to her about anything more substantial than whose turn it was to do the dishes.

Better for her to pull away and feel neglected than to start thinking of him as a thug, a drug user, a man with questionable moral principles . . . someone other than the man she'd married.

And the part about not wanting kids . . .

If she knew what he'd seen, what he'd done, some of the situations he'd found himself in, it was possible she'd have reconsidered her feelings on that particular topic, too.

He knew Jenna, and he knew she wouldn't have been able to handle some of the shit he'd seen or some of the possibilities of what could happen to a child in the cold, cruel environment in which they lived. Drugs.

Alcohol. Mental, physical, and sexual abuse. Kidnapping. Rape. Murder.

There was a laundry list of horrible things children were exposed to these days, and he'd be damned if he'd bring one of his own into this world. It would be like tossing a guppy into a tank full of piranha and expecting it not only to survive, but to thrive.

But it doesn't have to be that way, she would say. Gage could hear her voice as though she were standing right beside him, speaking into his ear. *We'll love our child. We'll protect him from anything bad. Keep our baby safe from every ugly, nasty thing that might hurt him.*

He gave a snort. Like that was possible. Unless they trapped their kids in a bubble and never let them out of their sight, there was no way a child could go through life without coming in contact with outside influences.

Bullying started as early as preschool. Drugs could creep in soon after. Molestation could happen anywhere, at any age. Peer pressure, petty larceny, low self-esteem that led to anorexia, bulimia, cutting . . .

It was enough to make a man willingly castrate himself. And how any woman could want to bear a child with those odds stacked against her, he had no idea. The shock was that Jenna and the rest of society didn't see it that way.

But then, they hadn't seen what he'd seen, had they?

No, he was right and he knew it. Which meant that if Jenna really did turn out to be pregnant, he was up shit creek without the proverbial paddle.

He would be forced to deal with impending fatherhood, deal with raising a baby in an environment no child should be subjected to. There was always house arrest and armed guards, he supposed. Maybe a tracking device embedded in the back of his or her neck.

Not a bad idea, and he knew where he could get one.

But he didn't need to resort to CIA tactics right away, he thought, straightening on the bed. Pushing to his feet, he took a deep breath and made a conscious decision not to borrow trouble just yet.

He had time to figure out what to do if one of those tester sticks turned positive. And with any luck, it wouldn't.

With a little luck—and maybe a few fervent prayers—this would turn out to be just a minor blip on his radar, and a lesson learned about accepting a cold beer late at night from an ex-wife with ulterior motives.

Knit 9

"Come on, pick up. Pick up."

As soon as Jenna had escaped from her dead-end argument with Gage, she'd headed downstairs and straight to the phone. If anyone could rescue her from her ex-husband's heavy-handed caveman routine, it would be Grace and Ronnie. After all, they'd led the charge to get her into this, they could certainly help get her out.

It took six rings, but finally Ronnie answered her cell phone with a muted, "Hello?"

"Help," Jenna said frantically, "I'm being held hostage by a raving lunatic who doesn't want a baby, but doesn't want me to have one, either."

"What happened? Are you all right?" Ronnie asked. She continued to whisper as though she didn't want anyone else to overhear her conversation.

"I'm fine, at least for now. But Gage got loose right after we talked this morning and threw a fit. No less than I expected, I guess," she admitted in a somewhat deflated tone. "Then he left, and I thought the worst was over, but *he's back*. He's back, Ronnie, and he's moving in. He says he's not leaving until I take one of the home pregnancy tests he brought with him and he knows for sure whether or not I'm knocked up. Of course, if I am, he may *never* leave. I may be stuck with him for the rest of my natural life!"

She made it sound like a fate worse than death, but deep down, a tiny voice was asking if that would be so bad. Would it really be so horrible to be stuck with Gage, possibly married again, raising a child together?

And the long and the short of it was no, it wouldn't be so bad. It might even be nice. That hadn't been her reason for jumping on board Grace's "baby, oh, baby" plan, but it might be a nice side benefit. After all, if Gage hadn't changed horses in midstream by declaring he no longer wanted to have children with her, they would probably still be married and she'd be bouncing baby number two or three on her hip by now.

But somehow this felt more disappointing than she'd expected. It wasn't the thrill and excitement of a couple wanting a child and celebrating its conception together. What had she been thinking trying to rope him into a life she wanted, but he definitely didn't? Oh, yeah, now she remembered. She *hadn't* been thinking; the tequila had.

"Are you okay?" Ronnie wanted to know. "Has he hurt you or are you afraid he'll hurt you?"

"Of course not," Jenna answered automatically. Gage would never hurt her—not physically, anyway.

"Then . . . I hate to do this to you, sweetie, but you're on your own. We're in the middle of a major meltdown over here."

Jenna jerked slightly in surprise, her pulse kicking up in concern. "Why? What's wrong?"

If possible, Ronnie's voice dropped even lower. "We

drove to Columbus to surprise Dylan and Zack, just like we'd planned. Except Grace was the one who ended up getting the biggest shock. She walked into Zack's room and found another woman in his bed."

Jenna gasped, her mouth falling open in disbelief, but before she could say anything, Ronnie went on.

"She was understandably upset. Insisted we leave, so we drove back home. She's spending half the time sobbing and half the time raging. I'm seriously worried she's going to hurt herself, hurt someone else, or make herself sick with grief."

"Oh, no," Jenna moaned. "This is terrible. I can't believe he did this to her. What a jag-off."

"To say the least," Ronnie grumbled. "You should hear the creative names Grace has been calling him. I knew she had a mouth on her when motivated, but she's been *really* imaginative today."

"Where are you? Your place or hers?"

There was an uncomfortable pause on the other end, and in the background Jenna could hear the sound of crying, punctuated by the occasional screech, peppered with thumps, bumps, and crashes. And once in a while, the deep, heartfelt bellow of Bruiser, Zack's mammoth Saint Bernard.

"Actually," Ronnie responded after a moment, "we're at Zack's place. She wouldn't let me take her anywhere else. And as soon as we hit the parking garage . . . she completely destroyed his Hummer, Jenna. Took a base-ball bat to it. I should have stopped her. I tried a couple of times, but an armed and angry Grace Fisher is kind of intimidating."

"Good God," Jenna muttered.

"I hope there were no security cameras down there,

or we're both going to jail. And don't think less of me for saying this," Ronnie went on, "but part of me thinks the bastard deserves what he gets. The other is just downright worried about Grace. She's acting crazed, Jenna. I've never seen her like this."

"Yeah, well, she's never had a fiancé cheat on her before."

"True. I'd probably feel the same way if Dylan ever cheated on me. And I'd go straight for all his dearest, most prized possessions."

Maybe it was shallow and petty, but Jenna concurred.

"I'm on my way. Don't let her hurt herself, Ronnie. If she starts going off the deep end or things get truly scary—"

"Why do you think I haven't left her alone? I can't decide if I should worry about her committing suicide or homicide. If Zack were here, I swear he'd have a skate blade buried between his eyes by now. Or his groin."

Jenna would have liked to laugh at that, but it simply wasn't funny.

"Give me half an hour," she said before disconnecting and racing back to the dining room to grab her purse.

After three steps, she came to a screeching halt and yelped in surprise. "Good Lord, Gage. Give a gal some warning next time, would you? Stomp your feet or whistle or something instead of sneaking up on me like that."

He raised a brow. "I didn't sneak. You just weren't paying attention. What's with the phone call?" he asked, indicating the cordless phone she'd left on the kitchen island.

It was clear he'd heard most, if not all, of her side of

the conversation, and she was so thoroughly offended with Zack on her best friend's behalf that she'd morphed immediately into "all men are scum" mode.

"Your *friend*"—she spat the word like it was cursed—"is an asshole."

Despite her charge and bitter tone, his face remained impassive. "Which one?"

"Zack, the two-timing dickweed. Grace showed up at his hotel to surprise him and found another woman in his bed. I'm headed over to help talk her down before the police show up."

She took a step forward and grabbed her purse, swinging the strap over her shoulder on her way to the front door. "They should arrest Zack for being a lying, cheating bastard," she muttered, somehow deciding that if she couldn't take out her derision on Zack himself, the nearest male—namely Gage—would do.

But when she banged out of the house, sans the satisfying slam of the front door, she frowned and turned around to find Gage standing on the porch behind her, gently closing the door she'd intended to rattle.

"What are you doing?" she wanted to know.

"Going with you."

She made a completely unladylike noise somewhere between a scoff and a snort. "I don't think so."

A slow, humorless smile stretched his lips until two rows of straight white teeth were visible in the glow of the porch light. Jenna took a breath, her heart skipping a beat as she realized he looked eerily like a rabid wolf, baring its fangs just before going for the jugular.

"I do," he replied, his tone remaining soft and perfectly regulated. "When I said I was sticking around until I knew for sure whether or not you're pregnant, I meant I'm sticking to *you*. Consider me your new best friend."

"I already have a best friend," she countered, crossing her arms beneath her breasts and belatedly realizing she'd forgotten to grab a jacket.

Not that she'd attempt to get past him and back into the house now. Not even if they were in the middle of a blizzard, in Antarctica, and her nose had just fallen off from frostbite.

"Two, in fact, but neither of them follow me around like my shadow day and night."

"A shadow," he repeated. "That's better. Consider me your shadow until you get your period or the stick turns blue, whichever happens first."

She narrowed her eyes, but couldn't think of a logical retort to his argument. Considering the determined tilt of his jaw, it wouldn't have mattered, anyway. Nothing she said would budge him, not when he got like this.

"Fine," she said, trying not to let it sound too much like a huff, even though she was frustrated enough to kick him.

Turning back toward the car, she slid behind the wheel, then stifled a grin as Gage struggled to climb into the passenger side and find a comfortable position.

He was so tall, his head brushed the roof of her tiny VW, and even after pushing the seat back as far as it would go, his legs were still bent nearly to his chest and bumping the dashboard.

"We could take my bike, you know," he told her, sounding slightly aggrieved.

"But you're *my* shadow, not the other way around,

and I don't drive a motorcycle," she quipped, turning the key in the ignition and putting her little Volkswagen in gear.

For several long moments, Gage didn't say anything, but she could almost feel him mentally grumbling. Good, it served him right. If he planned to follow her around for the next few days, making her life an abject misery, then she deserved to make him moderately uncomfortable from time to time, too.

She zipped down the gravel lane and picked up even more speed when she hit the main road. She didn't go over the speed limit, but she wasted no time in getting back to the city, wanting to reach Ronnie and Grace as quickly as possible.

Her mind was still spinning over the fact that Zack had cheated on Grace. Oh, he was handsome, and a jock, and famous to boot; and she knew professional athletes had gorgeous women hanging on them practically everywhere they went. But she'd thought Zack was different. She'd thought he'd sewn his wild oats already and was truly in love with Grace, ready to settle down and be a one-woman man.

Instead, it turned out he'd been leading Grace on. He apparently wanted to have his cake and eat it, too. Have Grace as his beautiful, clueless wife to make him look good in the press and with the home-and-family crowd while also continuing to lead a fast-and-loose bachelor lifestyle.

The jerk.

All men weren't selfish bastards, were they? There had to be a few decent fellows wandering around. A few guys who knew what it meant to be faithful.

Gage had been one of those men. One of the good

guys, who understood love and respect and monogamy. At least until—

A sudden thought popped into her head and she immediately scowled. Fingers tightening on the steering wheel, she cranked her head in his direction and demanded, "Did you cheat on me while we were married?"

Startled not only by her accusing tone and the question itself, but by the unexpected break in the silence of the car, he jerked his gaze to look at her, brows creased in the center of his forehead.

"What the hell are you talking about?"

Splitting her attention between him and the road, she said, "I want to know if you ever cheated on me while we were together. Is that why you suddenly pulled away and decided you didn't want kids with me? Was there another woman you wanted to be with instead?"

Is there another woman now?

It shouldn't matter. She shouldn't care. They were divorced, for God's sake. It was none of her business what he did or who he did it with.

She shouldn't care, she shouldn't care, *she shouldn't care*. But deep down inside, a teeny-tiny part of her did, dammit.

She didn't want to think about him being with other women.

Didn't want to think about him making another woman laugh, the way he used to do with her . . . A dirty joke, a funny face, a slight tickle while they were watching a movie.

Or another woman being the recipient of his romantic gestures . . . Flowers for no particular reason. A phone call in the middle of the day telling her to dress up and meet him somewhere after work for a surprise date. The occasional piece of jewelry or simply a soft kiss pressed to her cheek or temple out of the blue.

Yes, he'd been one of the good guys. Maybe not the perfect husband, but then, she probably hadn't been the perfect wife. They were both only human, after all, complete with their own individual foibles and insecurities.

But Gage had always made her feel loved and cherished and secure in their relationship . . . right up until things had started to go downhill. Was that because he'd found someone else? Because his loyalties had been divided?

She knew Gage—or had always thought she did, anyway. If there had been another woman he found attractive, found himself falling in love with, that could have accounted for his behavior toward the end of their marriage. Guilt might have explained his growing sullenness, his increased absences, his change of heart about having children.

If that was the case, Jenna thought she might just kill him. They weren't married anymore, but he still deserved to be punished.

"Don't be ridiculous," he responded in a voice that made her feel exactly that. But only moderately. The rest of what she felt was relief.

"There was no one else?" she asked softly. "You're sure?"

"I think I'd know if I were having an affair," he snapped, his annoyance at her line of questioning evident. "Jesus, Jenna, what kind of man do you think I am?"

For a second, she remained silent, her stomach still

tight, and then she said, "I don't know. I thought you were a man I could trust. I thought you loved me. I thought we shared the same wants and needs and views, and were going to be together forever. You blew a hole the size of a Buick in all of that, so how do I know what else you changed your mind about?"

At first he didn't respond, but there was a scraping sound in the dark space of the car interior that she thought might have been his teeth grinding down to nubs.

"I never cheated on you," he finally said in a low, dangerous voice. "I don't know what's going on between Zack and Grace, but don't pawn his misdeeds off on me."

Until that very moment, until she heard him actually mutter the words *I never cheated on you*, she hadn't realized that she'd been holding her breath, waiting. She wasn't even sure her heart was beating.

But now both her heart and lungs lurched back into action, sending her head spinning slightly and blood pounding through her veins.

"Fair enough," she replied when she was once again capable of normal speech. "When we get to Zack's apartment, though, I suggest you stay out of sight, because I doubt Grace will be feeling the least bit charitable toward anyone of the male persuasion. I wouldn't be surprised if she takes out her anger at Zack on every man within a hundred mile radius for months to come."

When they arrived at Zack's apartment building, the situation was even worse than Jenna had envisioned.

Because Zack was a high-profile hockey player, he lived in an upscale building, complete with security cameras and a uniformed doorman. The doorman had of course waved Grace and Ronnie right in when they'd arrived, aware of Grace's relationship with Zack. She had permission and a key, and had been there thousands of times both with and without Zack.

For Jenna and Gage, however, he insisted on buzzing up, and only let them past the lobby once Ronnie assured him both guests were expected and welcome.

Instead of the cacophony of wanton destruction she expected to hear as soon as they stepped off the elevator, they were met with only silence. Whatever disturbance Grace had caused when she'd first arrived had apparently passed. Either that, or Zack's neighbors had complained to the front desk about the noise and she'd been warned that if she didn't quiet down, the police would be called.

"You'd better stay out here," Jenna told Gage as they reached the door.

He nodded, taking up position against the opposite wall. Leaning back, he crossed his booted feet at the ankles and his arms over his chest.

"I'll keep an eye out for cops . . . or cheating ex-boyfriends," he said, proving that their minds had been running along the same track, at least partially.

Jenna turned the knob and let herself in, and at first the apartment didn't look much different than usual. Zack wasn't exactly a finalist for Neatnik of the Year to begin with, so half a dozen pairs of discarded shoes and well-used dog toys littering the entryway were less than remarkable.

But as soon as she got to the end of the short foyer, which opened to encompass a kitchen on one side and a giant open living area on the other, she realized that the normally messy room now looked as though a tsunami had hit it. Twice.

The living room was in shambles. Clothes were strewn everywhere. Cushions were missing from the sofa. Cords were yanked loose from the television, DVD player, Playstation, stereo, and everything else that required electricity to run. Zack's abundant and cherished hockey trophies were knocked off their display shelves. A few were broken, and one . . . one was rather creatively rammed head-first into the wall. A definite forfeit of his security deposit.

Making her way to the bedroom, she found Ronnie sitting on the edge of a chair in one corner, elbows on her knees as she patted a panting Bruiser with one hand and gnawed on the thumbnail of the other.

Grace sat cross-legged in the middle of the bed, photo albums and newspaper clippings spread all around her. Obviously she'd settled down somewhat. Or rather, she'd shifted from ranting and raving to quiet and dogged personal devastation.

Because in her right hand, she held a pair of scissors with bright red handles, and was using them to thoroughly and methodically cut the photos and newspaper clippings surrounding her into tiny, unidentifiable slivers.

Her face was streaked with tears and lines of what was probably supposed to be waterproof mascara. Her hair was a blond rat's nest, frizzy in some places, pulled straight in others. She looked like she'd been, quite literally, through the wringer.

"I tried to stop her," Ronnie said as soon as she spotted Jenna in the doorway. "I told her she'll be sorry later, but she won't listen to me."

"I won't be sorry," Grace insisted, not bothering to lift her gaze from her current project. "I could never be sorry. *Zack* is the one who's going to be sorry."

With that, she jumped up, grabbed an armful of the scrapbooks and paper fragments from the bedspread, and headed for the French doors overlooking a small balcony. Through the doors she went, night breeze ruffling the curtains behind her as she marched to the iron railing and pitched the records of all Zack's sporting achievements into the street.

Some of it floated gently downward like feathers. The rest fell and landed with a resounding *thunk*. Jenna winced, hoping there was no one walking along the sidewalk below who might become the unwitting recipient of a memento-induced concussion or the mother of all paper cuts.

"Grace, sweetie," she said softly as the other woman came back into the room. "Let Ronnie and me take you home. You'll be more comfortable there, and we can stay up the rest of the night talking."

"I don't want to talk. I want to hurt him."

Grace rushed across the plushly carpeted floor, throwing open the closet doors and yanking garments one by one off of their hangers. Casual shirts and slacks, suits, hockey jerseys, a tuxedo . . . she piled up as much as she could carry and stormed back across the room, tossing everything over the railing to join the rest of Zack's belongings on the street.

This was getting out of control. If they didn't stop her soon the cops really would be called, and Grace would likely be hauled away for destruction of property, littering, and breaking and entering, among other things.

On Grace's next trip inside, Jenna blurted out a question she knew would get her friend's attention. "Are you sure he cheated on you?"

As intended, the query drew Grace to a halt in the center of the room. Blond curls floated around her face as she turned on Jenna, eyes narrowed and blazing fire.

"Are you taking his side?" she demanded. "Do you think I'm making this up?"

If Jenna didn't know better, she'd swear she was about to be on the wrong end of a rotisserie spear.

"Of course not," she replied evenly, hoping to bring Grace's level of rage down just a notch. "But I wasn't there, so I don't really know what happened. Can you fill me in?"

Behind Grace, Ronnie slowly straightened in her seat, bobbing her head up and down. *Yes, yes,* she mouthed, *keep going.*

"He's a lying, cheating bastard," Grace spat. But she didn't move closer to the closet or back toward the balcony. "I went there to surprise him. Ronnie and I went there to surprise both of them."

Anger tinged her words, but there was sadness there, too, and her eyes glistened with tears. "She was in his bed, half naked, and he was in the shower. What does that tell you?"

"That he's a lying, cheating bastard," Jenna agreed. And then a second later, she wiped her brow with the back of her hand and said, "Boy, it's warm in here. Are you warm? I could use a drink, how about you?"

Grace blinked a few times, as though trying to follow the rapid switch in topics. No doubt she was so focused on her own misery that nothing else made much sense to her.

Jenna had been there a time or two herself. Not dealing with infidelity, but a betrayal all the same. When Gage had started pulling away and it had become clear divorce was in her future, she'd gone a little crazy, too.

For months, she'd walked around in a daze. She functioned, she communicated, she went to work and came home, went to her Wednesday-night knitting group and for drinks afterwards with her friends.

But the whole time, she'd felt removed from everyone and everything around her. Her entire focus, her every thought had been on Gage . . . how much she'd loved him, how much he'd disappointed her, the life they were supposed to have had together, and the life they now never would. Everything else was just white noise.

So she knew how Grace felt, knew what she was going through and the kinds of thoughts that were racing around in her brain.

She also knew that if she could just keep Grace distracted, she and Ronnie might be able to calm her down enough that she wouldn't do anything stupid or make matters worse.

"I'm sure Zack has something in the fridge. Help yourself," Grace told her distractedly.

Jenna gave a snort, crossing her arms beneath her breasts and cocking a hip. "No, thank you. I don't want anything from that jerk-off. And you shouldn't, either. You don't even want to be here, do you? I mean, why give him the satisfaction of knowing he's hurt you? When he gets home and sees this place, he'll realize how upset you were and probably get a kick out of it, asshole that he is."

It took a second for Grace to absorb what Jenna was saying, but then her eyes narrowed, widened, and narrowed again.

"You're right. Why am I even here?"

Behind her, Ronnie bounced to her feet, and Bruiser bounded up beside her.

"I'm better than this. I'm better than he is. He never deserved me."

"No, he didn't," Jenna concurred, because she knew it was what Grace needed to hear. And heck, it was probably true.

"Let's go somewhere else—your place or Ronnie's. You can even come out to Aunt Charlotte's and stay with me for a while, if you want."

Grace shook her head. "I want to go home. I want to drink wine, and eat Oreos, and sleep until I'm old and gray."

Both Jenna and Ronnie nodded, flanking their friend, each looping an arm through one of hers to lead her out of the bedroom.

"Sounds good to me," Jenna said. "We'll stop for massive quantities of wine and cookies on the way."

They had Grace halfway across the living room when she stopped, muttered, "Wait," and turned back toward the bedroom. Jenna and Ronnie raced after her, afraid of what she might be up to, but then gave mirrored sighs of relief when all she did was grab an old taped and battered hockey stick from the rear of Zack's closet.

Grace returned a second later, stick in hand. "This is mine now," she told them.

Jenna and Ronnie exchanged a glance, silently agreeing not to question or argue. They had Grace calmed down and moving in the right direction; that's all that mattered. If she wanted to steal a single piece of hockey equipment in order to stick it—pun intended—to Zack, they weren't going to fight her on it.

Gathering purses and jackets, they herded Grace toward the door, and Jenna made a point of getting there a split second before the others to frantically wave Gage away. Smart man that he was, he strolled a few yards down the hall and out of sight.

"Wait," Grace said again when they had her halfway out the door.

Both women froze, afraid Grace had changed her mind and was about to go back on a rampage.

But instead, she merely snapped her fingers and called, "Here, Bruiser."

The giant brown and white Saint Bernard, who had been only a couple steps behind them to begin with, padded straight to Grace, nudging her in the side with his nose and wet, panting tongue.

"He's mine now, too," she said to no one in particular, then turned on her heel and marched down the hall toward the elevator, the dog formerly known as Zack's trailing along at her side.

Purl 10

Thanks to a lot of well-mimed signals and hand gestures, Gage got the hint that Jenna and Ronnie were
carting an emotionally battered Grace off and away
from causing any more damage at Zack's apartment.
He took the stairs to the lobby while they headed down
in the elevator, then followed at a discreet distance as
they made their way out of the building and along the
sidewalk—at one point skirting piles of broken, torn,
and otherwise bedraggled items that looked as though
they'd once belonged to Zack—to the parking lot.

Jenna gently set her keys on the roof of her yellow
VW Beetle, silently leaving them for him as she passed
by and climbed into the back seat of Grace's car with a
much-worse-for-wear-looking Grace. Zack's dog rode
shotgun in the front beside Ronnie, strapped in and for
all the world acting like the human he thought he was.

It was funny, he thought, as he squeezed himself into
his ex-wife's sorry excuse for a motor vehicle, that Jenna
was suddenly leaving bread crumbs for him when only
an hour before she'd been telling him off and insisting

he wasn't welcome at her aunt's farm *or* to follow her back to town for this girlfriend crisis intervention.

But that was his Jenna. She might not want him around, but she would never abandon him downtown and without a viable mode of transportation, either.

Then again, she knew how much he hated riding around in her tiny tuna can with wheels. She was probably sitting in that back seat, laughing her ass off over the image of him stuffing himself inside. Steering wheel bumping his chin, knees pressed to his ears. He felt like he was driving a freaking clown car.

Despite his discomfort and wish for his bike, he followed behind Grace's much larger, more sensible sleek silver Lexus halfway across town to her equally sleek apartment complex. Taking his time, he parked a few spaces away from them, then sat and watched as the foursome piled out of the car and trailed into the building.

As soon as they disappeared, he climbed out of the bug to stretch his legs . . . and arms and hips and back and neck. If he'd had a cigarette, he probably would have smoked one, but since he tried to limit them to his undercover work only, he leaned his arms on the roof of Jenna's yellow jelly-bean car and tapped out a bored rhythm with the sides of his thumbs.

The thing about being a cop and working vice was that he was used to waiting. Nine times out of ten, his job involved sitting around doing not much of anything, watching for that one moment when he had enough evidence and the opening to make an arrest.

He used the time—most of it, anyway—to go back over the details of his cover and make sure there were no holes that might get him dead. Or to map out all the ways a bust might go down, also in hopes of minimizing casualties and not getting dead.

And sometimes, after he'd gone through all of that, he'd think about why the job was so important to him. The fact that he was making a difference and taking scum off the streets so they couldn't hurt innocent people like Jenna.

The only problem was, the longer he worked undercover and the more immersed he became with society's lowlifes, the more he came to think that what he was doing wasn't really making that much of a difference, after all. No matter how many thieves, murderers, sex offenders, or drug dealers he took down, more seemed to crop up. They were like the mythical Hydras; sever one head and another—maybe even two more—grew in its place.

So what was the point? If he wasn't really making a difference, if he wasn't truly keeping the streets safe for his wife and citizens like her, then why bother?

It wasn't that he didn't like his job or being undercover. There were parts of it that were downright invigorating. The secrets and lies. The role-playing. The delicate web of deceit that had to be woven around the criminal element. The heightened anticipation of the chase and eventual take-down.

When Jenna filed for divorce, though, it had made him stop and analyze his life, his decisions. He'd thought he was protecting her, keeping her at arm's length from what he did and the ugliness he saw on a daily basis.

But if what he was doing to keep her safe ended up pushing her away, then was any of it really worthwhile? It felt an awful lot like oiling the squeak in a hamster's wheel after the animal had already gone paws-up.

And with Jenna no longer around, he couldn't even be sure she *was* safe. He couldn't know where she was or what she was doing.

Oh, he wasn't one of *those* men. The possessive types who had to know where their women were every minute of every day for fear they might actually exchange a word or two with another human being. But he did like knowing that she never had any reason to wander into areas where she didn't belong and could get seriously hurt.

And yeah, if he could have cocooned her inside their house while they were married, he would have. Not to keep her in, but to keep every bad, negative element out.

She'd never understood that about him; his almost obsessive need to protect her. She'd thought he was simply becoming sullen, distant . . . that he didn't care *enough.*

Christ, could anything have been farther from the truth? He'd have taken a bullet for her. Still would.

What he wouldn't do was bring a child into the world—a world he was all too familiar with—when there was no way for him to guarantee that child's safety until he was old enough to take care of himself.

Smacking his palms flat on the roof of the Volkswagen, he muttered a short, colorful curse and took a step back.

But now Jenna very well may have taken that choice away from him.

A man should have the right to make his own decisions about whether or not he became a father. He shouldn't be dosed, bound, and used for stud service.

He'd learned the hard way, however—and on more

than one occasion—that people didn't always get their way. What he did or didn't want was moot at this point . . . or at least until they found out whether or not Jenna was pregnant.

Turning, Gage leaned his butt against the car, fingers curling and uncurling at his sides as renewed anger surged inside him.

He wasn't happy. He might never be happy about Jenna's actions and the way she'd used him, but that was water under the bridge, wasn't it?

The same as he'd learned that life wasn't always easy or fair, he'd also learned that you couldn't undo what had already been done.

So if it turned out Jenna wasn't pregnant, that would be great. Things could go back to the way they had been before she and her friends had hatched their devious little plan.

If she was pregnant . . . well, then he guessed he'd have to deal, just as he'd dealt with any number of other curve balls life had thrown at him.

He wasn't sure how, exactly, but he suspected it would take a hell of a lot of soul-searching and brain-melting mental contemplation. He'd have to pick up some parenting books, ask some friends on the force with families what to expect, what to do . . . how to feel. Because right now, he was fucking clueless.

Before he could work himself into too much more of a lather, Jenna appeared at the corner of the brick apartment building, moving swiftly in his direction. He straightened, but remained standing by the driver's side door until she reached him.

"Everything okay?" he asked.

She nodded. "Grace is sleeping. Not peacefully, and

she's got one arm wrapped around that hockey stick—which is apparently a beloved memento from Zack's childhood—and the other wrapped around Bruiser's neck, but at least she's finally getting some rest."

Careful not to touch him, she skirted past and opened the car door. "Ronnie's going to stay, but said she'd call if they need anything." She cocked her head, meeting his gaze. "I had visions of you standing out here all night, refusing to abandon your post, otherwise I'd still be up there with them, too."

Sliding into the driver's seat, she slammed the door and turned the key. Then, when she noticed he hadn't moved to follow suit, she lowered her window to glare at him again.

"Aren't you going to get in?" she asked. "I'd be happy to go home alone, but I don't know what I'll do with your bike once I get there, and it's going to feel strange walking around without my shadow in tow."

Face blank, he held her gaze a second longer, then started around the rear of the car. Only when he was sure she wouldn't see him did he let the ghost of a smile play over his lips.

Good ol' Jenna, always willing to take in a stray, even if that stray happened to be an overbearing, hulking, and thoroughly unwanted ex-husband.

It was the moans that woke him. Not sexy, encouraging moans like the last time he'd woken up in this narrow, less-than-comfortable bed in Charlotte Langan's farm house. Instead, it sounded like someone was hurt or scared. And since the only other person in the house with him was Jenna . . .

He tended to be a light sleeper anyway, but given

the weight of his thoughts these days, and the disturbing lack of noise out here in the middle of nowhere, he found himself tossing and turning more than usual. He'd never realized before how much the sounds of traffic several stories below, punctuated with the occasional siren or squeal of brakes, helped to lull him into unconsciousness.

Tossing off the single sheet that covered him, Gage padded barefoot down the hall, wearing only a pair of black boxer briefs. The well-traveled hardwood floor creaked as he made his way downstairs.

Stubborn woman that she was, Jenna had refused to sleep upstairs in a real bed. She didn't want to encroach on Charlotte's personal space by sleeping in her aunt's room. The only other guest room in the house was used mostly for storage and sported only a bedframe without a mattress, and he knew that much more than Hell would have to freeze over before she'd willingly spend the night with him in what had formerly been "her" room.

So she'd chosen to grab an extra set of sheets from the linen closet and sleep on the sofa in the sitting room. A sofa that had seen better days and looked about as comfortable as a bed of nails or pile of lumber.

He scratched a spot in the middle of his chest and shook his head. If he lived to be a hundred, he would never understand women . . . and he didn't think he'd understand Jenna if he lived to be a thousand.

He'd have been happy to slide over and welcome her into the tiny twin bed with him. He couldn't have promised it wouldn't lead to anything, but he *could* promise that if it did, there would be condoms involved.

Stepping into what passed as Charlotte's living

room, he saw Jenna stretched out on the red brocade settee. She'd kicked off the covers, revealing a pair of hot pink shortie pajamas with white, dime-sized polka dots all over them. The cotton-and-spandex material molded to her petite frame like a second skin, and he couldn't help but look his fill.

He remembered when she used to climb into bed naked and stay that way all night, but the PJs weren't bad, either. They were both cute and sexy at the same time, showing off her feminine attributes to perfection.

Jenna had always been self-conscious about her figure, he knew. She thought she was too short, too thin, and that her breasts were too small.

Gage had never been nearly as critical. Yeah, she was petite, but he liked that. He liked the fact that he towered over her, and that when he wrapped his arms around her and tugged her close, she nearly disappeared. It made him feel big and strong and powerful, like he could take on the world and protect her from anything.

And her breasts might not be as large as those most often seen in men's magazines, but he'd never had any complaints. They suited her, and had kept him plenty occupied when they made love.

Filed at the top of that invisible box of things he would never understand about women was the absolute perplexity that Jenna didn't recognize how totally hot she was. Even now, after the divorce, the whole forced seduction/baby issue between them, and with her sound asleep and him still groggy, she turned him on. The evidence of that was making itself known in the tenting at the front of his underwear.

He was about to turn around and head back upstairs,

reassured that Jenna was fine and apparently just mumbling in her sleep, when she moaned again and thrashed slightly on the sofa. Her arm flopped out to the side, nearly smacking into the edge of the coffee table. Her legs jerked, almost as though she were trying to run. And her head rolled back and forth on the pillow stuffed into the corner of the settee.

For a minute, he debated over waking her. It might put a halt to whatever bad dream she was having, but then she'd know she'd been crying out and that he'd heard her. He didn't want her to be embarrassed, and he most certainly didn't want her to notice the effect she had on him, even from a distance and while she was still asleep.

But if he left her alone . . . She jerked and groaned again, this time sounding even more frightened, more desperate.

Okay, enough was enough. Striding forward, he stopped beside the sofa and put his hands on his hips. "Jenna," he said, hoping the sound of her name alone would startle her out of her nightmare.

When she continued to struggle, he leaned down, fitted a hip onto the edge of the settee beside her own, and slid a hand around her shoulder. "Jenna," he tried again, giving her a small shake. "Honey, wake up. You're having a bad dream."

She stilled, her eyes popped open, and a second later, she was in his arms.

"Gage. Oh, my God, Gage." Her voice was thick with emotion, her chest heaving as she fought for breath. She pressed herself against his chest, arms squeezed around his neck like tentacles.

He didn't know what was going on or why she was

suddenly so willing to touch him when only hours before she'd insisted they sleep on completely different floors of the house, but he wasn't a man to toss aside a bit of luck when it came his way. Pulling her closer, he held her tight, his hands stroking her back while he inhaled the fruity scent of her hair where it tickled his nose.

"Aw, sweetie, it was just a nightmare. Nothing that should have you so worked up."

She pushed away a couple of inches to meet his gaze. Her face was pale except for two splotches of pink that colored her cheeks, and her eyes were damp and glossy with tears.

Raising a hand, he ran a thumb along the bottom of one eye and then the other, wiping away the wetness as best he could.

"What's wrong, honey?" he asked softly. "What were you dreaming about that was so bad?"

She shook her head and swallowed hard, fresh tears swelling to balance precariously on her lower lashes.

"It was you," she said in a watery voice. "I couldn't find you, and then when I did . . ." She took a hiccupping breath. ". . . you were dead."

He froze at her words, an unwanted but automatic snake of trepidation wending its way down his spine. Every cop knew that the end could come at any moment. They knew it, lived with it, but didn't let it keep them from doing their jobs.

Second only to his fear that something might happen to Jenna, though, was his fear that something might happen to him, resulting in her being left alone. Not just alone without him, but alone without someone to watch out for her and keep the bad things from touching her.

They might be divorced, which put him at a bit more of a distance than he had been before, but that didn't mean he wasn't still keeping an eye on her. He kept his ear to the ground, had surreptitiously convinced Zack and Dylan to watch out for her, and checked up on her himself when he could.

Without letting her know, of course. If Jenna found out he was still acting like an invisible commando bodyguard where she was concerned, she'd have his biscuits in a bag hanging from her belt . . . or attached to the ends of one of those fluffy boas she liked to wear.

So he didn't let her catch on. He remained at a distance, pretending he was a-okay with the divorce, and far removed from anything that had to do with her.

And whenever they bumped into each other or were forced to spend time together because of their mutual circle of friends, he played it cool, pretended she meant no more to him than any other woman he might pass on the street. He hoped he was pulling it off, because it was about as easy as sucking on a lemon and *not* making a face.

Still, he figured anyone, cop or not, would get the willies from being told they'd died in a dream. He only hoped her vision was the result of a vivid imagination and a spicy midnight snack, rather than any fortune-telling genes she may have inherited from the slightly wacky Langan side of her family.

"I'm fine," he told her, running his fingers through the short, black hair at her temples. He kept stroking her face and hair until she looked at him fully and the panicked, glazed expression started to fade from her eyes. "See. Flesh and bone and very much alive."

At that, her eyes began to water again and the petal-soft bow of her lips quivered. "I couldn't find you, and I couldn't find the baby, and then I did find you, and . . ."

He tensed at her mention of a baby. She hadn't said anything about that before, but apparently her dream had also contained an infant. Not so surprising, considering they both had baby on the brain these days.

"I was afraid I was going to find the baby dead, too, and I just couldn't handle that. I couldn't lose you both," she finished on a sob.

He grabbed her up and cradled her tight at the same time she threw herself against him. "Shh, it's okay. Nobody's going to die."

"You don't know that," she mumbled into his neck. "You always used to say that, but you don't know nothing's going to happen. You can't be sure."

His brows crossed at her sudden assertion. They weren't just talking about her dream now. They were talking about his job, and their failed marriage, and any number of thoughts and feelings and conversations that had passed between them over the years.

"Why are you worried about me now?" he asked softly. "We aren't even married anymore."

Jerking back, she fixed him with a hot, angry glare. And then she smacked him. Open hand, right across the bare chest.

"That doesn't mean I stopped loving you, you big lug. Or that I don't still care."

Her eyes blazed fire, and color was coming back to her face.

"I worry about you every day, on the job and off.

Why do you think it was so important to me that we start a family?" Her voice was still sharp, but now it was tinged with emotion, as well. "I want children, yes, but I also wanted a part of you growing inside of me. A little boy with dark hair, quiet intensity, and a dimple in his right cheek just like you have when you smile. A little girl with brown eyes, a sharp mind, and a stubborn streak two miles wide."

Something clenched tight in the area of his heart.

Maybe it was everything all rolled together and thrown at him out of the blue that caused his conscience to pinch, his chest to throb, and a knot of what he thought might be regret to grow in his gut.

He opened his mouth to speak, but the words stuck in his raw, dry throat. He had to swallow and lick his lips before trying again.

"You never said you worried about me."

Jenna rolled her eyes as though he were at the head of a class of dunces. "Of course I worried. Your job is dangerous, and it kept you away for weeks on end. Weeks when I never knew where you were or what you were doing. How could I *not* be concerned about you? How could I *not* have nightmares when you were away from me?"

"You've had this kind of nightmare before?" he asked, truly perplexed.

He'd never known her to have nightmares; not often, anyway, and not over anything more substantial than a scary movie they stayed up too late to watch. Then again, she was right about his undercover work taking him away from home for long stretches of time. How was he supposed to know how she slept when he wasn't in bed beside her?

It broke his heart to think of her crying out in the middle of the night, with no one there to comfort her.

Without *him* there to comfort her.

Dammit, he should have been.

He should *be*.

He'd always had regrets about their ruined relationship. But if he'd been sorry before, he now felt like a first-class heel.

He'd thought the reason for their breakup was based mainly on her desire for children and his refusal to give them to her. On the slow detachment that the recurring quarrel had caused.

Had he missed the bigger picture? Had there been more going on beneath the surface that he'd never seen, never known was there?

How many nights had she stayed up, wondering if he was all right and fretting over his safety?

How many times had he come home from an extended undercover case and *not* sat down to talk to her? Not hugged her, kissed her, filled her in on what he'd been up to or asked how she'd spent the days he'd been away?

On his part, he hadn't wanted her to know some of the specifics of what his job entailed. She didn't need to know that he'd just spent a month living in a crack den, peddling meth or heroin or cocaine to junkies on the street. Or that he'd spent days on end picking up prostitutes in sting operations and tracking down killers.

But it probably wouldn't have hurt for him to tell her that everything had gone fine and the bad guys they'd been after were now behind bars.

She'd married a cop, so she knew the basics of what being on the force entailed. Sharing some of the less-gory details wouldn't have been so bad. It wouldn't have scarred her any more than hearing about one of her students stuffing glitter up his nose or throwing up macaroni and cheese after lunch had scarred him.

Great. He'd been an idiot, and now that he'd figured that out—not his proudest moment ever—it was too late to do anything about it.

With a sigh, he ran his hand over her hair, kissed the side of her face, and then scooped her off the sofa and into his arms. Cradling her against his chest, he got to his feet and started across the room, back the way he'd come.

"What are you doing?" she asked, her voice still sounding thick and slightly hoarse from her crying jag.

"Taking you to bed," he said, and he didn't intend to take *no* for an answer.

Knit 11

The cold fear that had wrapped itself around Jenna's heart only moments before melted and turned into a pool of uncertain longing low in her belly.

Did she want this? Was she ready for it?

Tricking Gage into coming over and seducing him in a no-strings-attached effort to get pregnant was one thing. Sleeping with him when they were both alert and willing, with no ulterior motives, was something else entirely.

Rather than struggle or insist he put her down, she let him carry her up the stairs, enjoying the gentle sway and bounce as she rested against his chest and he took the steps carefully one by one. She told herself she was buying time to decide what to do.

Stay or go? Argue or capitulate? Be strong or give in just for this one night?

Spending the rest of the night in Gage's arms would certainly drive away the last vestiges of a nightmare she never wanted to experience again.

At the memory, a shiver of alarm trickled down her spine. She hated dreaming bad things about Gage.

Hated it when her subconscious created all kinds of terrible, horrific images that she wouldn't let herself think about during her waking hours.

Seeing him shot and bleeding to death in some dark alley. Seeing him surrounded by nameless, faceless lowlifes who obviously meant him harm.

And yes, even after they separated and divorced, she still experienced the occasional nightmare about his well-being.

Jenna closed her eyes where her head rested against Gage's strong, hard shoulder, and bit the inside of her lip to keep from groaning aloud.

She was such a mess! How did a woman her age, with her level of education and what she thought was a normal, decent amount of common sense, end up at the center of such a soap opera?

Oh, Lord. Her life was like a chapter out of some Latin-American *telenovela*. Maybe she should throw her head back, put a hand to her forehead, and start speaking in rapid Spanish. A good swoon definitely couldn't hurt.

Gage rounded the corner into the small guest bedroom, careful not to bump her into the doorjamb.

She was no closer to knowing whether or not she should go through with this, but it seemed the decision was being taken out of her hands. There was the small, narrow bed, covers thrown back and rumpled from his own few hours of sleep. The room was dark, with only a faint trace of moonlight spilling through the open curtains on the lone window.

And God help her, she actually found it romantic. Alone with her ex-husband in this tiny, cramped room, him carrying her up the stairs to bed like some medieval knight.

Sigh. If she hadn't slaked her lust with him multiple times only last night, she would definitely be thinking that she needed to get laid.

And maybe she did. Maybe she was like a plant gone too long without water. It had been so long since she'd had sex that last night had barely made a dent. She might need to do it again and again and again before her thirst would be assuaged and the color would start to come back to her leaves.

It was simple biology, really, and who was she to go against the laws of nature?

Mind made up, Jenna relaxed, let her body go slack, and breathed out a soft sigh as Gage leaned over to place her gently on the bed. Her eyes fluttered closed and she waited, taut with expectation, for him to follow her down, for the solid weight of his large frame to cover her, press her into the mattress, and for his lips to lightly touch hers.

Breathlessly, she waited.

And waited.

And . . .

What the heck was taking so long?

She let one eye open a crack and found him standing in the doorway, hand resting lightly on the jamb, his broad, bare back facing her instead of his . . . well, instead of his face.

" 'Night," he murmured, and started to walk away. "Sleep well."

Sleep well? *Sleep well?* What had happened to serving her a plate of piping-hot sex to drive away her bad dreams?

Hmph.

She sat up, *this close* to saying, *Hey, where the heck do you think you're going?! Get over here and make me scream, darn you!* but caught herself just in time. In a calm tone, she called his name instead.

He turned, arm still raised against the doorway. "Yeah?"

"Will you stay with me?"

It wasn't what she'd planned to say. But it slipped out all the same, and as soon as the words passed her lips, she knew they were right, that it was what she wanted.

He considered her request for a long, drawn-out moment, his chest yielding slightly as he seemed to make up his mind—possibly against his better judgment, if she was reading his body language correctly.

His arm dropped from the doorjamb and he turned back toward her. "Sure."

He slowly crossed the room, and she took the opportunity to admire his amazing physique, regardless of the silent message it might be sending. If attraction alone could have kept their marriage afloat, they'd have been celebrating their golden anniversary eons before she'd have ever considered leaving him. Because his body was, quite simply, beautiful.

Every line, every plane, every firm muscle and smooth expanse of skin. And the tattoos were sexy as hell.

The vine around his left bicep bulged when he moved. Even with the slightest motion, like crossing a room the way he was doing now. He didn't have to flex or posture for the black tribal cuff to come alive.

And lower, just above the waistband of his black boxer briefs, along his left side, were the colorful scales of a portion of the dragon's tail. Bright green, but with shades of other colors mixed in to give the illusion of iridescence and sharp black outlining.

She wanted to reach out and touch, the way she had last night, whether he knew it or not. She'd trailed her fingers over the bright orange flames gracing his right shoulder and down the narrowing end of the dragon's tail where it hugged his hip and pelvic bone and led directly to the portion of his anatomy that made him a most impressive male specimen, indeed.

Given his apparent reluctance at the moment, however, she wasn't sure he'd appreciate her pouncing on him and stroking him from head to groin. Not just yet, anyway, but with luck that would come.

So instead, she curled her fingers into her palm where they rested atop her thigh and scooted to the far side of the bed as he approached. He paused for a second, as though contemplating the wisdom of his next move, then fluffed the pillow against the headboard and stretched out beside her.

Even with as little room as the bed provided, they didn't touch. Jenna didn't know if it was by happenstance or design, but she didn't intend to let it pass for long.

Once he'd settled in and seemed to relax a bit, she shifted back and stretched out beside him. Very close beside him, resting her head on his shoulder and her calf over his lower thigh.

Reluctantly, he brought an arm up to brace her in place, his heat scorching down her back and around her waist. She draped her own arm lightly across his flat stomach and let her eyes drift shut on a sigh.

Oh, how she'd missed moments like this with this man.

Divorce definitely wasn't all it was cracked up to be. Everyone talked about how freeing it was. How great it was to be away from a bad situation, to start over, to experience true independence again.

For Jenna, divorce had just been awkward and lonely.

Yes, she'd been the one to file. And she still maintained that it was the right decision. At the time, there really hadn't been any other choice; things weren't changing and they couldn't continue on the way they'd been going.

She'd never been sorry for the decisions she'd made, but that didn't mean she wasn't sometimes sorry about the way things had turned out. It was one of those fun little hiccups in life that left a person smack-dab between a rock and a hard place.

Sometimes, when she was feeling particularly alone and the silence of her apartment started to close in on her, she actually wished her split from Gage had been more dramatic. If they'd gotten into ear-splitting, window-shattering fights . . . If Gage had a drinking problem, or she'd put them thousands of dollars in debt with extravagant shopping sprees . . . Maybe if things had gotten physical and he'd slapped her or she routinely used his six-pack abs as a punching bag.

Then divorce might have been a blessing. *Then* she might have enjoyed her newly single lifestyle and been like one of those footloose-and-fancy-free *Sex and the City* girls, going out clubbing every night and sleeping with every random man who came down the pike just to prove she was in charge of her own sexuality.

But the truth was, Jenna didn't want to be in charge of her own sexuality—not if it meant serial dating and sleeping around. And as much as she loved them, she didn't want to spend every night in some bar sipping Cosmopolitans with Ronnie and Grace, either.

She wanted this. This, and what she'd had with Gage before things had started to go downhill.

The quiet comfort of being with a man she loved.

The feel of warm arms holding her tight, and another body taking up space in bed with her—sometimes snuggled close, sometimes simply causing the mattress to dip and sway and let her know she wasn't alone.

The knowledge that somebody was going to be there when she got home at the end of a long day. Someone to ask how work had gone. Someone to kiss her cheek and tuck a strand of hair behind her ear. Someone to sit across the table from her while they ate dinner, or beside her on the couch while they watched the latest crime drama on TV.

If she told Gage any of that, though, he would think she was crazy. His immediate response would most likely be, *So why the hell did you file for divorce in the first place?* because he'd never really wanted or approved of the separation.

Her big problem at the moment, though, was how easy it was to forget all that when Gage was lying next to her, smelling so good and feeling like the best thing she'd ever had against her body.

Not counting the great sex from last night, of course.

Letting her eyes flutter open, she took in the broad expanse of his chest just beyond her cheek. His deep, even breathing and the steady beat of his heart beneath her ear lulled her.

Despite the tiny voice in her head telling her to keep her hands to herself, she slowly let her fingers drift along the outside curve of his pectoral muscle and up to his shoulder where orange-tipped flames shot from the mouth of the angry dragon.

"When did you get this?" she asked, reverently tracing the edges of the amazing artwork.

Gage's skin twitched under her fingertips, but he didn't move away.

"After the divorce," he said a minute or so later.

She didn't need to know that he'd started getting the new tat the day he'd signed the divorce papers. He hadn't been sure what type of design he was going to get when he'd walked into the shop; he'd only known he wanted something big that was going to take a good, long time to apply.

A neck-to-hip dragon that covered nearly his entire back had certainly fit the bill. It had taken months to complete, but the pain and long hours spent in the chair had helped to drown out every other thought racing through his brain. And it was hard to feel the hurt in his heart when razor-sharp needles were tapping ink into his skin.

"I like it," she murmured, not bothering to lift her head from his chest. Every word, every breath she took, reverberated against his flesh.

He'd have liked to say it didn't affect him, but if she slid the leg that was draped across his thigh just a couple inches higher, she'd realize that everything she did had an effect on him.

The perfume she wore that was a unique blend of wildflowers and citrus.

The way she painted her nails with clear polish so that they held a bit of shine, but never covered them with color. And contrastly, the way she always kept her toenails painted bright red or pink.

The clothes she wore that were reminiscent of the flower-children fashions of the seventies, but looked a hell of a lot sexier on her. The flowing blouses with tight jeans, or the occasional prairie skirt with a snug top. He knew she could be self-conscious about her diminutive figure, but as far as he was concerned, she had just enough on top to set any man's mouth watering.

The way she wore her hair—short and sassy, with just enough length for him to run his fingers through, to ruffle in the breeze, to tickle the inside of his thighs while she . . .

Yeah, um, better not to let his mind wander down that particular road or she wouldn't need to shift her leg at all to notice what was happening with him south of the border.

It was everything about her—the big and the small, the significant and the trivial. That's why, even after he'd put his John Hancock on those papers and they were officially divorced, he still hadn't been able to stop himself from having her name very carefully, very subtly worked into the central design of the dragon's body. So that no matter what choices she made, no matter what decrees were filed with the great state of Ohio, she would always be with him.

Always.

"Did I ever tell you how hot I think your tattoos are?" she asked, breaking into his thoughts. "Well, the two smaller ones, anyway, since you didn't have the dragon while we were together. But I always thought they were very sexy, and I wished I had the courage to get one of my own."

That surprised him. And sent his imagination running in all sorts of interesting directions. He could picture ink on Jenna. Something tiny and feminine on her ankle or hip or the swell of her breast.

The very thought heated his blood, had him thinking about getting her naked, and he figured he might as well give up on even pretending he wasn't half-hard beneath his Fruit of the Looms.

Well, what the hell. She was stretched out beside him, curled around him, and didn't seem to be all that concerned about keeping him at a distance, either literally or figuratively. Let her feel what she did to him and deal with the consequences.

Unfortunately, he wasn't sure whether to hope those consequences kept her dressed and at arm's length or got her naked and straddling him like she had last night.

"So what would you have gotten if you weren't afraid of needles?" He didn't ask where. He was afraid if she named one of those uber-sexy spots on her creamy flesh that he'd already envisioned, it would send him right over the edge.

"I'm not afraid of needles!" she exclaimed, sitting up slightly and turning to face him.

Even in the casual, sporty pajama set, she looked like a goddess. A pixie goddess with her lips tipped by a mischievous smile, but a goddess all the same.

"I just don't like pain. And what if I go through all that, then decide in three years that I don't really want a penguin on my ass?"

Gage raised a curious brow. "A penguin?"

Shrugging a shoulder, she said, "That was just an example. I was actually thinking of something more along the lines of a rose or a butterfly." She wrinkled her nose. "But those are boring, aren't they? I mean, everybody has rose and butterfly tattoos."

His hand cupped her arm just above the elbow, his thumb brushing slowly back and forth of its own volition. It had to be of its own volition because he would never—not since their divorce, anyway—voluntarily stroke her skin in what might be construed as an intimate gesture.

Would he?

"Arm cuffs and barbed wire are pretty typical," he replied, automatically flexing his bicep and wrist where one of each resided.

Her lashes fluttered as she glanced from the tribal band to the barbed wire and back. Then she reached to touch each with the fingertips of both hands—her left hand on his right wrist, her right hand on his left bicep.

"Yes, but very few people can pull them off as well as you do."

Before he could ask for clarification on that statement, she lifted her gaze to meet his. "I thought about using your name."

The emerald green of her eyes distracted him and he frowned as it took a second for her words to sink in. When they did, his stomach tightened and oxygen got stuck in his lungs.

His name branded in indelible ink somewhere on her body. Marking her forever as belonging to him.

He'd had no idea she'd considered such a thing . . . no idea she'd considered getting a tattoo at all.

On the one hand, he'd never pictured his pure, perfect Jenna marring her flesh with body art of any kind. Single ear piercings had seemed like plenty of decoration for her, and he'd never thought she needed—or wanted—more.

But on the other . . . Christ, the very thought of her letting herself be imprinted with his name, not only willingly, but happily . . . Of her cheerfully walking around with a label that told the world she belonged to him . . .

Even if it wasn't easily visible while she was dressed, she would know it was there. *He* would know it was there.

A stab of unadulterated pleasure and possession jolted through him, sending his heart thudding in his chest, blood slogging through his veins, and his balls tightening with desire.

He wanted to kiss her right here and now, then drag her off to the nearest tattoo parlor and see that she indeed had his name branded on her body before the night was over.

As it was, his grip had tightened on her arm and his shorts were tenting in a manner that couldn't be missed, not even by a blind woman.

But Jenna didn't act as though she noticed his physical reaction to her nearness or the confessions she was making one after another this evening. She simply continued to caress the lines of black ink on his wrist and bicep.

"Did I ever tell you how much I loved that you were a cop, too?" she asked in the same soft tone she'd been using since he'd placed her on the bed and tried unsuccessfully to walk away. "I was always so proud to know you were out there upholding law and order, helping people and keeping the community safe." A shimmer of sadness flashed across her face, but was quickly swallowed up by the small smile she forced to her lips. "It made *me* feel safe and protected."

The sexual heat that had been warming his blood by slow degrees over the last several minutes moved to his solar plexus and started to transform into an uncomfortable burning sensation.

All he'd ever wanted was to keep her safe. And according to her, she'd *felt* safe with him.

So how the hell could things have spun so far out of control? How could they have been married for three years, yet he'd never known she'd secretly wished for a tattoo—something as personal and distinctive as his name, no less? Or that she'd not only approved of but admired his choice of career.

Had she kept herself closed off from him so that he couldn't have been aware of these things? Or had he been the world's biggest idiot?

He suspected it was the latter. At the very least, he felt like an idiot. Like a man coming out of a decade-long coma to find that everything around him was strange and altered, and that life had moved on without him.

Was it possible that if he hadn't been such a fool, his relationship with Jenna might have turned out differently?

His gut said no. Just because he'd been clueless about a couple of things didn't mean there weren't still huge chasms of opposing opinions separating them. But she did have him reconsidering some of his previous trains of thought, some of the decisions he'd made and the beliefs behind them.

He raised a hand to stroke her hair, letting the soft black strands sift through his fingers. "All I ever wanted was to keep you safe," he told her in a rough whisper.

It wasn't easy for him to admit such a thing, not when he'd spent their entire courtship and marriage— hell, his entire life—being the strong, silent type. But if she could share some of the stuff closest to her heart tonight, in this dark, tiny room in her aunt's big old farm house, then so could he.

She leaned in, resting her torso against his chest and bringing her face so close to his own, he could feel her breath dusting his cheeks.

"You did. I was never afraid when you were around. Or when you were gone, because I knew you were out there fighting the good fight, and that if I needed you, you'd be there in a millisecond."

"Faster," he said past the lump growing in his throat.

She smiled at that, a gentle, angelic smile that reached her eyes and sent them sparkling. "Faster."

Relaxing across his upper body, she trailed her fingers around to the nape of his neck and toyed with the hair that was just beginning to grow out. Her touch tickled all the way down his spine.

Barely above a whisper, she murmured, "I always knew you'd be there for me if I was ever in danger, if anything was ever wrong."

He heard the pain in her voice, the words left unspoken, and felt a stab of guilt. "But you didn't think I was there for you the rest of the time, did you? For the everyday stuff."

In response, her lashes fluttered in a slow blink, her teeth nibbled her lower lip, and then she nodded.

His chest squeezed. Shit. He'd been such a fool. He'd screwed up their marriage in ways he was just now beginning to understand, and there wasn't a damn thing he could do about it. It was too late. The divorce was final and had been for more than a year. She was lost to him.

"I'm sorry," he said, the words grating as he forced them past a throat gone raw with emotion.

Her breathing hitched and a sheen of tears brightened her beautiful green eyes. "I know. I'm sorry, too."

And then she surprised him by covering his mouth with her own.

Purl 12

Gage's lips were warm and soft and reminded her of a thousand nights spent in his arms.

It should have mattered that they were divorced and had no business being in bed together.

It should have mattered that she'd taken advantage of him last night and he'd since vowed to stick to her like glue until he knew whether she was pregnant or not.

It should have mattered that kissing him, caressing him, making love to him would be the mother of all mixed signals.

It should have, but it didn't.

She didn't want to think about any of that right now, not when she was feeling more comfortable and content than any time in recent memory.

He let her kiss him, remaining perfectly still beneath her. His palms cupped her elbows, holding her in place, and his chest rose and fell against her, but he didn't deepen the kiss, didn't sit up and take over. Instead, he allowed her to run the show, kept his mouth slack while she nipped and licked and explored.

Oh, how she loved this man. It was like being a diabetic and having an overwhelming craving for chocolate éclairs, but knowing if she ate one, it might kill her.

Whoever said it was better to have loved and lost than never to have loved at all didn't know what the hell they were talking about.

It wasn't better, it was worse. So much worse, because now she knew what she was missing.

For this moment, though, she could have it again.

Last night had been wonderful, but it had been rather one-sided. This time, he was wide awake and would not only be a willing participant, but an active one.

And she didn't want to go back downstairs to the sofa or kick him out so she could have the bed. She didn't want to spend the night alone in this house, knowing he was only a few rooms or a stairwell away.

She teased the ends of his prickly, super-short hair, then let her fingers drift around to his neck and face. She stroked his jawline, with its layer of stubble making his cheeks rough.

That same five o'clock shadow scraped her skin as she dragged her mouth from his and began kissing everywhere else she could reach. Light, open-mouthed kisses that allowed her to take in every molecule of his scent and texture.

He smelled the same way he always had—delicious. His aftershave was one of those spicy sandalwood scents that reminded her of deep green pine forests, winter holidays, and isolated ski lodges with blazing fires in the hearth. Thanks to Gage, she was probably one of the only women on the planet who got turned on by Christmas trees.

She'd never told him that, but it was true. It was also

the reason she'd jumped his bones in front of the tree each Christmas Eve while they were married, and why so many of their decorations consisted of ornaments bought at after-Christmas sales. Rolling around on a tree skirt and banging into the Douglas fir a few dozen times did tend to result in broken candy canes and shattered bulbs.

And it had only taken her one Christmas morning of pulling those tiny, static-clingy silver icicles out of her hair and clothes and . . . other regions . . . to realize the wisdom of switching to a single string of garland.

She chuckled, thoughts of the past making her happy instead of sad for a change. Gage, she knew, had simply counted himself lucky to be getting lucky, and every time she came home with a different batch of decorations for the tree, he'd merely shrugged and chalked it up to one of those "woman at a clearance sale" things.

"What's so funny?" he asked in a low voice, and for the first time she realized his hands had somehow slipped under the hem of her pink tank top to skim the flesh of her midriff.

She shook her head, knowing she would never be able to explain, not in a few short seconds, and wanting to keep that particular memory to herself for a while longer.

"This won't change anything," he said when she didn't reply. "When we wake up in the morning, all of the same problems we've always had will be right there waiting for us."

The truth of his words pinched her heart, but they showed he'd been thinking along the same lines as she had. One night, one chance to experience again what they'd had during the early days of their marriage.

And then it would be over. The bright light of day would once again reveal all the sky-high hurdles between them that they couldn't seem to jump over or knock down.

"I know."

"And I'm not going away. You'll still have to put up with me hanging around until we know . . ."

He let the sentence trail off, but they were both well aware of what he'd been about to say. A flashing neon BABY sign might as well have been hanging from the headboard.

"I know."

His fingers continued to stroke her waist, her belly, the small of her back. Slowly, seductively, but his hands were so large that they covered a lot of space without needing to travel very far.

"It's up to you, Jenna," he murmured. "We can keep moving in the direction things are going, or I can get up and leave you alone. It's your call."

She shifted to lie more fully atop him, pressing her breasts into his chest and feeling the rigid length of his erection against her hip. It warmed her to know that even as aroused as he was, he had still offered to walk away.

"I don't want you to go," she said, rubbing her whole body lightly up and down against his.

He sucked in a breath and she saw the chords of his neck constrict. He nodded, almost imperceptibly, then in a grating tone said, "Fine. But you need to know that if I stay, I won't be tied down this time."

It was part warning, part threat, part reminder, and it sent a skittering of warmth blossoming low in her belly. Her throat was too tight, too dry to form words, so she merely nodded.

That was all it took for Gage's eyes to go from glittering with mild interest to blazing with sharp arousal. Both expressions were potent and intelligent, but only one was hot and smoldering with danger.

Luckily, she liked danger. She liked living on the edge.

But only with one person.

Only with him.

She returned her mouth to his jaw, letting her lips skate along the rough surface.

"You can be in charge this time," she whispered. "Whatever you want. However you want it. If you want to tie me to the bed instead, I'm game."

His fingers flexed in the flesh of her upper arms, and before she knew what was happening, she was flat on her back on the mattress with Gage hovering above her.

"I don't need toys and secondary fantasies," he told her in a voice rough with meaning. "When I'm with you, I only want you, just as you are."

His declaration brought a lump to her throat so that all she could do was swallow and blink back the sting of tears.

Gage wasn't the romantic sort. He'd never been one to bring her flowers or candy or plan something special for Valentine's Day. But once in a while he would utter something so beautiful, so heartfelt, he could have won a Mr. Romance competition against Prince Charming himself.

"It's a shame we couldn't work out our differences," she told him when she could finally manage non-wavering speech, "because we really are perfect for each other."

A flash of something dark and almost primitive passed over his face, but he didn't respond. Not verbally, anyway. Instead, with a growl, he grabbed her wrists and pinned her arms above her head, then ground his entire body against hers from chest to ankle while he took her mouth in a toe-curling, breath-stealing, bone-crushing kiss.

Gage couldn't decide what he wanted more—to wrap Jenna in about a thousand layers of cotton batting and cuddle her like a small child . . . or pin her to the bed and use his body to punish her for putting him through the wringer.

No one had ever been able to reach inside him and pull out his guts the way she could, and over the past couple days, she'd not only ripped them out, but tap-danced them straight into the ground.

He'd always thought guys who got mixed up in sex with the ex were . . . well, okay, yeah, lucky bastards as far as getting laid went, but also major morons. Once the marriage was over and the papers were signed, that needed to be the end, with both parties going their separate ways. Going back, even just for the occasional quick roll in the sack, was a bad idea. Bad with a capital B.

Lying in the cradle of Jenna's thighs hadn't altered his opinion, either. It was still a bad, bad idea.

But slap his ass and crown him the King of All Morons . . . damned if he was going to take the high road and walk away. He wasn't sure he'd have been physically able, even if he'd wanted to—which he sure as hell didn't.

So he'd take himself out back of the woodshed later. Probably whack his head against the wall a few hundred times and call himself every kind of name in the book, too.

Small price to pay, he rationalized, for another night spent with Jenna. Not tied to the bed at her mercy. Not being used in her misguided attempts to start a family. But making love with her the way they used to, the way he fantasized about while he was stuck on stakeouts or trapped undercover for weeks at a time.

His heart slowed its beat and his blood thickened, pumping like crude oil through his veins. Without warning, he pushed himself up and off the bed. Jenna made a startled, disappointed sound, which he ignored as he strode to his duffel where it rested on the floor in the corner and crouched to unzip the bag.

He found what he was looking for, then straightened and turned to toss the box on the bed. It landed next to Jenna's hip. Her eyes went to the label for a split second before she lifted her gaze to his.

"You know how I feel about this, and I'm not taking any more chances," he told her. Legs spread slightly apart and hands on his hips, his tone left no room for arguments. "We use them, or I go back downstairs and spend the rest of the night on the sofa."

In response, she sat up cross-legged in the middle of the bed, grabbed the box, and opened it at one end. Spilling the contents onto the mattress, she lifted a single small foil packet between two fingers and waved it in front of him.

"As long as you let me put the first one on."

Gage hadn't realized until that moment how still

he'd been holding himself, how rigid every muscle and tendon was—including his lungs, which suddenly sucked in a much-needed breath of air.

He didn't know what he'd have done if she'd refused. Burst into flames or crumbled into a pile of bones and ash, most likely.

But she hadn't refused, and he wasn't going to waste another second worrying about it. He'd rather just be grateful . . . and get down to business before she changed her mind.

He reached the bed in a single wide step, tangling his fingers in the hem of her pajama tank and yanking it up and off. She raised her arms to make the job easier and even tipped back on the mattress to let him strip her of her shorts.

He didn't take his eyes off of her as he quickly shucked his own boxer briefs and joined her on the bed. His big body covered hers, nearly swallowing her whole, and he held himself up on his arms to keep from crushing her.

The feel of her smooth skin rubbing against his own was like heaven, and something he hadn't known he'd missed quite so much until that very moment. He let the sensation sink in, etch itself into his memory, and warm him both outside and in.

It didn't take long, though, for more pressing desires to make themselves known. Between them, his penis pulsed and nudged forward insistently, as though it knew relief was only centimeters away.

"If you want the honors," he told her roughly, "you'd better hurry. I'm not promising to last much longer."

Jenna's lips pulled into a small moue. "Aw, poor baby. I thought big, strong men like you were supposed to have more staying power than that."

"Not where you're concerned," he bit out. Then he grabbed the wrist of the hand that held the condom packet and tugged it down toward her waist, closer to where she needed to put it to good use, rolling slightly to the side to give her room to work.

She chuckled, but didn't hold him in suspense. Tearing open the foil square, she removed the latex shield, placed it carefully over the tip of his throbbing dick, and rolled it into place.

Gage gritted his teeth, nostrils flaring as he fought to hold perfectly still, to not rush her or groan with delicious misery and risk slowing her down even more. Finally she finished, and he released a harsh breath.

Her hands moved to his shoulders while she laid there, staring up at him. Naked and welcoming and more beautiful than any woman had a right to be.

But he didn't want to get emotional about this. Didn't want to leave the door open to falling for her again, getting attached when there was no chance for reconciliation. He already had enough unfinished business to deal with where Jenna was concerned; he sure as shit didn't need more.

So rather than think, rather than take the time to enjoy the sight of Jenna sprawled beneath him, open and ready, he lifted her leg to hook around his hip and drove home in one long, forceful stroke.

As foreplay went, it wasn't exactly subtle or sophisticated. It didn't need to be. The second he pushed inside her, he knew she was fully aroused and more than ready to accept him. And if he were any more primed, he'd go off like a geyser.

Her other leg came up to hug his waist, linking at the ankles and jerking him that much closer, that much deeper. At the same time, her arms looped around his neck, tugging him down until their chests touched and her breasts were trapped between them.

He could feel the sharp bite of her nipples, the warm dusting of her breath on his face, her heart beating in tandem with his own. His fingers flexed in the flesh of her upper thigh and he leaned in to take her mouth in a hot, mindless kiss.

She kissed him back, her tongue warring with his while the rest of her body arched and writhed. Her movements enflamed him further, dragging a raw moan up from his diaphragm.

Sliding his hand around to cup her left buttock, he anchored her in place as he began to thrust. Slowly at first, savoring the in and out motion, the exquisite friction of hard against soft. Wet heat surrounded him, clutched at him, made him want to beg for mercy.

Rational speech was a little out of his reach, though, so he settled instead for deepening the kiss and deepening his strokes. Tiny mewling sounds emanated from Jenna's throat and her nails dug into his shoulders, letting him know she was right there with him. That the sensations building in his gut were also building in hers. That the flames licking their way up and down his spine were licking away at hers, as well. And whatever the female equivalent was of having his balls draw up in preparation for an orgasm to end all orgasms . . . well, that was there, too.

Her chest was heaving as she struggled to breathe, and finally she tore her mouth from his, sucking in gulps of much-needed oxygen. He followed her lead, then returned his lips to hers, kissing lightly before trailing his mouth along her cheek, up to her ear, down the taut column of her throat.

"Gage," she moaned when she could once again form coherent words. "Gage. Gage. Gage."

Hearing his name in that whispery, needy tone, from the lips of the woman he never thought he'd be with again, was like throwing gasoline on a brush fire. His temperature spiked, causing beads of sweat to break out all along his body, joining the fine layer of perspiration already there.

Her legs tightened around his waist, her arms around his neck as she rocked against him. Back and forth, harder and harder, grinding into his every thrust until they were both mindless and crying out for completion.

She came first, gasping, arching, gripping him like a vise. And since he'd only been hanging on, waiting for her to climax first, he let himself go.

His teeth clamped down on the muscle running between her neck and shoulder while his body convulsed with pleasure. He drove into her once, twice more, and then collapsed, feeling as drained and wrung out as an old dishrag.

He knew he was probably crushing her with his weight, but he couldn't seem to find the strength to move his pinky finger, let alone the rest of his two-hundred-plus-pound bulk.

She didn't seem to mind, though. Her arms and legs were still curled around him, and her fingers tickled through the short hair at the back of his head.

"Gage?" she asked after a couple minutes of near-silence, the only sound in the room that of their mingled breaths slowly returning to normal.

"Hmm?" He still hadn't lifted his head, still didn't have the energy.

"How many condoms were in that box?"

His brow arched and he summoned just enough control to lift his head a few inches to meet her mossy-green gaze. "I don't know. Ten, twelve, twenty-four. Why?"

"I'm just trying to plan the rest of my evening. And figure out how soon we might have to make a trip to town to replenish our supply."

It took a second for his sluggish brain to grasp her words, but when the meaning sank in, one corner of his mouth quirked up in a grin.

"I think we'll be okay for tonight." And if they ran out—tonight, tomorrow, the next day, any time, any hour—he'd simply hop on his Harley and cruise down to the nearest all-night convenience store.

He considered himself lucky that she'd been amenable to sleeping with him once—not counting last night's tie-me-up, tie-me-down, use-me-for-your-own-selfish-wishes scenario. The fact that she was open to going another round—maybe several more rounds while he was sticking to her like glue, anyway—made him want to get down on his knees and thank every god of every religion on the planet . . . and then some.

It probably wasn't smart. Probably wasn't the best way to maintain distance, keep that invisible wall of divorce and opposing views between them, but at the moment he didn't give a rat's hairy ass. That might have been the Little General exerting his will over any protests his frontal lobe might have been making . . .

But that was all right with him, too. Once in a while, it seemed, his dick had some damn good ideas.

* * *

Jenna stood at the kitchen table, watching Gage stroll toward the barn.

Letting him stay at Aunt Charlotte's with her—or at least stay without arguing, yelling, or giving him the silent treatment—probably wasn't the wisest move ever. Letting him make love to her night and day and noon and midmorning was more along the lines of something that qualified her for shock therapy treatments. At the very least, she thought she should have her head examined.

Then again, the thing that had set all of this in motion to begin with—that ever-so-bright idea of drugging him, tying him to the bed, and using him to get pregnant—should probably have been run past a psychological professional beforehand, too.

So, in essence, this was all Grace and Ronnie's fault. It had been their idea to start with, they'd badgered and cajoled her to go through with it, and if they hadn't, she wouldn't currently be in this mess.

Of course, "this mess" had her insides tingling like an electrified fence 'round the clock and had given her more bone-rattling, sense-zapping orgasms than she could count.

Literally. She'd lost track sometime after sixteen.

But she'd decided—admittedly, not necessarily with all of her brain cells functioning at top form—that a week of unfettered, uncommitted sex with her ex-husband wasn't the worst thing in the world.

For one, it was incredible. Not just good, not just enjoyable, but blow-the-top-off-her-head, leave-her-gasping-like-a-fish-out-of-water amazing. There had been times over the past few days when she could have sworn she'd lost feeling in her extremities.

Yes, they'd always had chemistry, and sex had definitely been one of the highlights of their married days, but she didn't remember it being *this* spectacular.

Maybe it was the illicitness of it all causing the extra sparks. The knowledge that they weren't married anymore, and therefore what they were doing was naughty, forbidden, taboo. And leading nowhere. It was hot, sweaty jungle sex just for the sake of hot, sweaty jungle sex.

For another, she was enjoying herself. She didn't mind staying at her aunt's farm while Charlotte was on the road traveling from craft show to craft show, and had been happy to agree when Charlotte had asked.

Sadly, she was used to being alone, and had long ago learned how to fill her time without feeling lonely. There was plenty of work to do just taking care of the alpacas, of course, but she'd also brought along a stack of paperback novels, a sack of yarn and needles, and notes in case she got around to starting on her lesson plans for the coming school year.

But having Gage around had turned out to be . . . kind of fun. She wouldn't have expected it, especially after the way they'd parted Saturday morning when he'd been so furious about being a pawn in her pregnancy plan. His sudden return and proclamation that he planned to shadow her every step until he knew whether or not they'd made a baby had immediately set her on edge.

She'd expected every second in his company to be excruciating. Instead, he'd not only seduced her and kept her in a very pleasant sexual haze, but he'd turned out to be quite helpful when it came to chores.

At first, he'd merely accompanied her to the barn and hung around watching while she cleaned stalls and put out fresh food, water, and hay. She hadn't minded, either. Her gym membership card had gotten a bit dusty lately, and she figured some nice, sweaty manual labor would be good for her heart and her waistline . . . and thighs and rear.

Plus, if her slightly pudgy, slightly creaky, slightly old aunt could run the place single-handedly, then surely she could do the same. And if she couldn't . . . well, if she couldn't, it was solid proof that she was a complete waste of human flesh and needed to hop on board the first UFO that tried to beam her up as a volunteer for their alien experimentation.

After a while, though, Gage had begun to pitch in. Bringing her a bale of hay here, helping to fill feed troughs there. Until eventually it seemed that Gage was doing most of the work and she was sitting back playing with the barn cats or petting one of Aunt Charlotte's beloved alpacas.

And through it all, she'd discovered something rather interesting about herself.

She'd discovered that she liked to watch.

It was no secret that her ex-husband was built like a god. A tall, muscular god, with wide shoulders, a narrow waist, and arms and legs the size of small redwood trees. He was like a sexy Paul Bunyan, and she had no doubt that he could palm any one of the alpacas milling around the pasture and spin it on the tip of his index finger, if he wanted.

He also had a firm, perfectly rounded ass that just wouldn't quit. Dressed most days in comfortably worn, nicely fitted jeans and black, white, or gray T-shirts that clung to his chest like a second skin, his muscles rippled with every move he made.

Bending over to scoop feed from the bin, his lats

stretched, the jeans tightened across his butt . . . and her mouth watered.

Hoisting a hundred-pound bale of hay, his biceps bulged, his thighs bunched . . . and her lungs refused to draw oxygen.

Stalking across the barn floor, the line of his shoulders and spine ran straight as a board and his hips swayed in that slow, lanky stride of his . . . and everything inside her turned soft and molten.

Whatever he was doing, she just stood back and admired the view. He was her own personal piece of eye candy, if only for the time it took for Aunt Charlotte to return and her to get her period. Which, surprisingly, suited her just fine.

Grace and Ronnie would be so proud. She'd always been the quiet one, the predictable one, the Good Girl of their trio. But shacking up with her ex-husband was none of those things. It was stupid and wrong and wicked, and possibly made her the official Bad Girl of the group.

A giggle escaped her, and she covered her mouth before her laughter could get out of hand.

Imagine that—Jenna Langan, a real, live Bad Girl. No one, she knew, would ever have expected it of her.

Funny how that made it all the more thrilling.

She liked being bad . . . within a certain structure and with a man she knew she was safe with. But still, considering her usual personality and past actions, she was being downright scandalous.

And right now, she felt like being the one to initiate a bit of scandalous behavior.

With heat unfurling low in her belly, she turned for the back kitchen door and slowly made her way to the barn.

A soft, upbeat tune met her ears and she started,

realizing the sound was coming from her own lips. She was humming. *Humming*, for God's sake. And her feet weren't so much moving one in front of the other as sort of . . . skipping along, almost as though she were floating on air.

None of these were good signs, and she would have to be very careful not to make too much of this time with Gage. Not to let any of it *mean* too much.

It was just sex. Really fantastic, scream-like-a-banshee sex, but just sex, and as long as she kept that firmly in mind, she would be fine.

Knit 13

Jenna sauntered into the barn, her eyes automatically adjusting to the building's dim interior. She tipped her head, listening for sounds of Gage and where he might be. A scraping noise from the rear of the barn drew her in that direction, and she realized he was doing a quick cleanup of the stalls before the alpacas were brought in for the night.

Tipping her head around the corner, she saw him working. His broad back. His strong, bare forearms and wide upper arms covered by snug black cotton. His long, denim-clad legs leading down to a pair of black leather boots.

She thought about making her presence known, knew she should offer to help . . . but it was such an attractive sight, she wanted to just sit back and watch. He was better than television.

Wandering over to a stack of hay bales in the center of the open barn floor, she sat down and waited for him to finish. A couple of her aunt's cats—all rescued, and all spayed or neutered because Charlotte didn't believe in adding to the animal overpopulation problem—came over to beg for attention, and Jenna happily stroked their bellies and behind their ears, sending them into choruses of loud, ecstatic purrs.

Several minutes later, Gage appeared in the doorway of the stall he'd been cleaning, leaning his shovel against the wall and his shoulder against the doorjamb.

"Looks like I'm not the only one who enjoys spending time in your lap," he drawled, a devilish grin tipping up the corner of his mouth.

Her cheeks flared with color, but she continued to meet his gaze. "What can I say? I'm a popular gal."

His smile slipped a degree, and in a low voice, he muttered, "So I've heard."

His response surprised her, and her eyes widened a fraction. "What's that supposed to mean?"

He shrugged his free shoulder, glancing past her rather than at her. "You've done a lot of dating since we broke up, that's all."

Ah, so that's what his sudden sullenness was about. "I am single now," she told him. "And who I date is my business, not yours."

"True," he reluctantly agreed, "I just didn't expect you to make the rounds quite so soon after the papers were signed."

"'Make the rounds?'" she repeated, a slight edge seeping into her voice.

"Yeah. You went out with another cop, a firefighter, a doctor, a Marine . . . What were you trying to do, give a one-woman salute to America's heroes?"

Anger simmered just below the surface . . . and then

disappeared as quickly as it had appeared. She should take his head off for that last remark, but darned if she didn't find him adorable instead.

"You're jealous," she said with a touch of humor.

His eyes narrowed. His lips thinned. "I don't think so."

"I do. Why else would you care who I dated, let alone keep track of them all?" A smile itched to spread across her face and amusement bubbled in her chest.

In contrast, Gage's scowl deepened. "I was concerned about you, that's all."

"Uh-huh." Setting aside the tabby who had been resting on her thigh, she stood up and wiped the seat of her lime-green Capri pants. She stepped forward until they nearly touched and tipped her head back to gaze directly into his brown eyes, gone even darker with displeasure.

Placing her palms flat on the hard wall of his chest, she said, "Well, I think it's sweet, whatever you want to call it. And for the record, I might have gone out with a lot of men these past few months, but I didn't sleep with any of them."

A tiny muscle at the corner of one eye twitched. "You didn't?"

She shook her head. "Not a one. The last man I slept with—not counting this weekend—was my husband."

A flash of heat flickered in his eyes and across his face. Bringing a hand to her chin, he cupped her jaw, stroking slowly back and forth with the pad of his thumb. A second later, he lowered his mouth and kissed her.

His lips were soft, but firm. Light but possessive.

She leaned into him, accepting what he offered and giving back everything she had in return.

"I haven't been with any other women, either," he murmured when they came up for air. "Just so you know."

His words made her gut hitch in a wave of unexpected happiness and relief, and she wrapped her arms around him even tighter, going in for another heartfelt kiss.

An hour later, after scaring off the cats and making a bit of a mess in the pile of hay bales, Jenna straightened her brightly colored peasant blouse and rewrapped the matching green boa around her neck while Gage tucked his T-shirt into his pants and buttoned the fly.

"I'm going into town tonight for my knitting group," she told him when he took her hand and tugged her to her feet. "Do you want to come with me?"

"Sure."

"I'm not riding on the back of your bike, so we'll have to take my little clown car," she said with a hint of humor in her voice.

He pulled a face, letting her know just how much he loved that idea.

"And I think Zack and Dylan may still be out of town, so you won't have anybody to hang out with at The Penalty Box. I'll understand if you'd rather stay here."

"Nah. I don't mind drinking alone. Besides, there's nothing here but cats, alpacas, and stacks of old craft magazines."

With a chuckle, Jenna said, "I think Daisy has a crush on you," referring to an adorable brown and white alpaca female who'd taken to following Gage around like a puppy whenever he was in the pasture or trying to herd them into their stalls for the night.

Rather than deny it, he grinned. "She was making eyes at me. If you're not careful, you might have some serious competition."

A jolt of something she didn't want to think too hard about struck her low in the belly. She also didn't want to think too long on his words, because—however lightly delivered—they implied there was more between them than truly existed.

"So when do you want to leave?" he asked.

She checked her watch, surprised to find it still on her wrist after the half-naked wrestling match they'd participated in earlier. "Soon," she said. "Maybe twenty minutes."

"That gives us enough time for another quickie," he replied.

Her eyes went wide and she turned a stunned expression in his direction. He wanted to do it again? So soon? She was lucky she could even walk after that last round.

He let out a bark of laughter. "Kidding," he said. "Just kidding. I can wait until we get back from town."

At that, she gave him the stink eye, and he laughed again.

"God, your face is so telling. I could yank your chain all day just to see what kinds of looks you'd give me."

Shaking his head—in amusement, she presumed— he cupped her chin with one hand and told her, "You go on in the house and get ready to leave. I'll get the mangy beasts bedded down for the night."

And then he kissed her. A quick, hard peck on the lips before he let his arm drop and headed back for the barn.

Carrie Underwood's "Before He Cheats" blasted from Grace Fisher's car stereo. For the past week—actually four days, eight hours, and forty-seven minutes to be exact, but who was counting?—she'd played the song over and over and over again, until the words seeped into her bones.

She could completely relate to the woman in the song who was taking revenge against her boyfriend by destroying his truck in the parking lot of a local watering hole while the jerk was inside cheating on her with some bleach-blond tramp. Especially since she'd done something poetically similar to Zack's beloved cherry-red Hummer after discovering another woman in his hotel room.

Grace wasn't exactly proud of some of the things she'd done that night. Oh, she was totally in the right, totally justified in her anger, her grief, her desire to punish the man who had hurt and betrayed her. No doubt about that.

And she wasn't sorry that she'd trashed Zack's apartment, either. Or flushed the two-carat diamond-and-platinum engagement ring he'd given her. Or stolen his dog. On the contrary, she only wished he had a second apartment she could have destroyed, had given her a second ring she could hammer and melt down to a pile of junk, and had a second dog she could abduct.

But she did sort of wish she hadn't made her abject misery and the details of her broken engagement *such* a public affair.

She'd always been open and honest on the air, which was what made her show such a hit. If she was having a good day, she shared her happiness with her audience, both in the studio and on the other side of the camera. If she was having a bad day, she used them to talk through it, and nine times out of ten found them more than willing to commiserate.

After all, everyone suffered from bad hair, chipped nails, lost contact lenses, and cramps, right? Letting her fans know she was as normal as the next person made her more human in their eyes, more like someone they would be friends with than an untouchable local celebrity.

This time, however, she suspected she'd gone slightly overboard. Not a lot, just a tad.

For instance, she probably shouldn't have gone on the air Monday morning with puffy eyes, a red nose, and streaked mascara because no matter how hard the makeup artist tried, she couldn't stem Grace's constant flow of tears or stop the makeup from running down her cheeks with them.

She also probably shouldn't have spent the whole hour ranting and raving and voicing her heartfelt desire for certain parts of Zack's anatomy to shrivel up and fall off. Or for him to contract a wasting disease. Or for the tramp he'd been with to break out in crusty, oozing sores so the world would know her for the whore she was.

That had been—perhaps, just a smidgen—over the top.

She wouldn't take it back, though. Nor would she take back the order for her program director to find guests and set up a series of men-are-scum shows for the very near future. She wanted to out the lying, scheming bastards who couldn't keep their dicks in their pants, and help other women like herself who had been lied to and betrayed by said bastards.

She also wanted to hang Zack upside down by his testicles and use his penis as a voodoo doll, but since he had a good eighty pounds on her and she hadn't yet figured out a way to hoist him up all on her own, she was willing to settle—for the time being, at least—for knowing that she'd done a good bit of damage to a handful of personal belongings that were near and dear to his heart.

Nosing her silver Lexus into a parking spot between two other cars, she folded down the visor and checked her appearance in the small mirror hidden there. She was at least *trying* to give a shit about her appearance again, but it had been a rough, ugly week.

Except for lipstick, her makeup was fine, so she applied another quick coat of high-gloss Ruby Slippers— a freebie from one of the major cosmetics companies in hopes that she would wear it on her show and possibly thank them publicly by name.

Her hair could use a little help, but running her fingers through a couple of spiky strands then scrunching in an attempt to curl a few others seemed to work.

What she needed was a spa day. Or at the very least, a trip to the salon. Her roots, which were a slightly darker shade of blond than the rest, were beginning to show.

Being an on-air personality, she didn't have the luxury of letting herself go. She was expected to have perfect hair, perfect skin, perfect nails, the perfect figure, and the perfect attitude to go with her perfect smile.

And ninety-eight-point-six percent of the time, she succeeded.

This week just happened to be one of the remaining one-point-four percent.

Her attitude ever since walking in on a half-naked Zack with a half-naked puck bunny had pretty much been "Fuck Zack, fuck her appearance, fuck the show, fuck the world."

Zack's constant attempts to contact her weren't helping, either. He'd called her cell and home phones—to grovel and beg for forgiveness, she was sure—so many times, she'd finally blocked his numbers. And everyone at work—hell, everyone she *knew*—had strict instructions not to let him anywhere near her, whether it was in person or through telephone calls, text messages, or candy-grams.

He was *persona non grata*, as far as she was concerned, and could go fuck himself, right along with his trail of willing bimbettes.

But because her attitude these days was somewhat less than perky and she had more important things on her mind—like how to torture and kill a man without leaving a trace—her hair and nails had pretty much fallen to the very bottom of her list of concerns.

Ironically, it was Zack's big, slobbery, pain-in-the-ass dog that had kept her sane and was starting to help her climb out of her deep, dark pit of despair.

Oh, Zack was still very much at risk of having an armed mercenary cut off the protruding parts of his body. She'd actually gone so far as picking up a copy of one of those magazines—*Mercenary Monthly* or some such—at a newsstand on her way home from work in hopes of finding a classified ad that read, *Will kill your cheating ex for cash.*

But before she'd had a chance to thumb through it, dumb old Bruiser had ambled up to the side of the bed, nudged her in the thigh, then hefted his way up to sleep next to her, his giant head and floppy, drool-covered lips resting in her lap. For the first ten seconds, she'd scowled and tried to push him away. Tried to figure out how to roll him off the bed and out of her room so she could lock the door.

She didn't even *like* the stupid Saint Bernard. She'd only brought him home with her because she knew it would kill Zack to find him missing. Even now, she imagined Mr. Hump-Anything-That-Moves pacing, tearing at his hair, bemoaning the fact that his beloved behemoth had been taken by his furious, and very possibly homicidal, ex-girlfriend.

It had taken only one glance from Bruiser's wide brown eyes to win her over, though. Well, that, and a deep, contented sigh and a long swipe of his wet tongue along her cheek. He'd done that, and she'd melted into a puddle of doggy-loving goo right along with the pint of Chunky Monkey resting on her bedside table.

She'd spent the rest of the evening cuddling with the big bag of fur under her favorite comforter while they'd both finished the ice cream and watched *Fatal Attraction* twice in a row. Of course, she'd had the presence of mind to cover Bruiser's eyes during the boiling bunny scene. Being a dog, he would probably *eat* a rabbit if given half a chance—heck, he ate socks, sneakers, and tennis balls on a regular basis—but she didn't want him to think she endorsed animal abuse of any kind.

The next morning, when she'd awakened with Bruiser still snuggled beside her, filling one side of the bed the way Zack used to, she'd suffered a brief moment of sadness. Most women, she supposed, would prefer to share their beds with a six-foot-six blond Adonis of a professional hockey player rather than a two-hundred-pound brown and white Saint Bernard with a drool stain the size of Jenna's Volkswagen under his right jowl.

Despite the damage to her fifteen-hundred thread count Egyptian-cotton sheets, there was something extremely comforting about having Bruiser there. His steady breathing, his soft fur, his radiating warmth. She'd wrapped her arms around him, given him a hard hug, and decided that life couldn't be all that bad if the sight of Zack's dumb dog could bring a smile to her face.

That name, though—Bruiser—would have to go. It reminded her too much of Zack, in a way that the Saint Bernard himself didn't. And she suspected a trip to the veterinarian was in their very near future. Breath that noxious simply could *not* be healthy.

So she would make an appointment to have her hair done. Maybe even her nails. And she would find a place that could do the same for Jethro.

Or Roscoe.

Or Chompers.

Well, she'd come up with something.

Grabbing her purse and knitting tote, she opened the driver's side door of her silver Lexus and headed for the front of The Yarn Barn. At the back of the store, she greeted her Wednesday-night knitting group and plopped down in the empty seat Jenna and Ronnie had saved for her.

Everyone else already had their projects out, needles clicking away as they knit and chatted and sipped lemonade from the small sidebar the store had provided for gatherings just like this.

Jenna was knitting yet another of her trademark boas. The feathery purple yarn ran through her fingers like water as she worked the set of large, plastic needles almost faster than the eye could see. She probably had two hundred boas in her own collection by now, but because she loved making them so much, she often gave bunches of them to her aunt Charlotte to sell at her craft booth—and this week, on the road. And they apparently went well, because Jenna was forever knitting them, and Charlotte was forever asking for more.

Ronnie, however, was using much smaller needles and a much sturdier yarn for the sleeve of a dark, smoky-blue sweater she was knitting for Dylan to wear during the coming winter.

"You're late," Ronnie said from her spot in the armchair to Grace's left. "Is everything all right?"

A stab of guilt speared her at the concern in her friend's voice. She knew Ronnie was worried about her. If their situations had been reversed and she'd been the one to witness Ronnie taking a baseball bat to Dylan's car and tearing apart his apartment, then crawling into her own bed to rail and wail for a day and a half, she'd have been concerned, too.

Frankly, Grace was lucky her friends hadn't called the men in white coats. Not that a few hours in a straitjacket and room with padded walls wouldn't have done her some good.

"Everything's fine," she reassured them. "Work has just been a little hectic lately, and my producer stopped me on my way out to argue about some upcoming show topics." The men-are-evil-and-must-be-shot segments, which she still maintained were timely and necessary to the fate of womankind.

Reaching into her bag, Grace removed a giant wad of thin, delicate white yarn already knit into several complicated pieces. Parts of what was supposed to have been her wedding dress. She'd been so excited about making it herself, instilling that love and excitement into every stitch.

On several occasions, Jenna and Ronnie had both offered to help, seeing how complicated the pattern was and fearing Grace wouldn't be able to complete it in time by herself. But Grace had declined. She'd *wanted* to do it all herself, to wear her own creation down the aisle.

Now, though, the idea brought her only pain and heartbreak.

Removing the miniscule needles from the piece she'd been working on last, she crossed her legs, sat back, and began tugging the end of the yarn to unravel the whole horrible mess.

"*What are you doing?*" Jenna shrieked, nearly jumping out of her chair when she spotted Grace's actions.

"I'm pulling apart my wedding dress," Grace answered, without emotion and without lifting her head. "And when I'm finished, I'm going to burn it, along with everything that asshole ever gave me, everything he left at my place, and every picture of him I can find."

While most of the women in the group didn't know about Zack's recent infidelity or the demise of their relationship, they caught on quickly—and wisely kept their mouths shut. Only Melanie, a young mother of two small children and one of their closer friends who often joined them for drinks at The Penalty Box after meetings, had the nerve to ask what in God's name was going on.

Ronnie attempted to fill her in as politely and with as few of the more gruesome details as possible. Grace wasn't nearly as discerning. She recapped the story in a voice sharp enough to cut glass and with a generous sprinkling of four-letter words . . . most of them used to describe the cheating Zack-Ass bastard.

By the time she finished, a pile of curly white thread lay at her feet, the physical embodiment of a metaphor for the unraveled mess her life and engagement had recently become.

Rather than feeling distressed over undoing all the hard work she'd put into the dress—and Lord, it *had* been hard work; tiny needles, whisper-thin yarn, and teeny, extremely complicated stitches—she found the harsh, repetitious yank-and-pull, yank-and-pull to be cathartic. She even managed to match her motions to the chorus of "Before He Cheats," which she was humming beneath her breath while the others chatted around her.

She hadn't been at it twenty minutes when she noticed the change. The air around her grew suddenly brittle, and there was a distinct shift to the sounds of the store that usually surrounded them.

And then there were the footsteps. Heavy, booted footsteps moving at a fast clip.

Grace's stomach tightened and a lump of something she preferred not to identify by name formed in her chest. She sat up straighter, steeling herself for what was to come as a dark shadow fell over her and the hot breath of doom blew on her neck.

"*You.*"

That one syllable was spoken so low and with so much venom, she was surprised she didn't die of odium poisoning right there on the spot. As it was, her skin did tingle and her pulse did kick up a beat.

Slowly and very carefully, she set aside what she was doing and turned in her chair to smile pleasantly up at a red-faced Zachary Hoolihan. He towered over her, chest heaving. He looked angry enough to spit nails, and she was frankly surprised steam didn't pour out of his ears.

Dylan stood on his left, just behind Ronnie's chair, looking distinctly uncomfortable. Gage stood on his right, looking . . . well, like Gage. Sort of big, intimidating, and expressionless. Between them, Zack put her in mind of Yosemite Sam, hopping around and blustering like a crazy person.

All week, she'd been imagining how she would act the next time she ran into Zack. And she'd known she would. Cleveland might have been a nice, big city, but it wasn't *that* big, and she'd expected he would make a point of tracking her down eventually to confront her about the damage she'd done to his car and apartment.

Payback, as they said, was a bitch.

"Are *you* addressing *moi*?" she asked in a voice so sweet, it nearly blew out her pancreas. Because damned if she'd let him think he'd gotten to her—aside from the recent acts of wanton destruction, that was.

"Damn right, I'm addressing you, Little Miss Smart-

Ass," Zack snapped. "You wrecked my apartment, stole my dog, and killed my car."

"Excuse me?" Her eyes went wide in practiced innocence.

"You. Killed. My. Car." He enunciated each word, spitting them through gritted teeth before resting both hands on the back of her chair and leaning in until they were nearly nose to nose. "You destroyed my Hummer."

"Your Hummer?" she asked in a voice she was pretty sure Shirley Temple had used in every one of her adorable little movies. "Did something happen to that big red beast?"

Zack stood back once again, but a vein had begun to throb at his temple and she thought he might be at serious risk of popping an embolism.

Good. It would serve him right, the jerk.

"You know goddamn well something happened to it. *You* happened to it. You broke into the parking garage at my apartment complex and destroyed my fucking Hummer! Then you broke into my apartment and went apeshit in there, too."

Grace placed one long index finger against her cheek, wishing now that she'd made a point of stopping at the salon *before* tonight's meeting. A beautifully manicured nail would have been just the thing to show Zack that she was doing fine without him. That she didn't care how many silicone-boobed puck bunnies he boffed.

Batting her lashes and pulling her mouth into a sympathetic pucker, she used her best Betty Boop impression to say, "But I thought you said your Hummer was *indestructible*."

If possible, Zack's face mottled an even darker shade

of red. His eyes were so wide, they were practically solid white with only pinpricks of blue at the pupils, and he looked ready to explode.

"Arrest her!" he burst out instead, pointing a shaking finger at her while nudging Gage in the ribs with his elbow.

Gage raised a brow, startled by his sudden demand. He glanced from Zack to Grace and back again. "What?"

"You heard me," Zack continued at a volume she suspected could be heard not only throughout the entire craft store, but at the other end of the strip mall where it was located. "Arrest her. Slap the cuffs on her, read her her rights, and drag her down to the pokey. I want her locked up for breaking and entering, theft because she took Bruiser, destruction of property, and just plain being a *bitch*." His tone lowered at the last and he delivered the insult as though it were supposed to be a great, painful stab to her heart.

Grace nearly snorted. After walking in on him five minutes after he'd Zamboni-ed some random tramp, being called a nasty name didn't make a dent.

Rising gracefully to her feet, she faced him full on, only the imitation-leather armchair separating them.

"I may be a bitch," she told him, her voice turning frosty for the first time since he'd walked into the store and started tossing around accusations, "but I'm a faithful bitch. You, on the other hand, are a lying, cheating bastard, who doesn't deserve a nice vehicle, doesn't deserve a nice apartment, and most certainly doesn't deserve a sweet little dog like Bruiser."

If Zack noticed her positive reference to the Saint Bernard when in the past she'd mostly complained about how big, stinky, and in the way he was, he didn't acknowledge it. Instead, he latched on to the rest of her diatribe.

A muscle in Zack's jaw jumped as he ground his teeth. Leaning forward until they were nearly nose to nose, he said, "For your information, I *didn't* lie and I *didn't* cheat. Something I'd have explained to you if you'd stop being pissed off for five minutes and answered your goddamn phone!"

"Oh," she replied tartly, "I suppose that bimbo was in your bed because she started choking on a salad shrimp during a promotional banquet and you decided to take her up to your hotel room to give her the Heimlich, right? And somehow during all the chaos, everybody's clothes just *fell* off."

"I didn't *take* her to my room," Zack insisted, eyes narrowed in growing frustration. "I didn't even know she was there."

"Yeah, and there's this great piece of swampland in Florida I'm thinking of buying for a summer getaway." She snorted. "I may have been dumb enough to date you for three years, but I'm not a *complete* idiot. You're lucky your Hummer wasn't set on fire, too."

"So you admit you did those things. I told you," he said, elbowing Gage again. "See, she confessed. Arrest her."

"I didn't confess to anything," she replied softly. "I was simply making a statement. If someone else feels the same way about you as I do and decided to mete out a bit of karmic justice . . . well, I say, Yay, them. And screw you, Zack."

Balling his hands into fists, he jabbed them on his hips and ground out, "Dammit, I *didn't* cheat on you,

Grace. You'd know that if you'd answer one of my phone calls and give me five fucking minutes to explain."

"You don't need to explain. I've got eyes to see and a brain that's fully capable of adding two plus two to get four. And you can spend your five fucking minutes fucking someone else from now on."

With that, she used her foot to rearrange some of the yarn on the floor that had gotten moved around and took her seat once again, returning to the job of unraveling as though none of the men hovering behind her even existed.

She heard grumbling, but couldn't quite make out what Zack was saying beneath his breath. Obviously, some of the wind had been taken out of his sails—something that should have pleased her, but didn't.

If she'd been home alone, she probably would have been curled up in bed by now with . . . Rex? King? Tonto? . . . and another pint of Ben and Jerry's. As it was, she was hanging on to her composure by a thread thinner than the yarn she was even now pulling loose from her wedding gown pattern.

Surprisingly, it wasn't anger that threatened to bubble over, but sorrow, and she hoped to hell Zack left before she burst into tears and let him know how much he'd hurt her.

Thankfully, he did, but not without a bit of prompting from his friends.

"Come on," Dylan said. "Let's get out of here. You'll feel better after a couple of beers."

"I'll feel better after she's behind bars," Zack quipped, and she could imagine a sneer twisting his lips. Ironically, his tone didn't seem to carry the same vehemence of only minutes before.

Even knowing he couldn't see the gesture, Grace raised a brow and calmly said, "And I'll feel better after you break out in genital herpes and your cock falls off."

Purl 14

"You hope he breaks out in genital herpes and his cock
falls off?"

Ronnie repeated the line for what had to be the six-
thousandth time, followed by her six-thousandth chortle
of laughter. This one just happened to be limoncello-
induced.

Jenna was sipping at her own bright yellow drink,
but even though Grace's parting remark to Zack had
been amusing, she hadn't gotten quite as big a kick out
of it as Ronnie apparently had.

After Zack had stormed out of the craft store with
Gage and Dylan in tow, the ladies had continued on
with their meeting. It had been a bit beyond them to
pretend nothing had happened, but Grace had staunchly
refused to comment on Zack's accusations, remarking
only on his infidelities and some of the less insane
ways she'd handled it.

Not that taking scissors to a man's hockey scrap-
book and abducting his two-hundred-pound canine
sounded particularly sane to anyone listening.

The women had all agreed, however, that she'd had

every right to toss his clothes into the street—which had then led to a discussion about the classic scene in *Waiting to Exhale* when Angela Bassett's character had stuffed everything her cheating husband owned into his car, doused it with lighter fluid, and set it afire.

Jenna cringed at the reminder, afraid it might be giving Grace fresh ideas. As it was, Grace took a tiny notepad out of her purse and jotted down the titles of every wronged-woman film the others in the group could recommend. *Waiting to Exhale*, *Fatal Attraction*, *Double Jeopardy*, and *Chicago* topped the list, but there were so many, Jenna thought she might have to confiscate Grace's video rental card before she got the chance to do any more "research" into the fine art of making a man's life a living Hell.

Soon enough, though, the meeting had broken up, and Grace, Ronnie, and Jenna had all agreed to head over to The Penalty Box for a drink. Even though she knew Gage would be there, waiting for her, Jenna felt the need to suggest that perhaps they go somewhere else. Because, of course, Zack would be there, too, and the way Jenna saw it, putting Grace and Zack in the same room together—even a very large room, filled with dozens of other people—was a recipe for disaster.

But Grace didn't want to avoid the Box, she informed them haughtily. She wanted to go there, order a martini the size of Lake Erie, and have a good time, if only to prove to Zack that he couldn't scare her away.

The Penalty Box had been their hangout for as long as Jenna could remember. Not just Zack's and Grace's, but the entire gang's.

Jenna's attention skimmed across the bar to where Gage sat with his friends. Zack was leaning on the round tabletop, wearing a deep scowl and sending the occasional scathing glance in Grace's direction.

Ronnie's boyfriend, Dylan, looked much more pleasant, sipping his beer and staring openly at the woman he loved. His gaze wasn't exactly scorching, but there was a definite heat there, and Jenna thought he was probably calculating how much longer he had to hang out with the guys and let Ronnie hang out with her girlfriends before he could pluck her out of the booth and drag her home for a long and thorough ravishment.

Truth be known, Jenna was thinking something along those lines herself. Gage's confession that he hadn't been with any other women since their divorce—and certainly not before, thank goodness—played through her mind. Even when he'd been free, even when he would have been well within his rights to date and sleep with other women, he hadn't.

Her heart gave a little flip at that, and at the knowledge that he was probably one of the most trustworthy men on the planet.

Gage chose that moment to look up, and their eyes met. She expected him to smile, maybe wink, but instead his expression remained stoically blank.

So much for trying to figure out how soon she could make her excuses and drag him home for some good old-fashioned slap-and-tickle.

Turning back to her drink, she used the tiny swizzle straw leaning against the side of the slanted glass to toy with the yellow liquid.

"Okay, you are entirely too quiet tonight," Grace remarked.

Jenna raised her head and gave her friends a crooked smile.

"Sorry, I was just . . ."—*feeling guilty*—"thinking."

Grace stole a glance over her shoulder. "About Gage the Wonder Stud?"

Heat flared into Jenna's cheeks.

"Oh, stop!" Grace chastised lightly, wrapping an arm around Jenna's shoulders and giving her a sideways hug. "Just because my life is currently circling the toilet bowl doesn't mean you shouldn't be happy. Look at Ronnie, she's positively giddy, and I only half want to strangle her."

They both turned their gazes to Ronnie, who was wearing a wide smile and staring off across the room at Dylan.

"It's sickening, isn't it?" Grace asked in a soft aside.

Actually, Jenna thought it was kind of nice. She remembered that part of the courtship ritual and how great it was to be head-over-heels in love, to have the world and every breath revolve around another person.

"All right," Grace said with a sigh, pulling her arm back and taking a long, strong suck of her quickly disappearing limoncello. "I can see I'm the only one having a down-with-men moment here."

"I'm sorry," Jenna told her, "I know you're having a rough time right now. I don't mean to be distracted."

Grace shrugged a slim shoulder. "That's okay. I'm getting kind of tired of talking about the cheating louse, anyway. It's taking up too much of my time."

She raised a hand to get their waitress's attention and signaled for another round of drinks. "So tell us what's been going on with you and Gage. And I sure as hell hope he *has* been a wonder stud instead of just some damn Shetland pony."

Jenna's face flushed with color once more. Not so

much from Grace's remark this time as the memories it invoked. Memories of exactly how wonder-studly Gage had been the past few days.

"Nothing . . . *much* has been going on."

Grace and Ronnie exchanged a glance before sly grins slid over both their faces.

"Oh-ho," Ronnie laughed. "That means *a lot* has been going on. Come on, Jenna, give us the scoop."

Jenna covered her eyes with a hand and gave her head a little shake. It wasn't that she didn't want to share the details of recent events with her best friends, but since she wasn't clear herself on exactly what was going on, she didn't quite know what to say.

"When last we checked in on Jenna and Gage, dear viewers," Grace murmured, bringing a curled hand to her mouth as though it held a microphone for her mocking narration, "they were shagging like howler monkeys and loving every minute of it. Let's catch up, shall we?"

She thrust the invisible mike at Jenna, and Jenna laughed. "All right, all right. Well, at least until this afternoon, we were still shagging like . . ." She trailed off, not quite able to say it.

Grace, of course, had no such qualms. "Howler monkeys."

"Yes." Jenna licked her lips, eyes darting away for a moment in embarrassment. "I'm not sure why, since we both know it's not going anywhere."

"I know why," Ronnie supplied, leaning back a couple of inches while the waitress placed a fresh drink in front of her. "It's because Gage is a gorgeous hunk of man and you've never really gotten over him."

"That's not—" Jenna began. But, of course, it was

true. She knew it, they knew it . . . heck, Gage probably knew it now that she'd jumped his bones six ways from Sunday.

Without the hope of getting pregnant, either, which had been her original goal and the whole point of molesting him to begin with. How telling was *that*?

"He insists we use a condom each and every time," she confided, tucking her head and playing with the straw in her new cocktail, but not bothering to take a sip. "And first thing every morning, he makes me take one of those home pregnancy tests. They've all been negative, of course, but he doesn't seem to believe me when I tell him it's too soon to find out if I'm pregnant or not. He still insists I pee on those stupid sticks and wait for them *not* to turn blue."

Ronnie made a *hmmm* sound low in her throat and both women's brows rose.

"What?" Jenna looked from one to the other, confused by their responses. "Am I missing something?"

It was Ronnie's turn to shrug. "I'm just wondering why a man who claims not to want kids is so obsessive about finding out whether or not you're pregnant. I mean, if the thought of fathering a child is so repugnant to him, you'd think he'd have taken off like his tail was on fire the minute he woke up and realized you'd lured him into a little forced procreation."

"Gage isn't that kind of man," she told them with a shake of her head. "I should have known better than to think he could just be a sperm donor. He would never abandon a child, even if its conception hadn't been entirely mutual."

"So what's going to happen if you are pregnant?" Grace wanted to know. "Is he going to stick around and help you raise the child, or does he just want to know you're pregnant before he takes off and leaves you to deal with it on your own?"

"I don't know," Jenna said. "We haven't really discussed it. And I don't see the point in worrying or making plans until we know there's something to make plans for."

A few brief seconds passed with only the sounds of the bar filling the silence—raised voices, clinking glasses, a baseball game playing on one television, mixed sports coverage playing on another.

Then Grace diplomatically put in, "All we're saying is that you and Gage never truly wanted to split up in the first place, and neither of you have ever really gotten over each other. Even you've admitted that much."

Jenna opened her mouth to protest, but once again her friends were speaking only the absolute truth, so what could she say that wouldn't sound either ridiculous or like an out-and-out lie? Clamping her mouth shut, she waited quietly for them to continue.

"So maybe," Ronnie said, taking over Grace's point of view, "Gage is sticking around because he's just as torn up over the divorce as you are."

"And just as *not* over you as you are over him," Grace added.

For several long moments, Jenna's pulse pounded in her ears as she considered what her friends were saying. Personally, she thought they were a little off base.

Time and time again, Gage had made it perfectly, crystal, plate-glass clear that he *did not* want children. On top of that, he'd made no secret of the fact that he was thoroughly pissed that she'd tricked him into possibly getting her pregnant, and now that they were continuing to sleep together, he wasn't taking any chances. If he could have wrapped them both in cellophane from head to foot and gotten the same tactile pleasure from the act, she suspected he would have done it.

The idea that he might be sticking around for more than frequent hot sex and to make sure she *wasn't* pregnant was alien to her, and something she couldn't quite stretch her mind around.

She was still mulling over what Grace and Ronnie had said later that night, on the ride back to Charlotte's.

Could they be right?

She cast a sideways glance at Gage, who was behind the wheel of her yellow bug. He hated the car, but seemingly hated being a passenger in the tiny Volkswagen even more. Apparently it was more masculine to *drive* a pint-size Beetle than be seen riding around in one.

Never mind that his legs were bent at an awkward angle, even with the seat pushed all the way back, or that the top of his head brushed the roof of the vehicle.

Jenna turned away, looking out the side window before she started laughing at his obvious discomfort and annoyance at being uncomfortable.

"Did Grace vandalize Zack's Hummer?" he asked out of the blue.

Then again, maybe it wasn't the size of her car that had his jaw locked and his knuckles turning white on the steering wheel.

Jenna licked her lips, debating how to answer. On the one hand, she had never lied to him, and just because they were no longer married and she didn't technically owe him any allegiance, she didn't want to start now. On the other, she felt a fierce need to be loyal to Grace and maintain her friend's confidence.

She cocked her head to study Gage's profile, and for the first time since they'd left the bar, he slowly turned his head to meet her gaze.

"I wasn't there, and I don't know the details, but yes," she murmured barely above a whisper. It hurt to hear herself admit it, to betray a friend's confidence. But almost as though she were possessed by a powerful, supernatural spirit, she felt compelled to tell Gage the truth, regardless of the consequences.

His eyes stayed locked with hers for a heartbeat longer before he gave a sharp, brief nod and returned his attention to the road.

The silence that followed made Jenna's skin hurt. She felt dizzy from lack of oxygen and her vision blurred with near-panic.

"Are you going to arrest her?" she asked desperately, chest heaving in the beginning stages of hyperventilation. "Or tell Zack so he can have her arrested?"

It seemed like an eternity until he answered, but finally he said, "Nah. Zack has more money than God. He can buy a dozen Hummers to replace that one, if he wants. And if he really did cheat on Grace, then I don't feel particularly sorry for him."

Jenna let her head fall against the cool glass of the passenger-side window, sucking air into her abused lungs.

After another couple of miles passed in silence and her brain was able to process the tail end of his reply, she turned back. "*Did* he cheat on her?"

Once again, he was slow to respond. Rolling his

shoulders beneath his tight black T-shirt, he said, "He says no. Swears that woman wasn't in his room when he went for a shower, and he doesn't know how she got in. He didn't even know she was there until Grace showed up and discovered her."

"Do you believe him?"

"There's no reason not to. He's never lied to me before, as far as I know, and he wouldn't need to lie to me about this. I'm not his mother or his wife or his priest. It's not my place to judge him. What he does in his private life is his business, whether I approve of it or not. He also knows that no matter what he tells me, I wouldn't repeat it to anyone else."

Which only made Jenna feel like more of a heel for having repeated something about *her* best friend that was meant to be kept in confidence. She nearly groaned as remorse pooled in her gut and threatened to swamp her.

"He's really torn up over it," Gage continued as they pulled into the gravel drive beside Charlotte's big, white farm house. He cut the engine, but made no move to get out of the car. Instead, he shifted to face her, lifting an arm to rest on the back of the seats. His hand dangled near her face and his fingers toyed with the ends of her hair.

"He's called Grace a thousand times, at least, but she won't answer—not even when he tries to fool the caller ID by using different phones. The doorman at her building won't let him in, and the guards at the television studio have strict orders to call the police if he sets foot on the property. That's why I thought it was a good idea for him to go over to The Yarn Barn tonight. I was hoping

Grace would give him a chance to explain, at least *listen* to his side before she cut him off at the knees."

"In case you hadn't noticed," Jenna murmured, "Grace isn't exactly the magnanimous type. Not when she's hurting and feels so strongly that she's been wronged."

He huffed out a breath. "Tell me about it."

Rather than lowering the level of tension in the tiny vehicle, the revelation that Zack may not have cheated on Grace after all only seemed to ratchet it up several notches. Jenna's chest felt tight and she could feel tightly constrained emotion radiating from Gage in an ever-growing ripple effect.

Rubbing her palms nervously along the outside of her thighs, she licked her lips and softly asked, "Are you angry with me?"

One, two, three seconds passed without a response. Then, just as quietly, he said, "Why would I be angry?"

For a moment, she thought about keeping her mouth shut. If he wasn't upset, maybe she shouldn't have drawn attention to the fact that he seemed to be. And if he was—well, it probably would have been smarter to pretend she hadn't noticed.

But the stiff jut of his chin told her *something* was wrong, and she would just as soon get to the bottom of it before they went in the house. Their relationship was stressful enough these days, there was no use tossing added kindling to the pile.

"Because of what happened at The Yarn Barn with Zack and Grace. Because I knew what she'd done, but didn't tell you."

"Why would I be mad about that?" he asked carefully.

"Well, it was a lie of omission," she admitted, "and I know how you feel about that sort of thing."

He mulled that over for a second before the flat line of his mouth relaxed a fraction.

"I understand why you did it. I don't even blame you; you were just protecting a friend. If Zack had admitted to an affair, I probably wouldn't have told you, either. But it did make me wonder . . ." His words trailed off for a moment and he shrugged. "Things between us were so ugly there at the end, the thought crossed my mind that this might not have been the first time you lied to me—by omission or otherwise."

Jenna's heart pounded against her ribcage like a jungle drum and a lump formed in her throat. She knew how he felt about liars. On his top ten list of sins that would send you to Hell, directly to Hell, do not pass Go and do not collect two hundred dollars, it was right up there with child sex offenders and people who talked in the theatre.

Swallowing hard in an effort to dislodge the knot in her chest, she thought back to everything that had passed between them over the years. Had she ever lied to him, be it a little white lie or a big, honking black one?

After a brief silence, she nodded and looked him directly in the eye as she murmured, "I have lied to you."

His already tense body tautened even more at her admission, every muscle going tight and a tic starting at the back of his jaw. When he spoke, his voice was thick with emotion. "Do I want to know?"

"I'm not sure. It's a pretty big one."

Gage's eyes slid closed, almost as though what she was about to say might be too much for him to handle.

When his eyes opened again to settle on her, his mouth twisted into a grim line and he said, "All right, I'm ready. Tell me."

The confession wasn't easy to get out, and it took her a minute. A minute to form the words. A minute to decide if this was truly a wound she wanted to open, a part of her heart she wanted to bare and leave vulnerable.

But he was waiting, and looking so earnest, she couldn't find it in her to back out now. Not just because her pulse was pounding in her throat or her stomach was doing handsprings at the speed of light.

"I lied," she began in a voice so low and shaky, she wasn't even sure he could hear her, "when I told you I wanted a divorce."

For a moment, it was as if all the air had been sucked out of her tiny Volkswagen bug. Neither of them moved, and Gage held himself so rigid, she wasn't certain he was still breathing. But she'd already started to tell him the truth, so she might as well finish it.

"A divorce was the last thing I wanted, but you weren't talking to me, were starting to shut me out, and I didn't know how to reach you. Nothing else I tried had worked, so I thought maybe demanding a divorce would shock you into realizing how much you'd changed since we got married."

Her gaze dropped to stare at her hands where they were clasped tightly in her lap, and if possible her voice grew even softer, more pained. "I expected you to say *No way in hell* and agree to counseling or something to work out our problems . . . not to nod and move out of the house, then sign the papers without a single argument when they arrived."

She hadn't intended to cry, had deemed herself well past the point of breaking down every time she thought about that period of her life and how much it had hurt to not only lose her husband, but to have him walk away as though their marriage was no more important to him than a piece of junk mail or an old pair of shoes. But that didn't stop tears from gathering at her lashes and spilling down her cheeks.

"Why didn't you fight for me?" she asked, then turned her head to face him full on. "Why didn't you fight for us?"

Knit 15

The ache in Jenna's voice, the sadness on her face, squeezed Gage's heart and tore it into a million tiny pieces. He would rather take a sucker punch to the rib-cage than see that expression on her face.

And he'd rather get kicked in the crotch a thousand times than be the cause of it.

But here he was, the main source of her grief and despair, of the tears pouring down her face.

What could he say? How could he explain that leaving her had been the single hardest thing he'd ever done in his life? That it had ripped his guts out and in many ways left him a shell of a man. Or that he'd had to get blind, stinking drunk before he could bring himself to put his John Hancock on those divorce papers.

He couldn't. Because if he tried, she'd wonder why he hadn't stayed instead, hadn't fought the way he now knew she'd hoped and expected him to, and he couldn't explain the driving force behind that decision, either.

So he did the only thing he knew he wouldn't screw up. He hooked a hand around the back of her neck, yanked her forward as far as their seatbelts and the min-iscule automobile would allow, and kissed her. With his lips and tongue and body, he tried to tell her what he couldn't put into words.

Jenna's nails dug into the muscles of his upper arms and she made small, desperate mewling sounds at the back of her throat. Sounds he answered with low groans of his own.

He shifted, trying to get closer, trying to draw her farther across the seat, but the damn seatbelt dug into his chest, his elbow hit the steering wheel, and the gearshift nearly cut off the circulation in his leg.

With a muffled curse, he pulled back, releasing Jenna—and smacked his head into the roof of the car.

"Fucking damn Volkswagen," he muttered, breathing heavily and rubbing the sore spots on his thigh and skull at the same time. "Why couldn't you buy a decent American car instead of this tuna can on wheels? I feel like freaking Frankenstein stuffed into a jelly jar."

Though her cheeks were still flushed with passion and damp from her tears, the tension of a moment ago seemed to have passed and Jenna's mouth curved just before she broke out laughing.

"It's Frankenstein's monster," she corrected in typi-cal schoolmarm fashion, "but you're right, that is sort of what you look like. Minus the bolts in your neck, of course. And this is a perfectly good car," she added staunchly, defending her bug like a mama dolphin de-fending her young, "just maybe not for a man the size of a grizzly bear."

His own lips twisted, and he had no choice but to chuckle along with her. After a minute, he unsnapped his seatbelt and pushed the driver's-side door open. "So let's get out of here before I start to cramp up and somebody has to chop off my limbs to get me free."

Rounding the hood of the car, he waited for her to collect her purse and knitting tote—a dark blue one with a sunflower on the front that she'd made herself—then took her hand as they walked to the house. Gage was glad she was no longer peppering him with questions about his state of mind when they separated, but he could have stood a few more hours of heavy petting in her front seat . . . even if it made him feel like a horny sardine.

She fitted the key into the lock, then opened the door and preceded him inside. One by one, she flipped on the lights, laying her bags on the table as she made her way to the kitchen.

"Would you like something to drink?" she asked, pulling open the refrigerator door and studying its contents.

Gage didn't know what he wanted. He wasn't thirsty, but a couple good stiff shots of Johnny Walker Black might help to numb the prickles of memory stemming to life low in his belly. Memories he didn't want to think about, and certainly didn't want to relive.

"No, thanks," he said, dropping into a straightback chair beside the table and resting his arm along the solid oak surface. He drummed his fingers for a second, then reached almost distractedly for her knitting tote.

A snowball-sized clump of bright purple yarn was sticking out of the top and he grasped it, slowly drawing the length of half-completed boa toward him. She'd completed two or three feet of the thing, but he knew from her burgeoning collection of homemade boas that she tended to like them quite a bit longer.

Despite the number of times he'd seen her wearing them, the number of times he'd unwound them from her neck, handed them to her while she was getting dressed, or simply moved them out of the way, he didn't think he'd ever taken note of how soft they were. This one felt like silk, and he couldn't seem to stop rubbing the feathery strands between his big, callous-rough fingertips.

When Jenna appeared beside the table and took a seat across from him, he jerked, then felt his face heat with embarrassment at being so distracted by the texture of a feminine purple boa that he hadn't heard her approach. She didn't seem to notice his discomfort, though; or if she did, she ignored it. Instead, she simply leaned back in her chair and took a sip from the small glass of orange juice in her hand.

"Remember the time you tried to teach me to knit?" he asked quietly, surprised when the question popped out of his mouth. He hadn't intended to ask it, hadn't even realized he was thinking along those lines.

She chuckled, and the action did amazing things to her breasts.

"Talk about a disaster," she said with amusement. "I think it took me a full week to untangle all the knots out so I could use the yarn again."

Rather than being offended or embarrassed by her recollection of his shortcomings, he took it in stride and found himself enjoying the teasing note in her voice. It was reminiscent of the days when they'd been dating or were newly married. The fun times. The happy times. The times before reality had sunk in and tainted every part of their relationship.

"Hey, I warned you I wouldn't be any good at it." He lifted his hands in the air, turning them one way and then the other. "These massive paws are meant for manly stuff like chopping wood and working on car engines."

Still grinning, Jenna shook her head, sending the short strands of her ebony hair bouncing. "Likely excuse. That's as bad as claiming cooking and cleaning are woman's work, when we both know men are as capable of boiling water and pushing a vacuum as anyone else." Her brow rose as though daring him to argue.

He might have been a fool about many things, but even he wasn't stupid enough to step on that particular land mine.

And then she upped the ante—practically called his manhood into question—by slanting him a sly glance and adding, "Dylan learned to knit."

The tone of her voice alone suggested she considered Dylan the more masculine of the two just because he'd managed to click two sticks together and somehow come up with a length of twisted yarn that loosely resembled a scarf.

So of course he responded in the only acceptable manner for someone of the Y-chromosome persuasion. "Dylan is a pansy."

Her eyes widened at that a second before she burst out laughing. "Oh!" she barked. "So Dylan is man enough to hang out with you and be one of your closest friends, but the minute he picks up a pair of knitting needles, he suddenly becomes a fairy, huh? I'll have to be sure to share your point of view with Ronnie the next time we talk."

Gage scowled, because he knew that's exactly what

she would do. Even if he took it back and proclaimed Dylan the manliest of men because he'd learned to knit, this exchange was still destined to become conversational fodder for their next Girls' Night Out or Wednesday-night knitting group—if not a good deal sooner.

After that, Ronnie would relate the tale to Dylan, and though he doubted Dylan would be upset by his remark, Gage suspected his friend *would* ride his ass about it from now until the next millennium.

"So teach me," he said, blurting out the first thing that popped into his head that he thought had a shot in hell of getting him out of the doghouse.

Her mouth went slack and she blinked like he'd just announced he enjoyed wearing ladies' underwear.

"Excuse me?" she asked, the words garbled with shock.

He shrugged a shoulder and kicked back in his chair even more, assuming a relaxed position. "I know you tried once, but I'm not sure my heart was in it. I was humoring my new bride. Try again, and I promise to take it more seriously. If you think you're a good enough teacher to pull it off, that is."

He added the last because he knew it would get her dander up. And sure enough, her spine straightened and she raised a brow, this time in acceptance of his challenge.

"Fine; let's go."

She stood up, grabbed her knitting bag and the half-finished purple boa he'd been toying with the entire time, and stalked past him toward the sitting room. He followed at a slower pace, wondering exactly what he'd gotten himself into . . . and what the hell had possessed him to bring up the ill-fated topic of knitting in the first place . . . before dropping onto Charlotte's old-fashioned settee beside her.

Jenna pulled the started boa, loose yarn, and two large white plastic needles out of the sunflower tote, then tossed the bag aside. "Are these big enough for your 'massive paws,' Sasquatch, or should I go out and chop down a couple of pine trees for you to use instead?"

He pulled a face and shot her a warning glance before palming the needles. "I think I can handle them."

But inside his head, of course, a small voice was warning him that he might have bitten off more than he could chew. He gave the yarn connected to the needles a sharp tug, testing its tensile strength and wondering if it would hold his weight if he decided to hang himself with it after he royally fucked up this little impromptu knitting lesson.

Idiot, idiot, idiot, his mind screamed. He should have kept his mouth shut. Or better yet, grabbed Jenna and pinned her to the wall, using his tongue for better things than talking himself into a corner.

A corner filled with knitting needles, frilly purple yarn, and an ex-wife who would never let him live this down.

Taking a deep breath, he tried to remind himself that he was a cop, for God's sake. Six-feet-three-inches, two-hundred-plus-pounds of solid muscle, capable of intimidating and smacking down some of the biggest, baddest bad-asses out there.

Five-foot-three-inch, hundred-and-twenty-pound Jenna was not going to intimidate or get the best of him, no matter how sharp her needles were.

"Okay," he said after a long, Zenlike moment, "I'm ready."

"You sure?" she baited, even as she snuggled closer, leaning right up against him and creating the start of a third long, hard stick for him to deal with. "There's still time to back out if you're afraid your big He-Man ego won't be able to handle the crushing defeat of knowing your 'pansy' friend can master a hobby you can't."

Eyes narrowed, brows lowered, and lips turned down in a frown, he met her gaze and drawled, "Bring it on, babe."

She gave him a look that clearly stated she didn't think this was going to go well, but she'd humor him for a while.

With a sigh, she said, "All right, this one is already started, so we'll just pick up where I left off and teach you the basic stitches."

From there, she proceeded to show him how one needle went through the first stitch on the other needle . . . how fresh yarn wrapped around that needle . . . how to draw the yarn through to create a new stitch . . . and repeat . . . and repeat . . . and repeat. It was definitely more complicated than it looked or sounded.

Some of his stitches might have been bigger than others, and his rows might not have been as neat and practiced as hers, but he didn't think he was doing half-bad. He was actually, amazingly, sort of even enjoying himself.

Of course, it didn't hurt that Jenna was warming him from shoulder to thigh. Or that the flowery scent of her perfume and strawberry fragrance of her shampoo were blending together to numb his brain and send his pulse pounding.

He'd been at the *insert needle, loop yarn, draw yarn through* thing for about an hour before he murmured, "You know, this is kind of sexy."

She lifted her head from where it had fallen to his shoulder, studying him through lazy, heavy-lidded eyes. "Sexy?"

"Yeah. You've got the whole thrust-and-retreat, trust-and-retreat thing going on. The soft yarn. The beautiful woman pressed against me. I like it," he said, slowing his stitches and letting his words sink in. "It's turning me on."

"Gage?" she replied in a low voice.

"Hmm?"

"Watching paint dry turns you on."

So much for lulling her into a sensual haze with his gentle, yarn-is-sexy speech.

"Only if it happens to be drying on your naked body."

To his surprise, she sat up straighter and leaned away from him, only to turn her body at such an angle that she was facing him. She lifted a leg and settled her knee between his spread thighs, leaning close enough that he had to release one of the knitting needles mid-stitch and use his free arm to circle her waist.

"Now that is sexy," she said.

Her hands went to his neck, then around to his nape where her fingers scraped over his short hair. He let his eyes flutter closed for a moment as a shiver of longing snaked down his spine and heat pooled in all the right places.

"Know what else is sexy?" she whispered just above his ear.

His mouth opened and sound came out, but it was

nothing more than a strangled gurgle. Later, he might be embarrassed about that. Now, he couldn't find it in him to give a shit. Not when Jenna was slinking around on his lap like a world-class stripper—something most men had to sacrifice a month's salary to get.

Translating the guttural noises he was making to mean, "No, darling, please tell me," she tipped his head back, waited for him to open his eyes and meet her gaze, then breathed, "This."

And before he knew it, the slick tip of her hot tongue was running from the base of his throat, over the hard ridge of his straining Adam's apple, up along his chin, and she was taking his mouth in a kiss that sizzled his skin, boiled his blood, scorched him down to the bone. It left him little more than a pile of ashes, at her complete and total mercy.

To hell with knitting lessons; he'd just gotten a better offer.

Tossing the needles and yarn aside like they'd suddenly morphed into a Japanese puffer fish in his hand, he grabbed her up, twisted them both around, and laid her beneath him on her aunt's red brocade sofa.

Jenna's arms and legs immediately encircled him, hugging him tight. He didn't think a breath of air could get between them as it was, but still he pressed closer, until her breasts were flattened against his chest and his growing arousal nudged the apex of her thighs.

Their kiss deepened, sending the air in the room from simply smoldering to darn near vaporizing. Every cell of his body was tight and ready, and he knew the same was true for her.

Sliding his hands to her waist, he moved them under her loose, flowing blouse and skimmed it up her midriff.

When the material caught on her arms, he reluctantly pulled his mouth away to order, "Lift," and waited for her to follow his instructions so he could yank the top off over her head and toss it aside.

That done, he returned to her lips. Licking, suckling, absorbing the taste and feel of her until it seeped into his bones and became a part of him.

Flicking open the snap of her bright green Capri slacks, he tugged and shifted until he could skim them from her legs completely, leaving her in only a simple white bra and panty set . . . and the strappy sandals tied to her delicate feet. Frankly, he just didn't want to take the time to deal with them, fumbling around with knots and strings and buckles.

Besides, he liked them. Liked the idea of having her naked beneath him, save for a pair of sexy heels at his back or up over his shoulders.

Trailing his lips across her cheek and down the column of her throat, he felt the rapid thud that mimicked the erratic beat of her heart. His own heartbeat was none too steady as he cupped her left breast in one large palm and ran his thumb over the hard ridge of her nipple beneath a layer of lace.

Her taste in underwear had always been simple. No leopard-print thongs or diamond-studded demi-bras for his Jenna. But her demure choices still managed to turn him on . . . probably more than any Frederick's of Hollywood get-up would have.

Something about Jenna's own inherent innocence wrapped up in the trappings of an angel, *knowing* what she was about to do with him—and allow *him* to do to *her*—was hotter than all the decked-out Playboy bunnies in Hef's Playboy Mansion put together.

Slipping his arms around her back, he unhooked the clasp of her bra, letting it fall away to reveal the pristine perfection of her breasts. The small, round globes wouldn't be winning her any wet T-shirt contests, which was fine and dandy with him, since he didn't want her entering any to begin with. But he'd always been plenty happy with her chest . . . and every other inch of her, for that matter.

Pitching the flimsy garment across the room to join the rest of her clothes, he buried his lips against one small raspberry nipple, then rolled it under his tongue. Jenna mewled in pleasure, her body arching beneath him.

Her every movement, every purr and whisper, sparked along his skin and coiled deep in his gut. Chest heaving, he jackknifed into a sitting position and jerked his T-shirt off over his head. He made equally short work of his boots and jeans, pausing only long enough to retrieve a condom packet from his rear pocket, before returning to hover above her.

While he was at it, he relieved her of her panties so that they were both blessedly naked, not a stitch between them—at least from the ankles up—except a thin layer of latex. Even that was more than he would have wished, and they both knew it might already be too late, but damned if he was willing to take the chance.

So he'd stick with the condom, play it safe, and thank his lucky stars that was the only barrier—the only physical barrier, anyway—keeping them apart.

He stroked her soft, supple skin, the textures of her body coming alive beneath his fingertips. Her arms, her throat, the narrow line of her back and curve of her abdomen. All came together to form a perfection of womanhood.

Jenna might not think so; like most women, he knew she had a few hang-ups about her appearance. But there was nothing wrong with his eyesight. He knew sexy when he saw it, and his wife . . . or ex-wife, rather . . . happened to be smokin'.

His gaze zeroed in on the neat triangle of dark curls below her navel, and even as she sighed his name, trying to draw him up for another kiss, he was sliding down. Charlotte's old-fashioned sofa wasn't exactly the most comfortable place to make out, but finding a better spot would take too long, and he didn't want to do anything that pulled his attention from her, not even for a minute.

Hitching her legs over his shoulders, shoes and all, he inhaled the warm, spicy scent of her arousal before nuzzling her folds and beginning a long, slow barrage of licks and kisses that had her wiggling and whimpering beneath him. He drove her up, up, up, taking no prisoners and giving her not even a second of respite before going straight for her hot button and sending her careening over the edge.

She screamed—his name, thank you very much, he thought with no small amount of smug male satisfaction—and her fingers clutched at what little there was of his short hair.

Shifting back up and over her, Gage pushed his aching cock into her warm, welcoming center while the thick, engorged tissue surrounding him still pulsed with her orgasm. That sensation alone nearly did him in.

For a minute, he remained perfectly still, afraid that if he moved, if she moved, if anything in the house or surrounding county moved, he'd lose it and not only embarrass himself, but miss the chance to finish what they'd started in a way that wouldn't have him banging his head against the wall the rest of the night.

Breath slowing, Jenna's eyes fluttered open and she met his gaze, lifting her arms to drape them almost negligently about his neck. The legs she wrapped around his hips, however, weren't nearly as slack. They hugged him tight and drew him in to the hilt.

"That was nice," she murmured, still looking sleepy and content, though he could feel her renewed interest in the tiny ripples stirring where he was buried deep.

One corner of his mouth quirked up in a cocky half-smile. "We aim to please."

She canted her hips, pulled his head down until his lips hovered mere centimeters above her own, and whispered, "Then aim higher."

He barely had time to release a strangled chuckle before their mouths locked and their lower bodies began an X-rated imitation of what they were doing with their lips and tongues.

With his fingers digging into the flesh of her hips, he pumped. In and out. Harder and faster. A little side to side that nearly made his head explode. It was too much and not enough all at once, sending the blood coursing through his veins.

He clenched his teeth, puffing short breaths through his nose in an effort to hang on just a minute longer, just a second longer, just a nano—

But Jenna wasn't helping matters, writhing and mewling and doing a million little things that urged him toward a speedy finish. And when she reached up to cup his buttocks and gave a squeeze, she might as well have touched a lit match to the tip of a stick of dynamite.

Fuck it, he thought, thrusting once, twice, and again,

before letting out a shout of completion. Clutching at him, Jenna let out a cry of her own, spasming beneath and around him, and making him glad to be a man.

Damn, life was good. Or at least—with the exception of not being able to stay with this woman forever— it sure as hell could be.

Hours later . . . hours and hours later, after he'd made love to her on the sofa, halfway up the stairs, then again when they'd reached the guest room bed.

It was far better than playing around with yarn and pointy plastic sticks any day of the week.

And between bouts of going at it like meerkats, they'd rested, pressed against each other like pieces of a jigsaw puzzle.

She was curled around him now, head on his shoulder, arm around his chest, leg thrown over his thigh. But he didn't think she was any more asleep than he was. Drowsy, maybe. Sated and comfortable, definitely, but not sleeping.

He was thinking about rolling over, kissing her from brow to ankle and back again, though he wasn't quite sure where he was supposed to get the energy.

Jenna shifted slightly, her breath warming him as she sighed.

"Gage?"

"Hmm?" he responded without opening his eyes, his arm tightening automatically at her waist.

"You never answered my question."

"What question?" he asked after a second. He tried to think back, but his brain was apparently so sex-zapped he had no recollection of a question left unanswered or a conversation left unfinished.

"From earlier, in the car," she continued softly.

It came back to him with all the subtlety of a baby grand falling on his head from twenty stories above. The car. Her tears. Her watery voice asking why he gave up on them so easily, why he hadn't fought to keep their marriage together.

The pain he'd felt then, seeing and hearing *her* pain, clutched him again, raking across the inside of his gut like razor blades, leaving him raw and bleeding.

How could it still hurt this much, for both of them, so long after the fact? The old adage that time heals all wounds was apparently a load of crap.

Time certainly hadn't healed anything for him. He'd missed Jenna every day since the split. Wished things could have been different every day since she'd asked for a divorce. Hated and came close to strangling every other man he'd seen with or even near her since.

He suspected the same was true for Jenna, otherwise she wouldn't have brought it up, wouldn't be pressing for an answer that had the potential to be even more distressing than the question itself.

And suddenly, he was tired. So fucking tired of it all.

Gage would give his life to protect her, but if she needed to know . . . They might have silently agreed to spend the week rolling around like ferrets on Ecstasy, but they'd also made it clear to each other that there was no going back.

This wasn't the beginning of a reconciliation. They weren't taking a stab at patching things up, only enjoying each other's company in and out of bed while they waited to find out whether or not she was pregnant.

So nothing he told her now was going to impact

their relationship one iota. She might cut him off, get her panties in a bunch and impose a no-more-sex rule. But that only meant they would go back to the way things had been that first day—he'd still stick around until she either got her period . . . or didn't . . . and she'd go about her business, ignoring him and making it clear he was an unwelcome addition to the house-and alpaca-sitting stint she was pulling for her aunt.

In the end, though, they would still be divorced, still go their separate ways. Well, give or take, depending on how the daily over-the-counter pregnancy test thing turned out.

With both sides of the *tell her/don't tell her* arguments warring in his head, he released an audible sigh, then heard himself ask in a low voice, "What does it matter now?"

Pushing away from his chest, she propped herself up on one arm to stare down at him. Her eyes glowed emerald-green even in the dim light of the bedroom, expressive as ever and telling him exactly how serious she was about this.

"It matters," she said barely above a whisper.

"I never meant to hurt you," he told her, wanting to be sure she understood that first and foremost.

Rather than nodding and simply accepting his statement as fact and a partial apology, she arched a brow. "Really?" was her equally arch response. "Because you did. Long before you moved out, you shut down on me, started pulling away. You made decisions about our life together without consulting me and wouldn't budge, simply expecting me to go along with them. When I tried to talk to you, you clammed up. You grew silent

and brooding and . . . turned into someone I didn't
know anymore. What I want to know is *why*."

The house was dark and quiet. He was drowsy and
sated from hours of amazing, spine-tingling sex. For
those reasons, or maybe a dozen others, his defenses
were down at the moment and he found he didn't have
the energy to fight her need to know.

"Because I loved you." *Because I still love you*, he
thought, but kept that particular confession to himself.
"And because I was trying to protect you."

Purl 16

Jenna blinked, having the strange urge to stick a finger in her ear and wiggle it, then ask Gage to repeat himself so she could be sure she'd heard him correctly.

"Protect me?"

Tugging at the sheet that had covered them both a few minutes ago, she pulled it up and held it in place over her bare breasts. "Protect me from what?" she asked.

"Everything."

It might have been only one word, spoken in little more than a whisper, but it hit her like a sledgehammer to the solar plexus. She tried to draw in a breath, to get oxygen to her deprived brain and other malfunctioning organs. But her lungs seemed frozen in her chest just as surely as her tongue was frozen behind her lips.

Pushing up into more of a sitting position against the headboard, Gage's earnest brown gaze drilled into hers. "I want to protect you from every single thing out there that might cause you harm or pain."

"I don't understand," she said, aware deep down of just what an understatement that was.

"You don't know how bad it is out there, Jenna. You don't know the kinds of things I've seen day in and day out since joining the vice squad."

Her mouth parted slightly as things began to click. Oh, she still had six or eight million questions she was dying to pepper him with, but what he'd just said sank in and so much of what had passed between them before the divorce suddenly made sense.

She'd started to notice a change in him only *after* he'd started working undercover. Before that, things had been fine. More than fine; they'd been deliriously, almost sickeningly (at least according to her friends) happy.

The silent treatment and growing distance between them had come directly on the heels of the physical transformations he'd adopted in order to fit in to whatever group he happened to be infiltrating that week or month. She'd never put two and two together before, but looking back she could clearly see the timeline of events as they'd played out.

But she still didn't understand *why*. What did one thing have to do with the other?

"I can imagine," she offered carefully, some part of her afraid that if she said the wrong thing, he might clam up on her again and they'd never get to the bottom of this.

"No," he told her firmly, the word whipcord sharp, "you can't. And I never wanted you to. I did everything I could think of to shield you from that world."

Jenna cocked her head, surprised by the vehemence in his tone, and as confused as ever by the direction this conversation was going.

"Why would I need to be protected from any of

that?" she asked him. "I'm not a porcelain doll, Gage. I may live in a nice section of town and lead a nice, middle-class life, but I'm aware that not everyone is so lucky. I read the paper and watch the news. I know what some of the conditions are like in the seedier sections of town, even if I'm not intimately familiar with them."

He regarded her in silence for a long, drawn-out minute before speaking. "It's worse," he said quietly, his eyes darkening and clouding over with something she couldn't quite identify. "The things you read about in the paper or hear about on the evening news . . . They gloss over the gory details. They don't show pictures of victims with needles stuck in their arms or lying in pools of their own blood. Children covered in bruises and living in drug dens so full of the stuff, you can get high off the fumes."

Her stomach fluttered—and not in a good way. It was ironic that he proclaimed to want to spare her the knowledge of what that world was really like, yet had just painted a vividly disturbing picture of exactly that.

She didn't think it wise to mention that fact, though. This was the most he'd talked about his job, about working undercover, in all the time she'd known him. She might not like what he was telling her, but she wanted to hear it all the same. Especially if it gave her some inkling of what had gone so wrong between them.

"I understand," she said. "I may not have seen those things with my own eyes, and I'm sorry that they happened, but I do understand. I also understand that you're one of the good guys. You're a superhero, out there fighting the good fight, doing what you can to stop the bad guys and help the innocents. What I'm not clear on—and forgive me if I'm being dense—is what that has to do with us."

Shifting on the bed, she brought her legs closer to her chest, resisting the urge to wrap her arms around her knees and show him just how vulnerable she was feeling. "You pulled away from me, stopped talking to me after you started working undercover. I see that now. But I don't see what one has to do with the other, or how you think you were protecting me by ignoring me, changing your mind about wanting children, distancing yourself from me emotionally . . ."

She trailed off when her voice started to rise and both anger and sadness began to creep into every word. Because what she really wanted to do was throw up her hands and scream, *What the hell does that have to do with anything? Why the hell did a handful of junkies and child-abusers cost me my husband and marriage?*

"How can I bring a child into the world, knowing what's out there? Knowing that every time he left the house, he'd be faced with drugs, alcohol, prostitution. Pedophiles and murderers. People who will do anything for a buck or their next fix, and have no compunction about using or abusing children to get them."

Jenna heard what he was saying, but she wasn't sure she comprehended it. Possibly because the words echoed in her ears, coming to her as though from the end of a very long tunnel. Her head buzzed, her vision clouded, and her heart pounded in her throat.

This had to be what high blood pressure felt like. Perhaps the early warning signs of a heart or panic attack.

"That's why you don't want a baby?" she demanded,

surprised when her voice came out steady and not nearly as *Taming of the Shrew* as she felt. "Because of what *might* happen? Because of a dozen or so negative *possibilities*?"

Mouth a thin line of anguish, he said, "There's some ugly stuff out there, Jenna."

"Without a doubt. There's ugly stuff everywhere, especially if you go looking for it. But you can't live your life in fear of it touching you."

Feeling as though she were about to crawl out of her skin, she pushed herself up and climbed over his legs to get off the bed. Giving the top sheet a mighty yank, she pulled it free of the bed and wrapped it around her so that it draped across the floor like a long-trained ball gown.

"What if none of that ever happened?" she turned to demand of him face-on. "What if we'd stayed married, had a child—*children*, even—and lived happily ever after? What if none of them ever got addicted to drugs or were molested or mugged on the street? It happens, you know," she charged in a tone growing ever more uncontrolled. "People all across the country lead happy, healthy lives, with solid marriages and perfectly content children, who never get caught up in any of those bad things you're so worried about."

Gage remained still on the bed, staring at her like a statue. Was he even listening to her? Did anything she'd said have an impact on him?

"We both grew up that way. Nothing awful ever happened to us. I mean, we used to joke all the time about our families giving the Cleavers or Bradys a run for their money, and how we wanted to create the same sort of environment for our own kids."

It wasn't entirely true that they'd grown up like sitcom children, of course. No family was perfect, and everyone had their own personal issues or baggage from the past, but not everyone had horrible, traumatizing, oversized baggage.

Jenna's parents happened to be stiff and stoic. Whenever the topic had come up, she'd described them as being the American Gothic version of the Cleavers. But she'd been well cared for, and no one had ever beaten, neglected, or molested her, and neither of her parents was an alcoholic, drug abuser, or even compulsive gambler.

And Gage had had an even more storybook childhood. His parents were fabulous. Jenna loved them to death, had been overjoyed to join their family—and had thankfully been welcomed with open arms by his mother, father, and siblings all—and had cried as much over losing such close contact with them as in losing Gage when she'd filed for divorce. Everything about his childhood had been perfect, from a mother who baked cookies and sewed Halloween costumes to a father who built him a treehouse and coached his Little League team.

Which only made it all the more difficult to wrap her mind around his current attitude about family and child-rearing.

"Things are different now," he told her, still morose, still holding tight to his horribly skewed point of view. "The world is a much more dangerous place now than it used to be."

"Maybe you're too close to it," she said, trying not to jump completely off the deep end. "You've worked undercover for so long and seen so much of the dark side of society that you can't see there are still good people out there. We're good people, Gage. We would love and protect our children, give them a warm home and a soft place to fall if anything ever did hurt them."

He shook his head. Sadly, it seemed, as though he wished things could be different, but still clinging tightly to his belief that having a baby meant one day losing that child to something painful and ugly.

Lowering his eyes to his lap, now covered by the thin, quilted spread her aunt kept on the guest room bed, he threaded his fingers together and shook his head again. "It's too risky," he rasped. "I can't take the chance."

She waited a beat, breathing slowly in and out, letting his final decision sink in. Anger bubbled in her belly, while at the same time a chill of sorrow spread through her veins.

"So that's it," she replied woodenly. "I don't get a say in the matter? You can't stretch your mind to believe that we could instill enough self-esteem and strong moral principles in our children that they wouldn't get mixed up in any of that stuff? You're going to trust that nameless, faceless strangers would wield enough power to hurt our kids before they're even born, but you can't trust the two of *us* enough to know we'd keep them safe and raise them right?"

He lifted his head to meet her gaze and the answer was clear. His eyes were bleak, splintering her heart into a thousand tiny shards. There was no changing his mind; she understood that now, even though somewhere, in the very distant back of her mind, she'd hoped and thought maybe, just *maybe* there was a chance.

Until that moment, however, she hadn't realized how

much pain of his own Gage was carrying around—because of his job, because of the things his job had forced him to witness, and because of the decisions they'd driven him to make.

She'd thought she'd lost it all when he'd pulled away from her and she'd been forced to ask for a divorce. Now she knew that wasn't true. She hadn't lost it all; he had. Because she still believed that good could win out over evil and had faith in humanity, while he . . .

He'd apparently lost faith in everyone and everything. Including her.

Including himself.

Gage got out of bed just as the sun was rising on the distant horizon, casting the sky in soft pink and orange and purple.

Not that he'd gotten a wink of sleep after Jenna had pressed him with the hard questions . . . and hadn't liked his answers.

He didn't think she'd gotten much rest, either.

There at the end, she'd had such a look in her eyes. A look of sadness, disappointment, and loss. It had clutched at him, squeezed him from the inside out and made him want to reach out. To grab her up, tug her back into bed, and hold her, murmuring reassuring promises until the sorrow faded from her eyes.

But he couldn't do that. He hadn't been able to offer a single soothing word, because everything he'd had to say had already been said. There was no changing his mind—no changing hers, either, he knew—and nothing was going to soften that blow for her.

Or the blow for him, especially after she'd looked at him that way, then simply turned and walked out of the room. She hadn't closed the door behind her, but she might as well have slammed it for the hollow, resounding heartache she left in her wake.

Gage straightened what was left of the covers before leaving the room and heading downstairs. He suspected Jenna had slept—or not slept, as was more likely the case—on the sofa after leaving him. He'd thought about following her, but what would have been the point?

So he'd stayed where he was and hoped she wasn't completely miserable, even though he'd known wishing for that was like wishing rain would fall up instead of down.

The stairs of the old farm house creaked as he took them slowly one at a time. He stopped in the entrance of the living room, but there was no sign of Jenna. No sheet or pillow on the antique settee. Not even the big, white plastic needles and purple yarn he'd tossed aside last night when things had still been good between them.

Good, *ha!* Before the conversation to end all conversations, things hadn't just been good, they'd been freaking fantastic. He could have gone on that way with her . . .

Yeah, well, if he'd been lucky, forever. But where Jenna was concerned, he didn't seem to be walking around with a four-leaf clover in his pocket. More like a black cat, a handful of spilled salt, and an upside-down horseshoe. Maybe even the number thirteen tattooed on his ass.

Turning away from the living room, he headed for the kitchen, but didn't find Jenna there, either. Her yellow VW was still in the drive, he noticed when he glanced out the window, so unless she'd taken off on foot, there was only one place left where she could be.

He considered going out to the barn after her, but was in no hurry for the confrontation he knew was coming. Silent treatment or screaming match, either way it wasn't going to be pretty.

There was coffee in the pot on the counter, so he poured himself a cup, then sat at the table to await Jenna's return. He tried not to think about last night's argument, but flashes flitted through his head. The words, the hurt, the ultimate outcome.

Just because he was responsible for ninety percent of it didn't mean he didn't have regrets. In a perfect world, he would change if he could. But the fact that this *wasn't* a perfect world was the very reason he couldn't change his mind, couldn't change anything.

He was on his second cup of coffee when he heard Jenna outside the back kitchen door. She stomped her feet to kick the morning dew off her shoes, then stepped inside, closing the door behind her and shrugging out of the light jacket she'd worn out to the barn.

When she turned from hanging the jacket on a hook beside the door, she saw him and froze. But only for a split second. She recovered quickly, averting her gaze and moving about the kitchen as though he wasn't there.

She could ignore him all she wanted, but he wasn't going away. Not yet.

They might be right back where they'd started . . . well, practically. Thanks to her friends and their little sex plan, they'd technically started out in bed, with Jenna on top of him.

Things stirred behind the zipper of his jeans and he clamped his teeth together to put a stop to any more of *those* wayward memories.

They might be *pretty much* back where they'd started, but he still needed some answers of his own before he could leave, no matter how cold a shoulder she might aim at him.

"I see you got yourself a cup of coffee," she said in a tone *this close* to being accusatory when she finally decided to acknowledge his presence.

"Yeah."

She carried her own cup to the table and sat down across from him. Hostility—or possibly hurt, disappointment, and any number of other emotions blended together into hostility—rippled off of her in waves. Her actions and body language all but screamed, *I'm not afraid of you. Look, I'll sit right here and act perfectly normal to prove it.*

And maybe she wasn't afraid—she'd never been afraid of him and he didn't want her to be, had never given her any reason—but she sure wasn't happy with him. Didn't want to be in the same room with him.

Same room, same house, same state. It didn't take a psychic to figure out that she'd have probably stripped down and done an Irish jig on the tabletop if she'd come in from the barn and discovered him gone.

After blowing softly on her steaming coffee and taking a couple of sips, she set her mug down and faced him square on. Her green eyes were shadowed, both beneath her long, black lashes and in their shimmering depths.

"I think you should go," she said quietly. The words were firm and forceful, but he noticed a brief, telltale quiver to her bottom lip.

His gut clenched, and every masculine instinct in his body screamed for him to get up, go to her, do *something* to end her suffering. But what could he do when he'd caused it all to begin with and wasn't willing to go back on anything he'd told her?

Nothing, that's what. Not a damn thing but sit there, hands fisted in his lap, fighting the urge not to leap to his feet.

"Go where?" he asked, not surprised when his voice scraped like sandpaper.

"Go," she repeated, the words steadier than his own. "Leave. Collect your things and get out."

"I can't leave," he told her. "Not yet."

"Why not?"

"You know why."

Her eyes narrowed, but in case she hadn't seen it before, he reached to his side and slid a box along the tabletop. The same box he'd picked up on his way out of the guest room and set aside when he'd first come downstairs.

"You can't be serious." Her shoulders went back and her spine snapped straight while an expression of disbelief crawled across her face.

He raised a brow, but otherwise didn't respond. She'd reacted the same way the first day he'd confronted her with a home pregnancy test and asked her to take it. Since then—after they'd wordlessly agreed to disagree and sleep together, anyway—she'd taken the boxes from him each morning and grudgingly taken the tests just to appease him.

So far, they'd each been negative. He wondered if his luck would continue to hold out on that score, or if he'd run out of pixie dust the same as he had last night in bed.

Grabbing the box from the table, Jenna pushed to

her feet. Her movements were stiff and jerky with fury.

"This is the last one," she said.

She might have been only five-foot-three, but her petite form still managed to tower over him while he remained seated and she stood like a sentinel only inches away.

"I'll take this, and then you're going to leave."

He opened his mouth to reply, but she stopped him with a shake of her head. "I'm not taking no for an answer this time, Gage. This is it, we're done."

Without waiting for his response, she stalked past him and climbed slowly up the stairs.

He stayed where he was, the knuckles of one hand turning white around his coffee mug as the seconds ticked by. He didn't know why he was suddenly so pissed.

This was exactly what he'd wanted, wasn't it? For the sticks to keep turning up minus signs so he could know Jenna wasn't pregnant and get back to his life, back to his job.

But the past few days had spoiled him, lulled him into a false sense of contentment. It had been so easy to push all the important stuff to the back of his brain and focus only on the fact that he was with Jenna again. They weren't fighting and were enjoying each other's company.

More than enjoying. A couple of times, he'd damn near enjoyed himself straight into a coma.

Now, though, reality was smacking him full in the face. His ex-wife was upstairs peeing on a stick that could very well show a positive sign this time. Then where would they be?

Nowhere he wanted to think about right now, that was for sure.

It wasn't in Gage's nature to bury his head in the sand over anything, but at this particular moment, he was happy to play ostrich rather than let his mind wander down all sorts of paths he wasn't ready to deal with. If he *had* to deal with them, he would—what other choice did he have?—but not until it was absolutely necessary.

Shifting in his seat, he tipped his coffee cup, which had only a couple of swallows left at the bottom. His butt was getting sore and his coffee had grown cold. How long had he been sitting here? he wondered. How long had Jenna been in the bathroom?

With a frown pulling down his brows and the corners of his mouth, he checked his watch. More than twenty minutes had passed since Jenna had stomped her way upstairs.

Well, she hadn't come back down, that was for certain. He hadn't heard her moving around up there, either, but then, he hadn't exactly been paying close attention.

The legs of his chair scraped across the floor as he pushed to his feet and started for the second floor. Jenna was nowhere in sight, and the bathroom door was still closed.

He debated going back downstairs to wait her out, then thought twice about it. The image of her sitting in there holding a little white stick with a plus sign on it flickered across his mind's eye and tightened the muscles low in his gut.

Shit. This possible impending-fatherhood thing was worse than a prostate exam.

Taking a deep breath and hoping trepidation didn't shrink his balls to the size of marbles, he leaned a shoulder against the jamb and rapped his knuckles softly against the door. "Jenna? You okay in there?"

A couple of muted scuffles followed his query and a minute later the door opened. Only a crack at first, then all the way as she stepped out into the hall.

"You okay?" he asked again.

"Fine." The reply was blunt and emotionless, but when she lifted her head to meet his gaze, he could see it was also a lie.

She wasn't crying now, but her eyes were rimmed with red, her nose slightly puffy and mottled.

His heart lurched. Was that a good sign or a bad sign?

Did he even want to know?

"Here," she said, thrusting the small white stick from the test kit at him. Her balled-up fist hit him in the center of his abdomen, driving the air from his diaphragm as his hand automatically came up to take what she was offering.

The instant they touched flesh to flesh, she released her hold on the plastic wand and yanked her hand away. He tried not to flinch, but felt her rejection like a two-by-four to the back of his knees.

"Congratulations, you win again," she said, her tone pinpoint-sharp and dripping with derision. "And you can save yourself the trouble of coming back here every day with another test, or calling and pestering me to take one, because it's no longer necessary. I just got my period, so there's no baby, and probably won't be one any time in the near future. Maybe never, thank you very much."

Her voice cracked on the last, and he caught the threat of tears brimming in her eyes just before she brushed past him and rushed down the stairs.

He'd thought he would be relieved when she finally got her period, when there was definitive proof that she hadn't gotten pregnant during their one night of unprotected sex.

Instead, he felt oddly disappointed. He wanted to run after her, but knew she wouldn't welcome his company at the moment, and had no idea what he'd say even if he did.

The best thing he could do now was thank his lucky stars and get the hell out of Fertile Valley before he did something stupid like kiss her, apologize, sleep with her again, or—God forbid—offer her another shot at his little swimmers just to wipe the look of devastation off her face.

No. He'd dodged the bullet once, he was not going to risk a direct hit next time around. It was done, finished, over with. Life could go back to normal . . . or at least what he'd come to accept as normal over the past year and a half.

And if he wasn't particularly happy, if he came home to an empty apartment and fell asleep in front of the television every night with only memories of better times to keep him warm . . .

Well, he could live with that. Especially since he didn't seem to have a choice.

Knit 17

Gage stood in front of his locker at the precinct, stowing his watch and trading his boots for an old pair of sneakers that had seen better days.

His team was going out on some undercover drug busts, so the faded jeans and white T-shirt he'd worn in could stay, but he'd add a skull-and-crossbones do-rag and a ratty, sleeveless denim jacket covered in scary-looking patches. That, along with his own personal body ink and a few other minor touches, should work to convince dealers he was up to no good and looking to score.

"Hey," Eric Cruz, one of his buddies and a fellow undercover officer, said as he came up beside Gage to open his own locker. "Glad to have you back."

"Thanks," Gage offered without much genuine sentiment. He'd only been gone a little over a week, but knew from experience that when one of the guys was missing from an op, you felt the loss and it altered tactical strategy accordingly.

Gage had expected to feel exhilarated by his return to work. He'd always enjoyed his job, gotten a thrill out of almost every aspect of it. It was a rush to go undercover and play a role that got the bad guys to trust him, then drop the hammer and put them in jail. It was exhilarating to organize a bust and be there for the take-down.

So, yeah, lately he hadn't felt quite as enthusiastic about it all, but when he'd first asked for time off to stay with Jenna, he'd been kind of pissed at having to leave. Then he'd decided that going away for a while might put things back in perspective and help him appreciate the job even more once he returned.

They hadn't been in the middle of anything big when he'd taken leave, either, which was a plus. But the thought of distancing himself from his team, of having something come up that he wouldn't be aware of, rubbed him the wrong way.

Then, after a while, he'd stopped thinking so much about what he was missing at work and had begun to simply enjoy relaxing, hanging out, and being with Jenna. He hadn't even minded helping out with the alpacas, despite the fact that the little buggers spit when they got scared. A couple of them had also trampled his toes and come damn close to making him sing soprano.

Once he'd been sure Jenna wasn't pregnant, though, and . . . okay, he hadn't left so much as been kicked out . . . he'd thought he'd be relieved to get back to his usual routine. Instead, he'd found himself dragging around ever since his alarm had gone off that morning. Both physically and emotionally, he just couldn't seem to generate a spark of interest in anything these days.

"You ready for today's op?" Eric asked.

"Sure," Gage responded automatically. "You?"

"Always, man. Gotta put the bad guys in jail and make the streets safe for innocent women and children."

It was a much-used line and common joke within the PD, but for some reason, hearing it this time sent a stab of something cold and painful through Gage's chest. His heart squeezed, and his ribcage seemed to tighten around his lungs.

Turning his head, he glanced at the inside of Eric's locker. Aside from a small magnetic mirror and CPD decal, the door and sides were covered in family photographs. Eric and his wife. His wife and three children. School pictures of each of the kids as they passed through several different grade levels. Eric, his wife, and the kids all together in front of a tree at Christmas.

He had a family, seemed happy, didn't appear to spend every minute worrying about what might happen. To them, or to him. Other officers—both in undercover or other departments—were married with children, as well, he knew.

How did they do it? How did they not go crazy with the knowledge of all the bad things that could happen to the ones they loved?

He wasn't afraid of much in this world—hell, as a cop, he'd faced just about everything there was to be afraid of—but the idea of losing Jenna to violence, to having her hurt in some way and being powerless to stop it . . . He'd rather have his guts ripped out and stomped on while his heart was still beating and he was alive and conscious enough to feel every twinge.

The idea of having kids with her and having to worry about them, too . . .

He broke out in a cold sweat and realized his hands were curled into fists at his sides.

Okay, this could not be normal. For the first time, he began to realize that maybe his concern for Jenna and their possible progeny might be slightly over the top. What other explanation could there be, since the other men in his unit, other men in his line of work, didn't seem to suffer the same reluctance to reproduce?

"Hey, Cruz?" he said in a quiet voice, the words scraping past his raw, dry throat.

"Yeah?"

He shifted back a step from the row of lockers and took a seat on the low wooden bench running between. "Can I ask you something?"

His tone must have alerted his friend that something was up because Eric's movements slowed and he cast Gage a curious glance. "Yeah, man, sure. What's up?"

"Your family. The wife and kids. They're good?"

Eric's face lit up, his mouth lifting in a smile as though someone had flipped a switch.

"They're great, thanks."

"And you don't worry about them?" Gage asked.

" 'Course I worry about them. But that's what this is for." He patted his chest, his palm covering the small gold cross he wore there. Always, whether it was visible or tucked inside his shirt.

Gage shook his head. "No, I mean *worry* about them. With all the shit we've seen, everything that's out there ready to take somebody down whether they deserve it or not . . . Aren't you afraid something will happen to them?"

For the first time, Eric turned to really look at him. If anything, the eye contact, the sudden intense scrutiny, made Gage nervous. He felt like enough of a pussy bringing this up to begin with; he didn't need a co-worker peering too deeply into his soul.

"I suppose if I stopped to think about it, I would,"

Eric replied. "But life's too short, man. I mean, anything could happen to any one of us at any moment. You could walk out of this building and get hit by a bus. I could trip on a shoe lace walking down the stairs and break my neck." He shrugged. "No one to blame. Nothing anyone did or didn't do to cause it, just an act of Fate."

"But bringing a baby into the world," Gage pressed. "There's some dangerous stuff out there. Don't you worry something will happen to them? To this innocent kid who has no way to protect himself? To your wife?"

"My wife can take care of herself," Eric said with a chuckle. "Hell, she scares me sometimes, so I have no doubt she could bring down any jerk-off who so much as looked at her funny. She can protect the kids, too, for that matter. But to be safe," he said, voice growing serious, "I've shown her a few self-defense moves. Taught her how to fend off an attack and not be too squeamish to kick a guy in the nads, if she needs to."

Gage thought about that for a minute. He'd seen Jenna pissed, and it wasn't pretty. No doubt she could take a man's head off at ten paces with nothing more than a book end. (Something he unfortunately knew from personal experience.)

For that matter, since she carried those damn knitting needles around with her ninety percent of the time, she could probably stab an offender in the eye, throat, stomach, groin, thigh . . . anywhere she could reach. And if he taught her how to do that effectively, how to use her keys as a weapon, her purse as a weapon, her entire body as a weapon . . .

"What about your kids?" he asked.

Eric considered that for a moment, then said, "You know, with the kids, you pretty much have to protect them twenty-four-seven the first few years. But there's not a lot to protect them from, street-wise, so you just keep an eye on them and make sure they don't swallow anything smaller than their eyeballs. After that, you start teaching them, too. You teach them to look both ways before crossing the street, not to take candy from strangers, to deal with bullies at school, say no to drugs . . . the usual."

"It's that easy?" Gage asked doubtfully.

"Not quite that easy, no," Eric admitted with a small shake of his head. "But if you do it right and raise them to see and understand the dangers, then you don't have to worry so much about them falling into something they can't handle." He paused for a moment, then gave a little *hmph* of sound. "I guess that's the real secret. You do the best you can to prepare them to handle whatever situations they might come across, then you pretty much have to let go and pray they make the right decisions."

The tightness in Gage's chest and abdomen hadn't abated, but his mind was running about a million miles a minute, and he was relieved when Eric didn't ask why he was suddenly so interested in all of this. He pretty much let the conversation dwindle on its own, then went back to prepping for their drug-bust operation, and Gage did the same.

Could it really be as simple as his friend made it sound? Oh, he knew raising a child wasn't a simple matter by any stretch of the imagination, but was it possible it wasn't the nightmare of hidden traps and dangers he'd envisioned? Folks had kids every day, right?

Yeah, one was occasionally found dead in a snow bank or wandering the streets alone. But a lot weren't.

And he could cross the fear of parental abuse right off the list, because there was no way he or Jenna would ever hurt or neglect one of their own children. If he had his way, he'd pretty much smother them in bubble wrap from head to toe the minute they were born, so even getting a paper cut would be virtually impossible.

It was too much to digest all at once, but Eric had given him something to think about. Given his rock-solid determination of the past couple years to avoid fatherhood and vulnerability at any cost, he considered that progress.

When Charlotte pulled her long, wood-panel station wagon up to her house, she'd been gone almost a full two weeks, was running on Zingers and Mountain Dew, and had to tinkle like a toy poodle.

Jenna's car, with its adorable magnetic daisies stuck all over, was nowhere in sight. Not that Charlotte was surprised. It was, after all, Wednesday night, and she only had about an hour to hit the potty, check her darling babies—oh, how she'd missed them while she was gone—unhitch the U-Haul from the car, and get to The Yarn Barn herself.

Throwing open the driver's-side door, she scooted around the front of the wagon, then hotfooted it into the house and headed straight for the bathroom before the little fender-bender in that expo building parking lot became only one of the accidents she had to account for from her time away.

After taking care of business, she came back downstairs and made her way out to the barn. Her babies were all tucked into their stalls for the night, dozing or enjoying some munchies. They looked healthy and fit, and Charlotte's heart swelled with relief.

Not that she didn't trust Jenna to take proper care of the sweet little beasts, but no one could look after them quite the way Charlotte did. She knew each of them by name, knew their individual quirks and personalities. Knew that all-white Snowball loved tiny pieces of apple and carrot, and that the black and white Domi (short for Domino) frightened easily. Really, really easily. And he didn't just kick or spit, as was typical of alpacas when they got nervous or scared, but his eyes went wide and he also piddled a tiny bit down his leg.

For that reason alone, she didn't race up to her baby boy's stall and shout the joy of her return. Instead, she waddled quickly but quietly to each stall to greet her darlings individually.

Pumpkin, one of her favorite light brown darlings, lifted her head, spotted Charlotte, and trotted over to the half-door with a wide grin on her long, narrow face.

Most people would probably say Charlotte was crazy, that alpacas couldn't grin. But Charlotte knew better—on both counts.

"Baby!" she exclaimed, throwing her arms wide to give the creature a giant hug.

Next came Sprinkles, Daisy, Snowball, Rascal, and finally Domino, all of whom got big hugs and kisses and tons and tons of super-special Mama lovin'.

She spent longer than she probably should have snuggling with her sweetie pies, but eventually she broke away, tossed them each a bit of extra hay for being such good furry babies, and reluctantly made her way back to the station wagon.

After dragging the bulkiest pieces of her luggage to just inside the house and unhooking the trailer hitch, she gathered her most recent knitting project onto the passenger side of the front seat beside her and cranked the engine. The ancient vehicle rumbled to life, purring like a big, happy jungle cat and lurching beneath her like an industrial washing machine.

Maybe this was why she'd had a thing for hogs in her younger days. The roar of an engine, the vibrating sensation that rippled through her entire body and set her skin to tingling. All that power. All that massive metal, with some big hunk of man perched on top.

Charlotte's cheeks turned rosy as a flush of heat stole through her body. The girls in her knitting group might think she was just a silly old woman, but she'd been a real chippy in her day. Oh, she'd never played fast and loose—she wasn't *that* kind of woman. She'd never teased the fellas just to get attention, either. But she'd had her fair share of suitors. And just like her niece, she'd had a bit of a thing for the bad-boy type.

If she'd been a few years—all right, decades, she admitted reluctantly—younger, she'd have probably set her hat for Gage herself. What a tall, tattooed drink of water he was, that one.

With a shake of her bright orange beehived 'do, she put the wagon in gear and backed out of the drive, setting off down the graveled road toward town at a fast enough clip that a giant cloud of dust and dirt blew out behind her, kicked up by her rear tires.

Thinking about Jenna and Gage made her wonder what had happened with the skein of yarn she'd left with her niece before going on the road. It was magic yarn, infused with special true love powers, so surely something wonderful had occurred by now, right?

Perhaps Jenna had met a nice young man and fallen madly in love. Granted, she'd only been gone two weeks, but Charlotte was a firm believer in soul mates and love at first sight. And with the extra-special yarn at work, drawing in suitable mates, anything could happen.

At five minutes after eight, she pulled into the parking lot of the strip mall where The Yarn Barn nestled snugly between a coffee shop and one of those ninety-nine-cent stores. She found an open space only a few spaces from the front door, grabbed her things, and hurried inside.

There was a skip in her step and a wide smile on her face, not only because she'd been gone for so long and missed her Knit-Witting pals, but because she couldn't wait to hear about Jenna's whirlwind romance. She just knew her niece would be grinning from ear to ear, bursting at the seams to share her good news.

The others had already arrived, filling most of the chairs that the store had arranged in a circle around a small coffee table for multiple crafting groups to use on different afternoons and evenings during the week. There was a crochet group, a quilting group, a sewing group, and even an appliqué class that met in the same space.

Several reusable ceramic mugs with The Yarn Barn logo on them sat on the low table, filled with both hot and cold drinks from the small refreshment area the store provided, and the steady, staccato click and clack of needles coming together could be heard over friendly chit-chat.

Charlotte loved that sound. It was a sound of comfort to her. Of home and happiness.

"Hello, everyone," she greeted them, taking a seat across the circle from her favorite members of the group—Jenna, Ronnie, and Grace. Of course, they were her favorites because she knew them best and spent the most time with them outside of their weekly knitting meetings.

Cries of "Charlotte!" went up all around, warming her right down to her toes. She'd only been absent from two meetings, but she'd really missed them, and it felt good to be back and to receive such a cheerful welcome.

"How was your trip?" Grace wanted to know after everyone had jumped up to hug her. And that nearly overlapped Ronnie's inquiry of "When did you get back?"

She told them all about her time on the road, becoming one with the highway and the big-rig drivers who made it their home. The truck stops where she'd eaten, and the rundown motels where she'd stayed. She'd been like Thelma on her way to meet Louise.

And then there had been the craft shows, which were held in giant fair auxiliary buildings or outdoors on the huge fairgrounds themselves. They'd bustled with crowds and been filled with vendors hawking every kind of craft and handmade item imaginable, and Charlotte had done a good bit of business for herself and others whose pieces she'd taken along to sell.

But the shows hadn't been nearly as exciting as the freedom of the road, moving from place to place, and feeling the wind blow through her hair as she raced along the interstates. With the possible exception of missing her babies and the Knit Wit meetings, she almost couldn't wait until next year to get back out there and do it all over again.

Although . . . come to think of it, she might have to consider either a new hairstyle or a hat of some sort. Maybe a helmet or set of scarves in different colors and prints. Because that wind blowing through the open windows of the wagon had really played havoc with her beautiful, bright red upsweep. If she hadn't used so much hairspray to keep it in place, and then to work it back into place each time she stopped to tinkle, she would have looked positively frightful at the end of every day.

It wasn't until she'd finished regaling everyone in the circle with stories of her adventures of the last two weeks that she realized Jenna had been unusually quiet. Well, not unusually quiet for sad, divorced Jenna, but unusually quiet for ecstatically happy, newly infatuated Jenna.

"So how did things go for you out at the farm, dear?" she fished. "Was everything all right?"

Did a gorgeous hunk of man get lost on that dusty old road and stumble to the door to ask for directions? Did you invite him in for a sip of tea to quench his mighty thirst and end up offering yourself on a silver platter, as well?

Her niece offered a friendly smile, but anyone with eyes could see it was forced.

"Everything was fine," Jenna assured her. "I took very good care of your babies."

"I could see that," Charlotte said with a nod. "I stopped by to check on them before coming here, and they looked wonderful. Thank you again for staying there with them these last two weeks."

The group lapsed into silence and Charlotte's dark eyebrows—which clashed drastically with her carrot-red hair—came together in a frown as she studied her niece even more closely. The lackluster expression, the slow, methodical motion of her hands as she knit at about one-quarter her usual speed.

Jenna certainly didn't *look* like she'd been bitten by the love bug recently. A flu bug, maybe. The bumble-bee of depression, possibly. But nothing close to a love bug.

Could it be that the yarn hadn't worked its magic this time around?

No. Charlotte wouldn't believe that. It had done such a marvelous job with Ronnie and Dylan—two people who'd barely been able to stand the sight of each other in the beginning—that she simply couldn't believe it wouldn't also work wonders for Jenna. Jenna, who was open and looking for love.

It felt like there were ants in Charlotte's pants as she tried to remain still in her seat and *not* ask what the Jolly Green Giant had gone wrong. Hadn't Jenna used the soft purple yarn she'd given her? Was that the problem?

Charlotte wasn't at all certain what the qualifications and nuances of the magical spinning wheel were, so it was entirely possible that simply *possessing* or touching the yarn wasn't enough to invoke its powers. Maybe one had to actually use it to create something before those powers were released. Maybe—as had been the case with Ronnie and Dylan—*both* parties had to touch and use it for the enchantment to work.

Lordy, Lordy, if that was the case, then they were in trouble, indeed. How many times could she count on

Fate bringing a man and woman together long enough to knit with a magic skein of yarn?

The fact that Ronnie and Dylan had done just that was a miracle in itself, and something Charlotte didn't think she could either count on happening again, ever in this lifetime, or manipulate into taking place.

Her heart gave a little lurch in her chest as another horrible thought struck. What if she'd done something wrong? What if she'd used the wrong type of fibers this time, or hadn't spun them quite right?

What if the beautiful, solid-oak spinning wheel that had been handed down through generations of women in her family and was reputed to be enchanted with the ability to create true love was nothing of the sort? What if it was just a solid-oak spinning wheel, meant to spin new yarn out of fibers, and nothing more?

A chill swept Charlotte from the top of her Lucille Ball head to the corn pads stuck to her toes. She'd been so sure the wheel was infused with magic. So sure she could help to bring about true love matches through a hobby she already adored.

But if the wheel was just a wheel, then that meant Veronica and Dylan working out their differences and falling for one another was nothing more than a fluke. A natural human occurrence.

How dreadfully boring and mundane.

It also meant that Charlotte had no hope of drawing Jenna out of her self-imposed shell and helping her to fall in love again.

Sigh. Perhaps she was giving up too soon. Thinking the worst before she had definitive proof that the yarn from the enchanted spinning wheel had failed. She needed details, doggone it, so she could get a better handle on what was going on and whether her machinations had made at least a small dent in her niece's love life—or lack thereof—or not.

Unable to stand the ominous silence a second more, she piped up and directed a pointed question in Jenna's direction. "Did you keep busy while I was away? I hope you weren't bored out there all by yourself."

Grace snorted, quickly lifting a hand to cover the rest of her laugh. Something was definitely going on here, Charlotte thought, narrowing her heavily lined eyes in suspicion.

"Actually, Charlotte," Ronnie offered, casting a chastising glance at her blond friend, "a lot has happened since you took off."

"Oh?" Charlotte asked, scooching forward in her seat a fraction, trying not to appear overly curious. "Like what?"

"Like discovering Zachary Hoolihan is a cheating dickwad SOB whose ass had to be kicked to the curb," Grace grumbled.

"Oh, my." Charlotte's eyes widened and her cheeks heated at the ferocity of Grace's statement.

Playing the part of levelheaded narrator, Ronnie quickly filled her in on Grace's discovery of her fiancé—*ex*-fiancé now, it seemed—in bed with another woman while on the road for a charity event with some of the other players from the Rockets team.

Grace scathingly referred to the other woman as a "puck bunny." For a moment, though, Charlotte considered asking her physician to fit her with a hearing aid because she thought Grace had said something very different. Something that started with a letter that came much earlier in the alphabet and wasn't any official hockey term that she'd ever heard.

"That's terrible," Charlotte offered. "I'm so sorry, dear."

Grace inclined her head and kept her mouth in a tight line, putting on a good show of remaining unmoved. But Charlotte didn't miss the telltale glimmer that filled her prettily madeup eyes. When she thought no one was looking, she sniffed, then wiped a finger beneath her lashes to remove any hint of moisture.

Poor Grace, Charlotte thought, her heart tugging in sympathy. She'd been so happy, so deliriously happy with that young man and all her elaborate wedding plans.

She'd even started knitting her own wedding gown, which Charlotte had been thrilled about. Not many young people would be willing to put the time and effort into such complicated projects, and she'd been eager to see the final results.

The miniscule needles and thin, white yarn were conspicuously absent at this evening's meeting, Charlotte suddenly noticed. And no wonder. If Grace's intended had stepped out on her, she wouldn't have continued working on any part of the wedding plans, either.

Through all of this, Jenna had once again remained ominously silent, keeping her gaze locked on the long aqua-blue boa she was knitting. *Aqua blue*, not purple. Not the yarn Charlotte had given her before she'd gone wheels up and taken off for adventure in the great beyond.

"And what about you, Jenna, dear?" she asked pointedly. Come Hell or high water, she *would* find out what had happened with her niece while she was gone. And where in St. Petersburg the enchanted yarn had gone!

In response to Charlotte's question, Jenna blanched, Grace chuckled, and Ronnie's mouth twisted to one side.

Hmm. Things just kept getting curiouser and curiouser.

"Our little Jenna had herself a booty call while you were away, Aunt Charlotte," Grace provided, her tone laced with glee.

Charlotte raised a brow as the color rushed back into her niece's face. She wasn't entirely clear on what a booty call was, but thought Grace's intonation and Jenna's accompanying embarrassment were pretty good indications that it was something naughty.

Continuing to act as diplomatic moderator for their little triumvirate, Ronnie calmly supplied, "Jenna and Gage spent a bit of time together while you were away."

"Oh, my goodness," Charlotte exclaimed. She certainly hadn't been expecting to hear anything like *that*.

"At last report, things were still going hot and heavy." Grace grinned and let go of her knitting long enough to flip a lock of blond hair back over her shoulder. She shot Jenna a lascivious, expectant glance and added, "We haven't gotten an update for this week yet."

"Actually," Jenna said in a tiny, almost voice, keeping her gaze glued to her needles, "he left, and he won't be coming back."

Everyone in the circle heard the pain in Jenna's voice, noticed the white-knuckled grip she had on her knitting and that she'd stopped stitching altogether.

"Oh, honey." Dropping her own knitting, Grace

dragged her chair closer to Jenna's side and took her hands. "I'm so sorry, I didn't know. And here I was being such a smart-ass."

"It's okay," Jenna murmured, although her watery voice and wavering words clearly revealed the claim to be a lie. "It was just sex, and we both knew it wasn't leading anywhere. It had to end sometime."

Ronnie, who had leaned in close to Jenna's other side and was rubbing comforting circles in the center of her back, whispered, "But you didn't want it to, did you?"

Jenna took a deep, shuddering breath. "It doesn't matter." Straightening slightly, she shook her head, sending her short, black hair fluttering. "Things were never going to work out. Not while we were married, and not now."

She lifted her gaze, which was wet with tears. "He's never going to change his mind. I don't think I ever really believed that before, but I do now."

"What did he say?" Grace wanted to know.

Jenna shook her head again and gave her two closest friends a meaningful glance that clearly said she'd share the details with them later, but wasn't ready to bare her soul just yet, in front of everyone. "Suffice to say I got the point this time. Loud and clear."

Inhaling dramatically, Grace wrapped her arm around Jenna's shoulders and squeezed her close. "We make quite the pair, don't we? Obviously we are not cut out to be involved with the males of our species. I say we swear off the opposite sex altogether," she announced with feeling. "We should start a 'Men are Scum' Club, where we sit around drinking girlie cocktails and discussing why testosterone is the curse of humanity and anyone with a Y-chromosome should be dragged into the street and shot."

At first, Charlotte didn't think Grace's good-natured teasing would have the desired effect. Jenna looked entirely too miserable to find anything amusing at this point.

But after a few minutes, she sniffed, wiped at her cheeks with the back of her hand, then raised her head to face Grace. "Can I be the president?"

Grace chuckled and hugged her again. "Absolutely. I'll be your vice president, and we'll have signs and buttons made up to promote the group. Our logo will be a twig and two berries with a big red line through them. No dicks allowed."

Laughter went around the circle, breaking the veil of tension that had fallen over the group. Slowly but surely, the women returned to their knitting, filling the area once again with the *clickety-clack* of needles on needles.

Grace and Ronnie, too, leaned back in their seats and picked up their respective projects.

"I think you're just looking for another excuse to toss back pretty-colored drinks," Ronnie shot in Grace's direction.

"Like I need an excuse," Grace retorted. Then, in a stage whisper aside to Jenna, she said, "Don't listen to her. She's been consorting with the enemy and is just jealous she hasn't had an epiphany about what assholes they are like the rest of us enlightened ones."

Ronnie raised a skeptical brow. "Until recently, *you* were 'consorting' with the enemy, too. More often than I do, I'd venture to guess."

Grace rolled her eyes and leaned forward to stick

her tongue out at Ronnie around Jenna, who sat between them. "But I have since seen the error of my ways," she proclaimed in a very put-upon tone. "That's why they call it an epiphany and why I'm *enlightened*, thankyou-verymuch."

From there, the conversation broke down into dirty jokes and the denigration of men, with Zack Hoolihan and Gage Marshall getting the brunt of the women's disgruntlement.

Charlotte was barely listening to any of that, though. She was much too wrapped up in worries over why the enchanted yarn hadn't worked.

It had apparently gotten Jenna and Gage back together for a short while—which certainly hadn't been her intention. She'd wanted Jenna to find a new man, not go back to the same one who'd already broken her heart once before. (Even if Gage was a nice enough young fellow otherwise.)

But if the yarn had gotten them back together, then it was supposed to *keep* them together. The spinning wheel was said to create yarn that brought true love, not temporary lust with a misery chaser.

This wasn't good, and it wasn't right, and there had to be something she could do.

Purl 18

"I think I fucked up."

Gage took a swig of beer from the bottle in his hand, doing his best to block out the noise around him. The raised voices of bar patrons, the competing programs playing on two separate televisions, the clanking of glasses from people drinking and waitresses filling or clearing orders.

It all clumped and clanged in his head, adding to the pressure there, making him wonder if he should drink more in an attempt to block it out . . . or drink less to keep the sensitive tissues of his brain from becoming so susceptible in the first place.

Zack and Dylan were with him—on their usual night, at their usual table—and had been since around seven o'clock. It was now nearing midnight, and Gage was pretty sure he could accurately predict that Jenna was *not* going to show up, after all. It was Wednesday night, her knitting group's meeting night, so she should have.

He'd followed the normal routine of meeting his friends with the sole purpose of being there when she came in with Ronnie and Grace. He wasn't entirely sure what he'd planned to do or say once she arrived, but he suspected it would have involved embarrassing himself in some fashion.

Now, though, he was sort of pissed that she hadn't shown up. Sure, she'd saved him public humiliation, but she'd also robbed him of the chance to see her, talk to her, do . . . something to make up for the way things had ended back at her aunt's place.

It hadn't been quite a week since he'd climbed on his Harley and headed back to the city, but it felt like months. Years, even. The longest four days of his life.

Every second of every minute since walking away from her—knowing it was really over and that they'd both finally said everything they had to say to each other—had made him feel worse. Made his insides tighten and his skin twitch.

If leaving had been the reasonable thing to do, he kept thinking, shouldn't he feel better about it? When a decision was right, it was supposed to have a calming effect. You were supposed to breathe easier and find inner peace.

All he'd found was one more thing to keep him up at night. One more regret to add to his ever-growing list.

This was one regret, though, that he wasn't sure he could live with. Each day that passed made him feel worse, made him wrack his brain for a way to fix what he'd broken.

Talking with his friends at the precinct had helped. For the first time in a long time, he'd opened his eyes a bit and paid attention to what was going on around him. Not job-wise, but deeper, in the personal lives of the men and women he worked with.

He'd spent years thinking law enforcement and family

didn't mix. Apparently, he was one of the few guys on the force who held that belief. Most of them were married; a lot of them, married or not, had kids. Many were divorced, sure—police work added a level of stress to relationships that most folks didn't have to deal with—but he had to admit that his observations mostly turned up happy, normal family lives.

So why couldn't he have that, too?

It was the first time he'd really let himself consider the possibility, and it didn't sit well because it meant he'd been functioning about fifty points shy of the average IQ. Jenna had tried to tell him that all along, tried to convince him he could be a good husband, a good father, *and* a good cop.

He hadn't believed her. Hadn't trusted her—or himself—enough to believe they could have everything. He still wasn't entirely confident of the feelings roiling around inside him, but he was coming around. He was starting to think maybe, just . . . maybe.

Which was why he'd wanted to see her tonight.

And why he was ready to admit he'd fucked things up royally.

"Oh, yeah?" Dylan responded. "What did you do this time?"

"I think I screwed up with Jenna."

Zack, who was prickly as a cactus these days and had been drinking at a slightly faster clip than his friends, made a sound deep in his throat. "Ha! Join the club."

"You screwed up with Jenna, too?" Dylan asked in an attempt to lighten the mood around the laminated table. He got a hairy eyeball for his trouble.

"You can't please 'em," Zack continued in a slightly louder voice than normal.

His words were becoming just slurred enough that Gage knew they'd have to take his keys and see that he got home some other way. "You buy 'em gifts, you give 'em a big ring, and you *don't* cheat on them, redargless"— which Gage took to mean *regardless*—"of what they might think. But do they believe you? No! 'Course not. They see one naked woman in your bed and aumotatically assume you banged her."

Slamming his beer down against the table, he nearly bellowed, "Well, I didn't!"

Dylan cringed, and several heads turned in their direction, but Zack didn't seem to notice . . . or care.

"We know that," Gage reassured him.

When he'd first heard about Grace's discovery of another woman in Zack's hotel room on the road, he'd figured Grace had every right to be upset and break off their engagement. Gage was kind of a stickler for fidelity in a marriage and loyalty in all other aspects of life. Friend or no friend, he could never back a cheater.

Once Zack had told them his side of the story, however, Gage's opinion had changed. He believed Zack when he said he hadn't invited that woman into his room—or his bed.

It wasn't Zack's ranting and raving and the accuracy of the details each time he recounted what had happened that convinced Gage of his innocence, but the obvious anguish in his friend's voice and demeanor. He was genuinely broken up about losing Grace; he loved her and had been faithful to her, no matter what she thought.

According to Zack, he'd been in the shower when both the strange woman and Grace had arrived at his hotel room. He'd answered the door when Grace knocked, but didn't know how the other girl had gotten in. A stolen key card, a bribed member of the housekeeping staff . . . determined puck bunnies seemed to constantly come up with new ways to get close to the players.

It had been a cruel twist of Fate that brought Grace to the door at that very moment. If she'd been five minutes later, Zack had told them more than once, the woman would have been gone because he would have kicked her and her already discarded clothes out into the hall the minute he found her in his bed.

It was something Gage knew Grace needed to know—whether she chose to believe it or not—but wasn't ready to hear just yet.

"Yeah," Dylan agreed. "And once Grace has a chance to calm down and really listen to you, she'll believe it, too. You just have to give her some time."

Zack let out another snort, then turned his attention back to the bottle in front of him.

"So what did you do to land in the doghouse?" Dylan asked, getting back to Gage's original comment.

Gage shook his head, running his thumb back and forth distractedly over the label on his Rolling Rock. "I'm starting to think I've been wrong about this whole 'no kids' thing."

"Whoa." Dylan's eyes went wide and he rocked back an inch or two in his chair. Even Zack dragged himself away from his wallowing long enough to stare dumbly.

Gage felt his face heat at such close scrutiny.

"That's quite an about-face. What changed your mind?" Dylan asked.

"I don't know exactly," Gage admitted, avoiding his friends' intense gazes by keeping his own eyes slanted down at the tabletop. "I was so sure it was a bad idea.

That refusing to have children and letting Jenna go was the right thing to do, the best way to keep everyone safe."

He drew in a deep breath and threw himself back against his chair. "But I miss her. Being with her again reminded me of how things used to be and how lousy I've felt this past year and a half without her. Then I went in to work and started to notice how many of the other guys have kids and happy marriages. Other UCs, detectives, beat cops, the members of SWAT."

Lifting his head, he met Dylan's gaze, then Zack's. "So if they can do it and aren't afraid something awful will happen to their families, what am I so worried about?"

Dylan leaned in, resting his elbows on the table. "That's what we've always wondered. We tried to tell you that just because bad things happen, it doesn't mean they'll necessarily happen to you. Or Jenna or any kids you have."

Gage's mouth curled into a self-deprecating grin. "Yeah, I'm getting that. I don't think I wanted to hear it before, though."

"You don't *think*?" Zack countered. "You were like the Great Wall of China any time the topic came up. I always thought you were afraid something would happen to you and you'd end up leaving Jenna alone to raise whatever children you'd had, but I didn't think it was worth ruining your marriage over."

He paused to take a swig of his drink, shrugging a shoulder as he lowered the bottle back to the table before continuing. "I figure it's better to be with the person you love for as long as you can than be without them forever." Swiveling his head from Dylan to Gage and back again, his eyes crossed and he said, "That made sense, right?"

Zack might be well on his way to fall-down drunk, but a few of his brain cells were still functioning.

"Yeah," Gage mumbled. "It does."

He didn't want anything to happen to him, to leave Jenna—or any children they might have—alone. And he sure as hell didn't want anything to happen to them. But being apart was clearly making them both miserable.

What was the point? Why should they be divorced and miserable when they could be married and happy for as long as they were blessed to be together?

They—*he*—had already wasted too much time, idiot that he was; he didn't want to waste any more.

Pushing to his feet, he dug out his wallet and tossed a couple bills to the table. "Can you get him home?" he asked Dylan.

Dylan looked surprised, but said, "Sure. Where are you going?"

"I have to find Jenna. I've got a couple years' worth of stupidity to make up for."

As far as plans went, it could have used a bit more . . . planning.

He'd stalked out of The Penalty Box full of gusto and determination. It wasn't until he'd reached his bike and was strapping on his helmet that he realized he didn't have a clue where Jenna was.

Thank God no one had been in the parking lot to see him remove his helmet, climb back off the bike, and walk back into the bar two seconds after he'd walked out.

To their credit, his friends hadn't laughed at him—
at least not until after he'd left again. Well, Zack had,
but Zack was three sheets to the wind and would have
laughed at his own shadow at that point.

After asking Dylan if he had any idea where Jenna
might be or where the girls might have gone after their
knitting meeting since they hadn't shown up at the
Box, his friend had pulled out his cell phone and called
Ronnie.

Without telling her why he wanted to know, he'd
found out that she and Jenna had gone to Grace's apartment for a couple of post-meeting, non-Penalty Box
drinks before heading home. Gage hadn't stuck around
to hear the rest of the conversation, but had headed
back out, this time with a destination in mind.

Now he stood outside Grace's apartment door, wiping
his sweaty palms on the thighs of his jeans and hoping
his heart didn't jump out of his chest before he got a
chance to tell Jenna everything he needed to say.

Sucking in lungfuls of oxygen, he braced his feet
slightly apart and lifted a hand to rap on the door. He
was about to knock again when the door flew open and
Grace stood there, staring up at him. She was dressed
in some floor-length white satin nightgown with a matching robe. With her blond hair and full face of makeup,
she looked for all the world like a Marilyn Monroe
wannabe. Stick one of those long black cigarette hold-
ers in her hand and she could have been a twenties
starlet.

"Hey, girls," she called back over her shoulder, "it's
a dick. Should we take a vote on whether or not to let
him in?"

Something told him she wasn't calling him a dick

because he was an ace detective, but considering *audacious* was one of Grace's regular settings, Gage didn't waste time trying to decipher her comment.

A second later, Ronnie appeared a few feet behind her—still fully dressed in the skirt and blouse she'd worn to work, thank goodness.

Gage breathed a silent sigh of relief at the sight of her. Of the three of them, she hated him least at the moment and was probably his best shot at acting as a voice of reason with the other two.

But instead of smiling and telling Grace to let him in, Ronnie's eyes narrowed and she crossed her arms over her chest. "I think we should let Jenna decide," she said in a voice that swept over him like a blast from the deep freeze.

Uh-oh. This might not be as easy he'd hoped.

A second after that, Jenna walked into view. She was wearing a pair of dark blue jeans with pink appliqué butterflies running down one leg and a white, scoop-neck top with a butterfly high toward one shoulder. And the boa around her neck of course matched every shade of pink and white in the outfit, bringing it all together in Jenna's own unique style.

A fist clutched his insides as he took in every detail, from her ruffled black hair to the painted pink toenails peeking out through the open toes of her wedge sandals.

She looked good . . . but she looked sad, and he vowed to do everything in his power to wipe the pain from her face.

"I need to talk to you," he said, meeting Jenna's gaze and speaking past the other two women who stood between them.

A heavy silence followed his words. He waited for her reply, but the longer she took, the more blood pounded through his veins.

Finally, Grace pushed away from the door and headed for the kitchen. "Since it doesn't look like you'll be leaving, can I get you a drink?"

He heard ice cubes falling into a glass and dragged his attention away from Jenna long enough to watch Grace stroll back toward him, drink in hand. She offered him the tall, clear glass of light brown liquid, and he nearly reached for it. God knew his mouth was as dry as the Gobi Desert.

At the last minute, though, he stopped himself, curling his fingers into his palm. "No. Thanks," he told her slowly.

Lifting his eyes to meet hers, he saw a sparkle of amusement there and one corner of his mouth curved in response. "I learned my lesson last time. I'll get my own beverages from now on."

"Smart man." She returned his amused half-smile with one of her own, then raised the glass in mock salute. "You might want to pass that tip along to Zack, by the way, because if I ever get the opportunity to slip anything into his drink, it *won't* be a few harmless sleeping pills."

That came a little too close to a threat on someone's life for Gage's cop sensibilities, but he wasn't here to referee a lovers' dispute; he had enough problems of his own along those lines.

Turning back to the matter at hand, he fixed his gaze once again on Jenna. He didn't care if he sounded weak or ridiculous, he needed her to talk to him, to *listen* to him.

"Please," he implored, tucking his thumbs self-consciously into two front belt loops. "Just for a minute."

She exchanged glances with her two friends, but gave a stiff nod and started toward the doorway. Stepping into the hall, he shut the door on Grace and Ronnie to afford them a bit of privacy.

His breath hitched and the heart inside his chest literally ached, it was beating so fast and so hard against his ribcage.

Jenna, who had moved closer to the opposite wall to put some distance between them, didn't seem to be having such problems. She was practically glaring at him, arms still crossed staunchly beneath her breasts and her lips pressed into a flat, humorless line.

"What do you want, Gage?" she asked in a tired voice.

He'd done that to her. Put the sorrow in her eyes and the slope of defeat to her shoulders.

Swallowing past the lump in his throat, he said, "I'm just going to jump in here, because I've wasted enough time already."

Deep breath. A lick to dry lips while he tried to get his thoughts in order.

"I messed up, Jenna. You were right about everything, and I was too damn thick-headed to see it."

She didn't respond, simply stood there watching him, waiting for him to finish—or get to the point, whichever came first. To keep from grabbing her and pulling her in for a long kiss that might help to absolve him of his sins, he shoved his fingers into his pockets.

"I was a fool, Jenna. I was afraid of losing you to some of the things I've seen out on the street. So afraid that instead of holding you close and appreciating every minute we had together, I let it scare me into letting you go and letting our marriage collapse because of it."

He thought he saw a flash of interest in her eyes and prayed he was on the right track, prayed he could convince her to take him back.

"I was wrong. Wrong and stupid and foolish, and every other word you can think of that spells I-D-I-O-T," he admitted with a sorry shake of his head. "It took me a while—too damn long, I know—to realize that I can't control what *might* happen. In the words of a man smarter than I apparently am, any one of us could walk outside and get hit by a bus tomorrow. It wouldn't have a damn thing to do with our jobs or lifestyles or what kind of people we are."

Dropping his head, he studied the black of his boots against the nondescript beige of the industrial hallway carpeting for a second, then took a deep breath, met her gaze again, and barreled on.

"I hate the thought of going through the rest of my life without you. Without ever knowing a minute of happiness because you aren't there. I don't want to live without you or without the children we'll have together. I can't tell you I won't still worry—or have moments of sheer panic, frankly," he added with a crooked, self-deprecating smile, "but I don't want what I've seen as a cop to steal our future. Not for one more minute."

Holding himself rigid, he waited for her reaction, waited to find out if his revelation had come too late to win her back.

And, dammit, he couldn't tell. Her face remained impassive, her eyes narrowed with skepticism, but not giving anything away.

This was not going as well as he'd hoped, he thought

with a mental cringe. On the way over, he'd envisioned
the reaction his speech would receive. He'd tell Jenna
he loved her and wanted her back, wanted a happy marriage and children with her, after all. And she would be
so delighted and overwhelmed that she would give a
little shriek of joy, throw her arms around his neck, and
kiss him silly.

Clearly he'd made an error in his calculations.

The seconds ticked by in his head like the echo of
a gong, and then it hit him: *He hadn't told her he
loved her!*

Shit. Mental head slap.

He'd been so focused on letting her know he'd come
to his senses and wasn't going to let fears about the future keep them apart any longer that he'd forgotten the
most important part.

"I love you," he blurted out.

Her eyes widened slightly at that, but if it was due to
the declaration itself or the force with which he made
it, he couldn't be sure.

"I love you," he repeated at a slightly lower decibel
level. "I've always loved you, Jenna. Never stopped, not
even when I signed the divorce papers and walked
away. The last year and a half without you has been . . ."
He thought about it, then blew out a frustrated breath.
"I'd say 'hell,' but Hell is Disney World compared to
how miserable I've been."

Risking the pain of rejection that he knew could still
come, he took a step forward and grasped her elbows.
Her arms slid away from her midsection and fell to her
sides, and he tugged her closer until they touched chest
to chest.

Staring down at her, he whispered, "I'm sorry. I've

put you through so much and wasted so much time. But I want to make it up to you. I want to spend the rest of my life making it up to you, if you'll just give me the chance."

His diaphragm constricted as he ran out of air. That was it; that was all he had in him. If she was going to forgive him and take him back, then she'd have to do it now because he didn't know what else to do or say that might win her over. The ball was in her court, and all he could do was wait.

Unfortunately, the silence was killing him, scraping along his sensitized nerve endings like nails on a chalkboard.

And her expression gave away nothing. Her eyes were still dark and unreadable. Her lips were still drawn into a thin, tight line.

Fearing it was over and that his heartfelt speech had come too late to break through the thick wall of protection *he'd* put there to begin with, he released his hold on her arms and took a step back.

There was no pain, not yet. It was like that sometimes with trauma. Shock set in first, numbing the body and momentarily blocking the pain receptors in the brain. But soon enough, reality would kick in, and the knowledge that he'd lost Jenna again—just when he'd finally gotten his head on straight—would be agonizing.

He took a step, half-turning to begin the long, endless walk down the hall and away from her. He prayed she'd go back inside Grace's apartment before his knees went weak and he did something less than manly like collapse or break down in pathetic sobs.

"You want babies?"

Her words came to him like an echo from inside a dark tunnel. At first he thought he'd imagined it, then he wasn't quite sure he'd heard correctly.

Turning back around, he found her standing right where he'd left her, looking at him expectantly. She hadn't slipped back into Grace's apartment, and she apparently *had* asked him a question.

The most important question.

"Yeah," he said, feeling a hitch in his chest that threatened to work its way up his throat. "I want babies. But not just any babies. I only want babies with you."

Finally, he knew he'd said the right thing. Jenna's eyes filled with tears, her lips quivered, and she launched herself against him before he could brace himself for the impact. He stumbled back a step, but caught her and anchored them both as his arms came up to wrap around her waist.

A ball of warmth burst low in his belly and spread out into every cell of his being. He hadn't fucked up, after all; at least not permanently.

She'd listened to him, believed him, and—thank You, Jesus—forgiven him. The only time he could remember feeling this good or being this happy was on his wedding day.

He didn't think he should mention it yet, but he intended to get her down the aisle again as soon as possible. And if she wanted to get started immediately on the baby-making part, he was ready, willing, and more than able.

After a few minutes of simply standing there, holding each other close, Jenna lifted her face from his neck and fixed him with narrow, serious eyes. "Never,

ever do that again!" she told him in a watery voice, then gave his side a pinch for good measure.

"Ow." He squirmed away from her lethal claws, then asked, "Never do what again?"

"Put me through something like that," she nearly shrieked. "The silent treatment, the divorce, the not knowing what the heck you want and putting me through the wringer. Never, ever, ever—"

She came at him again with those two dangerous fingertips, and he jumped quickly to one side before she could make contact.

"I won't," he assured her. "I promise."

With a slightly less homicidal demeanor, she snuggled up to him again, and he was more than happy to snuggle back.

"You were so sure when you left, so certain you were making the right decision. What changed your mind?" she asked, leaning into the circle of his arms at her back.

He thought about it for a moment, then replied slowly, "I think I finally . . . opened my eyes. After being with you again, then leaving you again . . . God, that is something I *never* want to repeat, let me tell you. I don't think my heart could take it." He shook his head, then made himself get back on track. "Anyway, I started to notice that a lot of the guys on the force have wives and families. They don't shut themselves away from their loved ones or walk around petrified something will happen to them."

She lifted a brow and annoyance started to seep back into her gaze. "Isn't that what I've been trying to tell you all along?"

He made a face. "That would be the part where I admit to being a little dense."

Her expression darkened even more. "A little?"

And then she pinched him. Again.

"*Ow.*" He rubbed at the poor, abused spot on his side, then said, "You'd better take it easy. If you keep battering me like that, I might not be in any shape to knock you up tonight."

Her lips twitched with the urge to grin, but she held back, intent on holding his feet to the fire a while longer.

"Who says I want you to knock me up tonight?" she replied smartly, tipping her head in that come-hither way she had that used to drive him crazy—in all the very best ways.

"You've only been angling for kids for two or three years now," he reminded her. "I figured you'd want to get started. And I, for one, am looking forward to some pretty amazing makeup sex." He waggled his brows for emphasis.

She chuckled. "I'm okay with the makeup sex, but I think we should go a little more slowly with the rest. I want to be sure this is going to work out and that you're not going to *change your mind again.*" She growled the last and aimed her curled fingers at his ribcage.

He sucked in his gut to avoid more potential bruising. "I won't, I swear."

Seeming to accept his word, she said, "And then I'd like to get remarried before we start having kids."

"This from the woman who drugged me and tied me to the bed in an attempt to get pregnant?" he asked, brows lifted in doubt.

Her mouth twitched guiltily. "That's when I thought I was going to be alone for the rest of my life and didn't want to spend it childless. Now that I know you're going to be there . . ."

She made the pinchy motion again and he rolled his eyes, grabbing her wrist and laying her palm flat on his chest so she couldn't use it against him.

"I'm not in as much of a hurry. We have time."

It wasn't what he'd expected—part of him had expected her to jump his bones right there in the apartment complex hallway—but it sounded good to him.

With a grin, he leaned in to kiss her. Slowly at first, then deeper, until she was pressed to him like cellophane and his arms were bound around her so tightly, he was afraid he might break something.

When they pulled apart a long, long while later, he touched his forehead to hers and whispered, "So what do you say we go home—your place or mine, I don't care—and at least get started on that makeup sex?"

She stepped into him again, arms around his neck, and gave a little hop, wrapping her legs around his waist. She trusted him to catch her, like so many times in the past. Which he did, by curving his hands under her butt.

"I say yes. I may even let you tie me to the headboard this time," she teased just above his ear before giving it a tiny love-nip and then moving downward.

Her naughtily whispered words and her mouth on the side of his throat sent his cock jutting upwards, straining against the fly of his jeans. He was trying to hold on to his control here, but she'd be lucky if he didn't toss her down right there in the hallway and strip her bare.

Between voracious, soul-stealing kisses, he managed to grate out, "Shouldn't you tell your friends we're leaving?"

She gave a half-hearted nod and he steered her none-too-steadily over to Grace's door.

Jenna tapped, then yelled out, "Everything's fine."

Kiss.

"We're leaving."

Lick.

"I'll call you later."

Suuuck.

While his legs could still carry him, he headed for the elevator at the end of the hall. From her heightened position in his arms, she reached down to punch the button with her thumb, then turned back to him. Their gazes met and he saw his love for her reflected in those mossy-green depths.

"I love you," he murmured, wanting to say it again and again so she knew the words were true.

Releasing her hold on his neck, she ran her hands through his short hair and whispered, "I love you, too. And we're going to make it work this time."

"Yes, we are," he agreed with a knowing grin. "Yes, we are."

Bind Off

It worked!

It worked, it worked, it worked!

Charlotte did a little jig, discoing around the antique spinning wheel as though it were her partner on the dance floor.

The wheel *wasn't* defective. The yarn *hadn't* failed in its true love mission.

Oh, glory! Oh, joy!

Slightly out of breath from her exertions, she slowed her steps and took a seat on the stool of the spinning wheel.

She'd lugged the giant piece of equipment back down from the attic . . . . left it in her bedroom for a day or two to give her creaking bones a rest . . . then dragged it the rest of the way to the living room. Her intention had been to ready some new fibers and spin a new skein of yarn for her niece in hopes of undoing whatever bad mojo the first skein had brought about.

But now she didn't have to, because Jenna had arrived at tonight's knitting meeting with a smile on her face that could have lighted Lakefront Stadium. She'd been floating on air, bursting to share the news that she and Gage were back together.

Apparently, a lot had happened since Charlotte had last seen her niece.

Good things.

Wonderful things.

Enchanted-yarn-working-its-magic kind of things.

And Charlotte was absolutely certain now that the yarn was responsible for bringing both Ronnie and Dylan and Jenna and Gage together. How could it not be when Jenna had brought the feathery purple yarn with her tonight to finish a boa she'd begun while Charlotte had been away . . . and Gage had come to stay with her out at the farm?

Charlotte had been delighted, but not the least bit surprised, to hear it—as well as the fact that Gage had wanted to learn to do a bit of knitting and *that* was the yarn Jenna had used to teach him.

It was the story of Ronnie and Dylan's love affair all over again. Definitive proof, as far as Charlotte was concerned, that the wheel and its yarn had the power to do exactly what her mother and grandmother and her mother before that had always claimed.

She was so excited, she had to tinkle again.

A few minutes later, she returned to the sitting room and took up position behind the spinning wheel. Now that she knew—really, really *knew*—she had her work cut out for her.

The yarn she created with this spinning wheel was clearly powerful enough to draw two people together despite seemingly insurmountable obstacles. But could it find a way for Grace to forgive Zachary?

Normally, Charlotte would never suggest a woman

return to a man who'd cheated on her. Oh, no. Bodily harm and immediate neutering, maybe, but never forgiveness.

According to Jenna, however, Zack swore he hadn't been unfaithful. There was a story there about a female fan sneaking into his hotel room on the road and Grace choosing that unfortunate moment to surprise him, but he swore up and down he wasn't guilty. And because Charlotte trusted Jenna, and Jenna trusted Gage, who believed that Zack had possibly been wrongly accused, Charlotte was willing to suspend judgment.

Grace was too deeply mired in grief at the moment to listen to such a tale, though. She needed time . . . and perhaps a bit of supernatural intervention.

Threading the readied fibers—which she'd dyed pink this time—into the wheel, she slowly started to work the pedal, started to work the soft alpaca fur into a tight, artful strand of yarn.

Grace might not be ready to forgive Zack just yet, but hopefully once Charlotte gave her a bit of enchanted yarn, she would be.

Or perhaps the wheel had someone else in mind for the lovely television star.

If that was true, then Charlotte would accept it, of course. The important thing was that the yarn drew Grace to her true love and gave them a lifetime of happily ever after.

And with Charlotte's sneaky little fairy godmother help, that's exactly what she was going to get.

JENNA'S BOAS

*(which can also be used as restraints during hot sex
with a current or ex-husband)*

Materials:

Size 13 knitting needles

1 1.5-ounce skein of feathery "eyelash" yarn
(any color)

Directions:

Cast on 16 stitches.

Knit every row until boa is one yard long or reaches
desired length.

Cast off and weave yarn ends into fabric of boa with
crochet hook.

Read on for an excerpt from the next book
by Heidi Betts

Knock Me for a Loop

Coming February 2010 from St. Martin's Paperbacks

Charlotte Langan's late-model station wagon, complete
with faux wooden panels running the full length of
both sides, rumbled beneath her, sending pleasant little
ripples into her feet, up her short legs, and along the
narrow line of her vertebrae. The heat was turned up
full blast in an attempt to counteract the brittle cold of
Cleveland, Ohio, in mid-December.

Holiday decorations were up already—and had been
since just after Thanksgiving—lining the damp streets
and filling lighted storefronts. Christmas was one of her
favorite times of year. The colors and raised spirits and
festivities. Not to mention presents! Whether she was
giving or receiving them, oh, how she loved the presents.
What other time of year did a woman have such a bona
fide excuse to shop until she dropped?

Flipping on her right turn signal, Charlotte maneu-
vered her car—which she imagined handled much like
a refrigerator on wheels—into the lot of a local strip
mall, then began to drive slowly up and down the rows
of cars already parked there. Using the steering wheel

for leverage, she hoisted herself up and forward for a better view as she peered through the windshield searching for an empty spot.

When she finally found one near a brightly lit overhead lamp, she pulled in—it only took six or eight tries— cut the engine, and set the parking brake. Because a woman could never be too careful, and the parking lot *was* on a slight, probably fifteen-degree incline. Then she grabbed her knitting tote from the passenger side of the seat beside her and climbed out of the station wagon.

Frigid air swamped her, and she tugged the hood of her thick, fluffy fleece coat up and over her head, tightening the strings until she was sure she looked like the Jolly Green Eskimo . . . or maybe a giant lime popsicle.

Her bright purple faux UGG boots splotted against the slick asphalt as she goose-stepped her way across the lot and pulled open the door to The Yarn Barn. A wall of blessed heat smacked her full in the face as soon as she stepped inside, and she sighed with warming pleasure. Loosening her fuzzy hood and tugging at her thick, hand-knit alpaca mittens, she made a beeline for the back of the store, where the rest of her Wednesday-night knitting group would be waiting.

Because The Yarn Barn hosted a number of craft groups and craft-related classes throughout the week, a large meeting nook had been set up in the rear. Several mismatched chairs were arranged around a low coffee table, and there was a refreshment area off to the side, complete with snacks and both hot and cold beverages.

At the moment, there was nothing Charlotte wanted more than a steaming cup of cocoa clutched between her ice-cold hands, but she would settle for the familiar

KNOCK ME FOR A LOOP   303

comfort of her size eight needles and the warm caress of the alpaca fiber yarn she was using to knit a long, variegated cardigan as it ran through and around her fingers with every stitch.

Already, she could hear the staccato clack of needles clicking together beneath the voices of the women who were gathered and busily working on their respective knitting projects. A sweater here, a scarf there, and several pairs of slipper socks to keep toes toasty over the long, cold winter or be stuffed into stockings for Christmas.

"Aunt Charlotte!" Jenna cried, catching sight of her over the top of one of the backwards-facing chairs.

Sitting in that chair was the strikingly beautiful Grace Fisher, who turned along with everyone else to watch Charlotte's approach. "I swear, Charlotte, you look more like a troll doll every time I see you," she quipped.

Charlotte chuckled with amusement. Some people might have taken Grace's remark as an insult, but Charlotte was delighted with the description. From the moment Grace had first tossed out the comparison and then gifted Charlotte with one of the little plastic figurines to show her what she was talking about, Charlotte had been hooked.

That doll had been the first of what was turning out to be quite the troll collection. She had one with yellow hair on her mantle, one with blue hair on the dresser in her bedroom, one with green hair on the back of the toilet in her bathroom, and the one with flame-orange hair that Grace had originally given her hung from the rearview mirror of her station wagon, where she could admire it on a regular basis.

She just loved the little buggers. Like Cabbage Patch

dolls, they were so ugly, they were cute, and she'd
made it one of her goals in life to get her own bright
orange, bee-hived hair to stand as tall as theirs. She
was close, too—only a few inches to go.

"We were beginning to wonder when you'd show up,"
her niece said as Charlotte struggled out of her oversized coat and let it drop to the floor beside an empty
chair. Patting the well-shellacked dome of her hair to
make sure the hood hadn't done irreparable damage,
she took a seat and pulled her craft tote onto her lap.

"Sorry. I got busy with my babies and lost track of
the time," Charlotte told them, referring to her beloved
pack of alpacas.

That wasn't entirely true, of course. She'd finished
feeding and bedding down everyone in plenty of time,
but when she'd returned to the house to collect her things
before leaving for the weekly knitting meeting, she'd realized she didn't have the skein of pink yarn she'd made
for Grace.

Special yarn.

Very special yarn.

A year ago—give or take a few excitement-filled
months—Charlotte had almost by accident stumbled
across a delightful secret. The solid oak spinning wheel
that had been handed down through the women in her
family for generations was *magic*. Not run-of-the-mill
magic, either, but the very best kind—the kind that
brought true love.

Charlotte had grown up with her mother and grandmother telling her stories about the enchanted, true-
love spinning wheel, but she'd thought they were just
that—stories. It wasn't until recently that she'd remem-

bered the old wheel, hidden and collecting dust in a corner of her attic. She'd dragged it downstairs (no easy feat for a woman of her somewhat advanced age and limited height), cleaned it up, and used dyed fiber from her own alpacas to spin a skein of soft black yarn that she'd then given to Ronnie, one of the young women in her knitting group.

At the time, Ronnie had been head over heels in hate with a man who wrote for a competing local newspaper, and Charlotte thought they would make the perfect guinea pigs for her enchanted spinning-wheel test run.

When that had turned out better than great—Ronnie and her beau were now living together, and Charlotte expected a wedding announcement any day—she'd used the wheel to spin another skein of enchanted yarn. Fluffy and purple this time, for her own dear niece, Jenna, who had been divorced and miserable. Charlotte hadn't expected Jenna to reconcile with her ex-husband, but since the two now seemed deliriously happy together and were planning to tie the knot a second time just before Christmas, she certainly wasn't going to complain. As far as she was concerned, that simply proved that the spinning wheel *did* bring true love to those who used the yarn it created.

Now there was one more person in need of the wheel's very special powers.

Poor Grace. Another of Charlotte's favorite knitting group members, she was such a lovely, vibrant woman. And she'd been even more lovely and vibrant in her happiness over being engaged to Zack "Hot Legs" Hoolihan, the star goalie for the Cleveland Rockets and one of the city's homegrown heroes.

Happy, that was, until she'd walked into Zack's hotel room one day last summer while he was on the road with the team and found another woman in his bed.

Though Charlotte had been out of town at the time, she'd heard the whole sordid story when she got home. Zack denied any wrongdoing, but Grace was adamant that she wasn't blind and knew what she'd walked in on.

According to Jenna and Ronnie, Grace had gone a bit crazy after discovering her fiance's infidelity. Charlotte had seen her mini-meltdown firsthand when Grace had gone on the air of her self-titled local cable television show, *Amazing Grace*, and spent the entire half-hour ranting and raving about the perfidy of men in general and Zack in particular. And apparently she had also taken a baseball bat to Zack's red Hummer and gleefully tossed his clothes and assorted other belongings out his sixth-story window.

Although Charlotte couldn't blame Grace for being upset, she thought such blatant destruction of property was a little over the top. Especially since Zack just as publicly and vehemently proclaimed his innocence.

Though she tended to side with Grace on the matter—after all, they were both women who knitted, and knitting women needed to stick together—Charlotte wasn't sure exactly what to believe. As with most disagreements, she suspected the truth lay somewhere in the middle.

What *was* clear, however, was that Grace's life was in desperate need of some divine intervention. A little sprinkle of fairy dust to help her get over the pain of her *dis*-engagement . . . and hopefully find love again.

That's where Charlotte came in.

Just call her Match-Makin' Mama, she thought with a silent giggle.

She'd dyed more of her babies' soft, beautiful fiber a bright, bold pink, and then used her family's secret, enchanted spinning wheel to weave a wonderful skein of yarn just for Grace.

Which was why she couldn't possibly have left the house this evening without it.

But she'd found it, thank goodness. Right where she'd left it, too—in a wicker basket beside the sofa in her living room, along with several other homemade balls of yarn.

Now she simply had to find a way to slip it to Grace some time during their Knit Wits meeting and ensure that she put it to good use. Otherwise, the magic that the spinning wheel infused into the yarn would never get a chance to create a true love match.

And it *would* work. Of that, Charlotte had no doubt. The wheel's yarn had worked twice before, and she was certain it would work again for Grace. After all, the third time was, as they said, the charm.

Around her, the gals chitted and chatted, discussing their weeks and their latest knitting projects, and men. Men always seemed to be a popular topic of conversation, whether the group was admiring a specific physique or bemoaning their fickle, infuriating hides.

Being the eldest member of the group—and, sadly, the one most removed from a romantic relationship of any kind, unless she counted her enormous love for her alpaca babies and barn cats—Charlotte tended to sit back and enjoy the animated conversations rather than offer her own opinions about the opposite sex.

Girls these days . . . Charlotte was far from being a
prude, but some of the stories her knitting buddies told
could strip the Garnier Summer Wildfire #968 right
off her hair and send it blooming in her cheeks. Not
that she would ever let them know their banter tee-
tered on the far side of her moral alphabet. (As in Triple X-Y-Z.)

In her day, young women didn't make time with as
many young men as they apparently did today. They
also didn't share the intimate details of their relationships with anyone who would listen.

But Charlotte considered herself a modern, sophisticated woman, so she took it all in, and even made a few
mental notes for herself. Not many—she was too afraid
her eyes would go blind and her fingers would burn
down to the bone if she tried to write them out. And
granted, she hadn't had the opportunity to put her wom-
anly wiles to the test in quite a long time, but one never
knew when Prince Charming might come galloping—
or in her case, shuffling—into one's life.

Luckily, not everybody was as miserable in her love
life as Grace and Charlotte.

A few were married and raising families, including
Melanie, who tried her best to get away from her two
small children long enough to attend the weekly knitting meetings.

A few were college-age girls who were enjoying their
youth too much to tie themselves to any one boy yet.

Then there was Jenna, who was jump-out-of-her-
skin, the-hills-are-alive-with-the-sound-of-music in
love with her ex- and soon to be re-husband, Gage. Always had been, and the whole world knew it. It had just
taken a few years of misery, a premature divorce decree,

a couple pints of tequila, and some magic yarn to get them both back on the same page.

And Ronnie was right there twirling around on the hillside with Jenna, glowing so brightly over her happiness with Dylan Stone that she practically burst into flame every time someone mentioned his name.

Charlotte's gaze slid to Grace. Ronnie was telling them about the past weekend, when she'd gone away with Dylan to a remote mountain cabin. Apparently the temperature had been too low and there had been too much snow on the ground to do much more than stay inside in front of a blazing fire. Charlotte rather suspected that had been the point to begin with. Why else would anyone leave the frosty temperatures of Cleveland in the middle of winter to vacation in an even more glacial location?

Charlotte also suspected she was the only one who noticed how uncomfortable Ronnie's story was making Grace. Though a smile was firmly painted on her lips, it was strained and the attempt at outward amusement didn't reach her eyes.

If Ronnie knew that her animated account was causing her friend even a modicum of discomfort, she would have clammed up in a nanosecond, but Grace was so good at hiding her emotions and playing the part of a perfectly coiffed, perfectly content public figure that she had everyone around her fooled. Even her best friends.

They didn't call her "Amazing Grace" for nothing, after all.

But Charlotte saw. And she knew that no matter how hard Grace pretended to be over the devastation of her broken engagement, in reality it was still tearing her up inside.

Not for long, though. God and true-love magic willing, Grace's shattered heart would soon be mended.

Almost before she knew it, the hour had drawn to a close and everyone started tightening stitches and rolling up loose yarn, putting away their works in progress. Butterflies fluttered in Charlotte's stomach as she saw her opportunity.

Jumping to her feet, she hurried to shrug into her coat and sidle up to Grace before anyone else could join them.

"I have a surprise for you, dear," she said quietly, reaching into her bag for the carefully woven skein of silky-soft pink yarn.

Grace's gaze lowered as she reached to accept Charlotte's gift, and Charlotte noticed that the polish on Grace's perfectly manicured nails perfectly matched the tint of the yarn.

Oooh, this was wonderful! It had to be a sign. A sign that this particular skein of magic yarn was, indeed, meant for Grace.

"That's so sweet. Thank you, Charlotte."

The words were sincere enough, but they didn't carry Grace's usual flare of enthusiasm. Everything about her these days was muted, as though a bubble of unhappiness surrounded her.

"Make yourself something special with it," Charlotte suggested, wanting to press and make sure Grace started using the yarn as soon as possible. "Maybe after you finish that pretty sweater you're working on now." Which only had one more sleeve and some trim work to go.

Lips curving in a half-hearted smile, Grace leaned down to buss Charlotte's cheek. "I will. Thank you again."

Well, it wasn't exactly a blood oath to begin knitting with the new yarn before the clock struck midnight, Charlotte thought with a mental sigh, but it would have to do. Now all she could do was cross her fingers and her toes and hope to heaven the enchantment of the ancient spinning wheel held true and worked its wonderful magic once again.